The Intergalactic Adventures of
QUEEN BEA

♛

BOOK ONE

Jeanne Gransee Barker

Seattle
U.S.A.

This is a work of fiction. Names, characters, businesses, places, events and incidents are either the products of the author's imagination or used in a fictitious manner. Any resemblance to actual persons, living or dead, or actual events is purely coincidental.

For more information visit www.jeannegranseebarker.com.

Cover design by Jeanne Gransee Barker. Cover photo courtesy of iStock Photography.

ISBN-13: 978-0692358962 (print)

For Kylie, my bright light
who inspires me every day.

Acknowledgments

I'm so grateful to all those who have been invaluable on this book's many-year path to completion. To my parents, who made me believe I could do anything I put my mind to. To my early readers, my brother Tom and my cousin John: Thanks for encouraging me to get this out of my computer and into the world. To the Geek Goddesses—Ruth Maxwell, Phoebe Kitanidis, Barrie Bartlett—who provided gentle accountability, emotional support and key critiques: Without you, I'd still be on Chapter 10. I miss your regular guidance and hope I can finish Book Two without you. To Kylie, whose low-blood-sugar antics sparked me to create these characters while waiting for our Spiro's pizza: Your old-soul witticisms never cease to amaze and encourage me. And to my brother Mark: Every time I faltered you were there. You are the most positive person I know. Your attitude and approach to life are inspiring. When I grow up, I wanna be just like you.

Prologue
Thirteen Years Ago

The tiny house was warm and dark. Ed Vaslow—as he was known here—lay on his bed staring at the ceiling. Something wasn't right. He could feel it in the air, an undefined tingling on his skin. Out the window he saw a familiar blue flash on the horizon. It flickered for an instant and then was gone. There wasn't much time now.

Moving as fast as his old bones allowed, he got up, dressed and slipped into his well-worn leather loafers. After pulling on his thick cable-knit sweater, he picked up a small black device from the dresser and put in his pocket, feeling the weight of it settle.

Without turning on the lights, he went into the living room. Taking a packet of papers out of the desk drawer, he reread his note of explanation and double-checked that every legal aspect was covered, then tucked them into the very bottom of the diaper bag. The kitchen was next. The cupboard was full of neatly stacked jars of toddler food. Winter squash was her favorite. He took all three jars of that. And the little sausages—she loved those too. Tears pooled in his eyes. He scrubbed them away and refocused his attention on his task.

He went into the baby's room. Baby—he had to stop calling her that. At two years old, she was a little girl now. It was quiet save for the rhythmic purr of breathing through her tiny, slightly stuffy nose. He'd miss that sound. He opened her dresser drawers and took out a couple of extra outfits and diapers. By the time he was done, the diaper bag was so full it wouldn't zip.

A crooked smile formed on his lips from behind his scruffy gray beard. He leaned over the sleeping child and looked one last time—a look to last a lifetime. He'd thought about this. Prepared for it. The Parkers were good people. They'd do the right thing. He could sense it. She'd be safe there. Without him she'd have a better chance.

Vaslow had prayed that this backward blue planet would be among the last sectors explored. Alas, luck had not traveled with them. Though the child was not trackable at her young age, he was. He knew what he had to do. He'd just never imagined it would be so difficult.

The little girl, clad in her thick fleece pajamas, hung like a rag doll as he lifted her, not rousing from her deep sleep. He'd been lax in his training while caring for the girl; his weary muscles no longer liked to bend and lift at the same time. "You're getting so big, sweetheart," he whispered softly in his native tongue as he moved her. He was too old for this mission and too damn cantankerous. They had known that when they asked him. That's what made him a perfect choice. But in the end it was a gamble and they'd lost.

The girl on one shoulder, Vaslow slung the diaper bag strap over the other and went out the back door to the carport. Through the trees, he could see a light. Maybe they were still awake. That would make it easier.

He strapped the sleeping toddler in her car seat and backed out of the driveway without turning on the headlights. Moonlight reflecting off the dusting of snow gave almost enough light to see. He drove the short distance through the woods to where the subdivision began. He knew it was just a matter of time before they built right up to his door. That mattered little now.

As he pulled into the driveway, he saw a kitchen light was on in the back of the house. He took the child out of her car seat and grabbed the heavy diaper bag, shuffling carefully up the snow-glazed steps. He knocked on the door, firmly but not so loud as to wake the other sleeping children.

A woman in a flannel, floral-print robe answered the door, face knitted with concern. "Ed? What has you out so late?" she asked. Her husband watched from the kitchen doorway behind her.

"I'm sorry to come at this hour...and with such an imposition." He looked intently at the sleeping girl on his shoulder as he spoke. "But I've got nowhere else to turn."

"Is everything all right?" Mr. Parker asked, stepping up next to his wife.

"No, it's not. My daughter—her mother—has just been taken to the hospital and I need to get there right away. I hate to ask, but can I leave her with you until I get it sorted out?" He met their eyes, pleading. It was a lie, like the note, but one he could live with.

"Of course," Mrs. Parker said, reaching for the child. "Hon, you get the bag." She scooped the child towards her in a fluid, natural motion. "Ed, don't worry about her. Take as long as you need. We'll be fine. We'll take good care of her."

"Thank you." Vaslow's voice broke as he felt the cold seep into his now vacant arms. He started to say something more, but couldn't form the words. He just nodded and turned to leave.

Once out of the subdivision, on a vacant stretch of road overlooking his house, he pulled off to the side. Head in his hands, he let the tears come. He was a warrior, damn it—an old one, granted, but a warrior nonetheless. Never had he imagined that child would melt his heart. He raised his head and looked at his house. It was faint, but he could see the blue light scanning the inside of his living room. No, it wouldn't be long now.

Chapter 1: The Gift
Winter, Present Day

Bea Parker sat on an orange crate on the flat section of roof outside her second-story bedroom window, absentmindedly twirling a lock of her thick, red hair while she tried to figure things out. Tiny flecks of white floated down from the midnight-blue sky. It was late for the first heavy snow. Through some weird trick of meteorology, Elmhurst and the rest of the suburbs on this side of Chicago had gotten less snow than those north and east this year. Usually there was plenty of snow on the ground by now.

The dream had woken her up again, leaving her with the creepy feeling she was being watched. No matter how many times she told herself it was just a nightmare, the feeling wouldn't leave her. The probing gaze of the shadowed figure lingered, the face melting from one shape to another so she couldn't quite get a fix on it. And the hollow voice that went from high to low still rang in her ears. She couldn't remember what he—she—it—said, but it crept into her mind and she couldn't shake it. Unable to fall back to sleep, she'd decided to crawl out her bedroom window onto the roof—the only place she could be alone to think.

The exact same dream had woken her up several times over the last week. Maybe this crazy dream was her mind's way of trying to sort out her messed-up life.

Crystal snowflakes landed gently on her nose and cheeks; they felt like frozen grains of sand. It wasn't packing snow, so there would be no snowmen tomorrow. She was too old for that anyway. It was just as beautiful, covering the brown grass and empty flowerbeds, making everything look new and fresh. She loved how the shapes of things looked so different when they were blanketed by the soft white. Everything changed so quickly, just like her life. But instead of becoming crisp and clean and new like the snow, her life had just come unraveled.

Last week everything had been normal. It wasn't perfect or anything, but she had no complaints, none that really mattered anyway. Living with Uncle Pete, Aunt Lucy, and her cousins was all she'd ever known. It seemed normal to her. She'd been there since she was two and couldn't even remember her mother, never thought about life before this. But now, with one stupid move, she'd learned that everything she'd ever known was a lie.

All because of the dumb extra credit for her report on crystals. If she hadn't been such a dork she could have lived her whole life without knowing. She'd decided to bring in the geode quartz Uncle Pete had given Aunt Lucy when they were dating. Her aunt had been busy rushing to finish an acorn costume for Teddy's school play, so Bea went to look for the crystal herself. In the back of her aunt and uncle's closet, behind the wicker sewing basket, Bea found a tattered manila envelope with her name typed on it. She opened it up and saw a bunch of legal documents and a yellowed piece of notebook paper tucked on top. Bea took it out and read it.

> *Dear Mrs. and Mr. Parker,*
>
> *Perhaps this is the biggest thing one could impose upon another, and I ask this knowing the weight of my request. In getting to know you, I have seen that your goodness and compassion are beyond measure. I feel you are the only ones in this world I can turn to. I am entrusting Bayatrice, the*

soul of my world, to your care. I must leave town immedi-
ately. By the time you read this note, I will already be gone.
I would give any price to be able to raise her myself, but my
circumstances are desperate. I ask that you find it in your
hearts to raise her with the love and care I have seen you
bestow upon your own children.

As the child's legal guardian, I have had all the forms pre-
pared in advance in the event that you decide to honor my
request. If you choose to help this child, you will be protect-
ing a treasure more dear than you could ever know.

Sincerely,
Edward Vaslow

Bea couldn't believe it. At first she thought it had to be some sort of misunderstanding. She wasn't Bayatrice. But all the other papers in the file had her name on them: Beatrice. Why was this Edward Vaslow her legal guardian? Why wasn't her mother, Gloria Parker, mentioned anywhere? But as she thought about it, her past all began to unravel. There were no baby pictures of her, no pictures of Beatrice with her mother. Her aunt and uncle never talked about her mom—they always changed the subject when she brought it up. She'd thought it was because talking about it made them sad. So she never did. But in an instant everything had changed. It all made sense. They'd been lying to her for her whole life.

When Bea had run to her aunt and uncle crying, they started crying, too. They said how sorry they were, how they never meant to hurt her. Bea's guardian had been a kind old man, but he hadn't told them anything about her birth family. Uncle Pete had explained they thought it would be easier for Bea this way. They told her they didn't have to raise her, that they chose to; that no matter what some piece of paper said, she was a Parker; and that they loved her with all their hearts.

At first Bea thought this explanation was enough, but in the days since finding the letter she'd begun to question everything about her life and the people in it. All the differences between her and her cousin Patty clicked into place. Patty had always been so popular, so sure of herself. Maybe all along, on some deep level, Bea knew that she really didn't belong and that's why she wasn't cool or funny like Patty.

Bea turned and looked through the window, and saw Patty sound asleep on the matching twin bed across from her own empty one. Her cousin's creamy complexion was so different from Bea's face, with its odd freckles that seemed to be running off it rather than centered on her nose and checks. She'd shared this room with Patty for as long as she could remember, but now the pesky feeling that she was really just a guest had been planted in her head and she couldn't make it leave.

Bea looked back to the yard and the newly white landscape. The snow brought a richness to the quiet night. She loved the way the world sparkled in the blue glow of the streetlights. Even as she pushed one problem out of her head, another was ready to step in and take its place.

Her birthday was only days away. She tugged on the too-short sleeves of her fleece robe from last Christmas and wrapped her arms around her thin, boyish frame. On top of having been lied to her whole life, there was something definitely wrong with her body. She was going to be fifteen, and though she was impossibly tall, she still didn't have her period or boobs. The doctor had said to "just let it take its course," whatever that meant. Patty, who was three months younger, had gone through puberty almost two years ago. This was getting ridiculous. Maybe it would never happen. Maybe she would spend her entire life pretending she was normal, knowing on the inside it was all a lie.

Bea prayed Aunt Lucy would keep her promise about not throwing her a party. It would be so embarrassing. Now that Bea really looked at her life, she could see that all of the kids she and Patty hung out with were really just Patty's friends, not hers. Bea couldn't blame them.

She had all these ideas in her head, jokes, and quick comebacks, but the problem was she could never get them to come out of her mouth. Instead she'd spent her life playing the sidekick to her popular cousin. She was the wannabe to Patty's queen bee. That was her, "Wanna Bea."

She did what she was supposed to, dressed like everybody else, smiled when she should, but the actions didn't feel like they belonged to her. If she didn't fit in, it wasn't anyone else's fault. Nobody teased her or treated her badly. They hardly noticed her.

The snow continued to fall, and the cold traveled up her sleeves and settled into her body. Taking one last look, she stood, and wondered if this feeling of not belonging was just like the snow: coming and changing everything, but just for a moment in time. When she turned to go back inside she couldn't believe what she saw.

The window was closed.

In the summer the window always stuck open and they had trouble getting it to slide down at all. Bea tried to raise the window by pushing up with her palms flat against the glass, but it wouldn't budge. Now what?

Bea walked to the window above Patty's bed and tapped on the glass. Tigger, their orange tabby cat, lifted his head, but Patty didn't move. Bea slapped the window frame with the flat of her hand. Still nothing. She tried it again, harder, with quick short slaps. Patty slept so soundly that she wouldn't wake up unless Bea was loud enough to wake the whole house.

The last thing Bea needed right now was to get grounded. She looked through the window to her waiting bed. Why couldn't she have just stayed there? There was no other way—she'd have to shimmy down the gutter to get the spare key and go in through the back door. She had done it before; she could do it again. But it wasn't thirty-degree weather before and she'd been wearing rubber-soled gym shoes. Bea looked down at her feet, clad in froggy slippers from last Christmas. What had her aunt been thinking, buying matching pairs for Patty and her? Why couldn't she have gotten the thick-soled Uggs she had wanted but Patty hated?

It didn't matter. She had to get off the roof.

Despite her height, Beatrice was very light, bird-like even. For once she was happy about that fact. She took a deep breath and held it. In one long exhale, she blew all the air out of her lungs and bent down to take her slippers off. She stuffed them down into the deep pockets of her robe. The cold was like little knives on the bottoms of her feet. She reached over the edge of the roof and felt for the gutter. Once she found it, she turned around and stretched one leg over the edge and wrapped it around the cold metal. Thank God she was wearing pajamas rather than the extra-large T-shirt she usually wore. She threw her other leg over and wrapped it around as well. Ingnoring the burn of the cold metal, she tested her weight to make sure her feet would stop her from sliding out of control, and then lowered herself off the roof entirely. Inch by inch, she moved down. She could do this. She tried not to look at the ground far below her.

Down six feet, she reached the first seam in the metal. Its sharp edge made contact with Bea's right foot, sending searing pain into the ball of her foot and up through her entire body. She didn't mean to, it was an involuntary reaction, but her foot pulled away from the gutter. Her other foot didn't have enough traction to hold her and she began to slide down, fast. Her pajama leg ripped as it caught on the metal. She made the mistake of looking down. Her heart beat against her ribs, her grip loosened, and she went flailing toward the earth. The sparkling white snow rushed up at her with amazing speed.

As she made impact with the ground, she saw a flash of blue on the horizon. The light flickered and faded in an instant. The air was knocked out of her with a sucking sound. She tried to breathe and nothing happened. It was as if her lungs were stuck. She tried harder, blood pounding in her ears. Then she remembered. It was like the time she was thrown from that horse at camp—all except the flash of blue. She sat up, holding perfectly still. Calm, calm, calm. Her lungs began to loosen their rigid grip. She waited. Don't rush. And slowly, she took a sip of air. It stung like fire. Relieved despite the pain, she sat in one spot, cold and wet seeping through her pajamas, until breathing came easily again. When she moved, everything hurt. Her leg was bleeding. Her foot was bleeding more. Her ribs felt like they were wrapped in barbed wire. But she was pretty sure nothing was broken.

Brushing the snow from the bottoms of the blocks of ice that were her feet, she put her frog slippers back on with trembling hands. Her body moved like old Mrs. Anderson from down the block. How many times had Bea gotten trapped behind her in a narrow aisle at Hal's Grocery? She would have more patience with the old woman's shuffling in the future. She reached for the lone brick in the planting bed, lifted it, and retrieved the spare key. Her hands were so cold she had to steady one with the other to get the key in the lock. The whoosh of dry heat against her cold-burnt face when she opened the door made her feel safe again.

She put the key back, kicked the snow off her slippers, and limped upstairs. The only thing she wanted to do was fall into her bed, but she knew she had to clean up first.

In the bathroom with the door shut and only the nightlight on, she peeked under the torn fabric of her pajamas. The blood on the jagged skin had already started to crust over. Band-aids, big ones, were needed here. She dug through the medicine cabinet and pulled down the supplies. Any of the disinfectants were going to sting like hot coals, but she couldn't risk telling her aunt in a week's time that she had an infected knee. Cotton ball ready, she took a breath and poured antibacterial liquid on her knee first, then her foot. She bit her lip to keep from yelping. The pain of cleaning the cuts was almost worse than getting them.

Back in her bedroom, she pulled an XXL Bulls T-shirt out of the drawer and slipped it on. She stuffed the torn pajamas into the back of her closet. She would figure out what to do with them in the morning.

As her back hit the mattress, she felt a sharp pain in her side. There was a box in her bed. No, not a box, a present. Even in the dark she could see the sheen of the deep-pile, red velvet bow, feel the weight of the jacquard-print paper. There was a simple tag with a short note written in an elaborate script. It read:

Bayatrice,

Follow the initial instructions and this device will tell you what you need to know about where you come from.

It is of the utmost importance that you show it to no one.

That spelling of her name, Bayatrice, just like on the note with the papers in her aunt and uncle's closet. Oh God, did her aunt and uncle put this here to make up for what had happened? Did they know she'd been out on the roof? No, they would be up waiting for her if they did. And she sensed they wanted everything about her past to disappear. They would never bring it up on their own. Why would anyone put a gift—a gift with her birth name on it—in her bed in the middle of the night? And how would they have gotten in? That thought creeped her out.

She hopped out of bed and poked her head out of the bedroom to check the front door. Leaning over the railing on the landing, she could see it was still locked. The back door had been locked. Maybe she was in shock and just imagining this.

Back in her room, Bea was almost surprised to see the package still waiting for her. Of course, Patty would have slept through its arrival. She would have slept through marching band practice. Whatever it was, someone clearly meant for her to have it. So what could she do but open it? She sat on the edge of her bed with her back to Patty and pulled one end of the bow. The dense nap of the velvet rubbed against itself as she tugged. The ribbon loosened and then fell away under its own weight.

The box wasn't actually wrapped. It was covered with the textured paper, giving it not only an elegance but also stiff, durable sides. She lifted the box top and the bottom slowly slid out. And there it was.

But what was it?

Fitting snugly into a velvet-lined tray was a round-cornered rectangular chunk of shiny black plastic, a bit larger and thinner than her aunt's iPhone. No, not plastic. Glass? No...something else. It was some sort of...device, she concluded, but not like anything she had ever seen before. Bea picked it up. It was at least five times as heavy as an iPhone. She turned it over in her hands. It was cold and completely smooth, one solid piece with no seams, like tumbled-polished black stone. There were no instructions anywhere. She checked the floor in case they had fallen out. Nothing.

She was so tired now. Her mind was racing, but she couldn't force her body to keep up. She set the device, whatever it was, back into its box, tucked the mysterious gift under her bed and fell soundly into a dreamless sleep.

Chapter 2: Sick Day

Bea woke to find Patty standing over her, saying something. Bea blinked and tried to concentrate, but couldn't keep her eyes open. But Patty was persistent.

"Bea!" she yelled, stomping her foot. "Bea, you have to wake up! We have school." Too tired to answer, Bea rolled over. Patty bellowed towards the door. "Mom, something is the matter with Bea. She won't wake up." Patty gave Bea's shoulder one last shake before going back to dressing herself.

Aunt Lucy dashed in and sat on the edge of the bed, buttoning the last button on her blouse as she spoke. "Bea, honey, aren't you feeling well?" She felt Bea's forehead. "You don't feel warm. You've got to get up now." She patted Bea's knee, lovingly trying to stir her. The light touch was like a hot poker on Bea's wounded knee. The burst of fire made Bea sit bolt upright.

"Oh, you are in there." Aunt Lucy laughed. "Wow, you were really out." She paused. "Are you with us? Everything okay?"

Bea blinked and it all rushed back to her—the fall, cleaning her cuts, hiding her torn pajamas, the gift, the note. She forced a smile, as if her body didn't ache or sting. "Oh, yeah, I'm fine."

"You're sure you're okay?" Aunt Lucy's brow knitted. "You look a little pale. You shouldn't push yourself if you aren't feeling well. I don't want another massive bout of bronchitis like you had last year."

"No, really—" Bea began to say she was just fine, because that was what she did. Lived between the lines. It was a reflex, like your knee being tapped in the doctor's.

"Uncle Pete and I have to go into the office, so you'd be alone. Would you be okay with that?"

Patty jumped in, as always, answering the question whether it had been asked of her or not. "Like hello, mom, we're almost fifteen."

"Well, I know you two are all grown up," Aunt Lucy said, swallowing a smile, "but it's still okay to want to have someone around when you aren't feeling well."

Bea looked into her aunt's face. It wasn't Bea's being sick that her aunt was worried about. Ever since her "discovery," her aunt and uncle had gone out of their way to be nice to her, put her name first when they called everyone to dinner, making sure she was a part of every conversation. It was totally annoying, since she hated being the center of attention. She was pretty sure that wasn't the effect they were going for.

This last week had been so messed up. She hadn't been able to focus at school. The teachers at St. Ignatius frowned upon "daydreaming on school time," a phrase that had *never* been aimed at her before finding those stupid papers. And now with the device and a note offering information about her past? She wouldn't be able to go five minutes without getting caught with her mind wandering. "Being alone is great. I mean…I'm not really feeling well and I wouldn't mind if I had to stay here alone." She spoke slowly and low, hoping she sounded more believable than when her oldest cousin, P.J., faked being sick.

Aunt Lucy stood and gave Bea a half-sad smile. "I'll call the school."

The next forty minutes went on forever. Teddy got into a battle with Patty outside their bedroom door about whether he could come in to say goodbye or not. Maybe Patty's intentions were good, but the volume of the conversation made Bea think it was more about Patty being in charge than concern for her. She heard P.J. say, "Come on, little man, we'll check on her when we get home…I'm sure she'll make it 'til then."

"Feel better, Beezy," Teddy's small voice called to her as he was ushered away.

With that they all went downstairs. Could people eat any slower? What were they doing down there, remodeling the kitchen?

Her head was on the verge of exploding in anticipation when they all finally packed up and left. Patty had run back in for her forgotten cell phone, but then they were all gone.

Bea got out of bed and ran to the window to check the driveway, just to be sure they had really left. Her legs couldn't move fast enough to get her across the room to retrieve the gift from under her bed. She lifted the dust ruffle, and it was really still there.

Tigger barely stirred as Bea pushed him to the foot of her bed. She grabbed the box and slid it across the gritty hardwood, inadvertently bringing some stray dust bunnies with it.

The box opened with a gentle whoosh and she lifted the thing out of its neatly fitted velvet seat. She checked again for instructions with no luck.

In the daylight, the present was even more amazing. The velvet was deeper and richer than she had noticed last night, the black of the device like a bottomless pool. She clutched it in her hands and it was still cold, much colder than the room. And today, as she held it and stared into its surface, it also seemed to…tingle. She had to be imagining that. Juggling it between her hands, she noticed that there seemed to be a certain way that the weight of the thing settled best in her palms: widthwise, one hand on either side, fingers underneath, with her thumbs free to move across its face.

She sat holding it like that, contemplating what it was and where it had come from.

Then it happened.

It didn't just tingle—it pulsed. Startled, she dropped it on the bed, jostling Tigger. *What is this thing?* All sorts of sci-fi horror plots ran through her head—thanks to P.J.'s insisting the family watch Alien Thrill Theater every Friday night. Mind melding and pod people came to mind.

That was just stupid. Of course whoever left it had to know about her real family. They had used her name the way it was written on the note from that Ed Vaslow guy. The note with the gift had said it would tell her about "where she came from." Besides, if it were a plot to take over the world, they certainly wouldn't choose some practically-invisible, fourteen-year-old from the middle of nowhere. Whatever this thing was, it definitely had something to do with her past.

Maybe if she told Patty, the two of them could...but she stopped herself there. Bea knew exactly what would happen. Patty would take over solving this mystery and Bea would be left watching from the sidelines. Her whole life had been entangled with Patty's—her cousin who wasn't really her cousin. It wasn't fair that Patty knew how to flirt with boys, how to put together cool outfits, how to crack jokes that everybody laughed at—things that Bea couldn't even imagine for herself. No, she had to start trying to figure things out on her own... beginning with this. Bea picked up the strange gift again and clutched it to her. This device might hold answers that her aunt and uncle couldn't—or wouldn't—give her.

She sat on the bed turning it over, shaking it, examining it. Nothing. It was just a lump, like a cell phone with no face or buttons. When she held it steady, it naturally sank into that comfortable sideways position between her palms. As she brushed the smooth cool surface with her thumbs, she heard a noise downstairs, then a jiggling of the door handle. Someone was trying to get in the front door. Aunt Lucy always locked the door. But Patty had come back in... There was a soft thud against the front door. What if whoever had left this thing here was coming back for her? They had gotten in before. She jumped into her bed and pulled the covers over her head. How dumb was that? She wasn't a little kid anymore; hiding wasn't the answer.

As much as she wanted to know about her past, she wasn't crazy about the idea of being kidnapped by strangers, no matter what they knew about her. She hopped out of bed and threw her comforter over the device, ran to the closet and pulled out Patty's softball bat. Grabbing it with both hands, she started toward the door. Wait. She might not be a baby anymore, but she wasn't Jet Li either. She heard the front door unstick from its weather-stripping and start to slide open. Her heart was pounding. Still holding the bat, almost hugging it, she pulled the door open and ducked behind it. She heard footsteps, big heavy footsteps.

Bea held her breath. Through the crack between the door hinges, she could see a dark figure moving—in her house! She squeezed her eyes shut and pulled the bat closer to her.

"Bea, I'm home!" Uncle Pete called out.

Bea's tense muscles melted and she slid down the wall, still shaking. She could hear him on the steps. She came out from behind the door, leaving the bat on the floor, and stood in her doorway.

Uncle Pete continued to talk as he reached the top of the stairs, opening a piece of mail. "Hope I didn't scare you, but my meeting was canceled. Thought you might like some company." He stopped on the last step and stared at her. "You look awful. You're white as a ghost." Bea rushed toward him and threw her arms around him, crumpling the letter in his hands. Uncle Pete kissed her forehead. "You're freezing and clammy."

"No, I'm fine, really." Bea's voice was soft and shaky as she pulled away, more embarrassed than anything else. Geeze, all this stuff was really messing with her brain.

"Yeah, fine, right. Back to bed. I'll get you some tea." He turned Bea around and gave her a gentle push in the direction of her bed. She obeyed willingly. No matter what had happened in the last week, he still felt like family, safe and warm. But he had *lied* to her. She didn't know what to feel. It hurt her head to think about it.

Her cell phone vibrated on her nightstand, the rhinestone case making it skitter across the hard surface. It was a text from Patty: "r u bettr?" Bea shut the phone without replying. Just something else to make her head hurt.

She really needed to lie down.

Her hand slipped beneath the covers and tucked the device under her pillow as she flopped into the bed. She closed her eyes and waited for Uncle Pete to come back with tea.

***

Next thing she knew she was waking up and the sun was already low in the sky. There was a cold cup of tea on her nightstand. How long had she been out? It was already three o'clock. Everybody would be home in an hour. The entire day was almost gone and she wasn't any closer to understanding the device.

Bea got out of bed and went to the edge of the railing on the landing. She stuck her head out as far as she could. Through the den door, she could see Uncle Pete in his recliner in front of the TV, with an open newspaper across his chest. He was sound asleep.

At least she had an hour.

She went back to her bed and pulled the device from under her pillow. Tigger looked up at her as she jostled the bed. "Okay, cat, you are sworn to secrecy," she mocked, feeling like she was taking this all too seriously. He looked up at her with heavy-lidded eyes and curled back up into a fur pillow.

Wincing as her knee bent, she sat cross-legged and got the thing into the last position she'd been holding it. Looking hard at the surface, she felt it start to pulse right away—but this time she held on. It hummed an odd otherworldly-sounding *bwoomm-bwoomm*, and then its face began to glow a black-purple, in rhythm with the pulse. She felt the smooth surface begin to expand in her hands. The sides where her thumbs were stretched down to fill the hollows of her palms. The whole device was growing. It was now three times its original size, as big as her diary. The material it was made of didn't get any softer—it was still as rigid as metal—but now its thin shape was warm against her skin. The dark glowing haze began to clear, revealing a brilliant blue screen with multicolored symbols she couldn't identify.

She absentmindedly brushed one of the symbols in the center with her thumb. It was made up of light, but she could *feel* its shape. Suddenly the blue shimmered and faded and an image of a slate-colored stone wall appeared. It filled the whole surface, edge to edge, except the sides where her thumbs were. The picture held still for an instant and then began to move, and Bea felt as if she were walking along a wall. It was the most realistic movie she had ever seen, better than 3-D. It felt like she could just put her hand right into the screen and touch the stone.

After a few seconds, the wall ended, opening up onto an enormous room full of elaborately dressed people. The outfits they were wearing were unlike anything Bea had ever seen before—lots of iridescent blues and greens, and the colors of the ladies' dresses moved and changed as if they were TV screens. The men wore silver mesh vests over radiantly colored shirts with long pointed collars. Women and men were adorned with intricate, elegant jewelry with gems so luminescent they could have been powered by batteries.

The room itself was unlike anything she'd ever seen, either—a watercolor dream. Swirls of hues dancing on—no, *in*—the walls. They looked as if they weren't solid at all, but translucent, maybe just made up of whims of light. The incredibly high ceilings were decorated with expansive geometric metal sculptures that resembled dragonfly wings, gracefully fluttering and hovering above the crowd. Musicians at the front of the hall were playing gleaming metallic instruments that they never actually touched, but which they seemed to control with sweeping arm movements and swaying. Everyone was laughing and smiling.

On a platform near the orchestra stood a man and woman, more finely dressed than anyone else, wearing simple crowns on their heads. Maybe a king and queen? The queen was holding a plump, giggling baby, bouncing it on her hip as she spoke. Wherever Bea looked she could focus in on things at will. Whatever this device was, it was very cool—so much more realistic than any smart phone or tablet she had ever seen.

She shifted her gaze to the windows and that scene filled her vision. The images were even crisper and clearer than they'd be if she were there in person. Outside the glassless pane window were wispy clouds in a sea of sky, bluer than the sky ever was in Illinois. She had a close-up view of the finely etched metal, bent into too-perfect curves. She could faintly hear music and chatter. She turned back to look at the baby, and the whole of the room swept past her vision, as if she were controlling a movie camera. The baby was round and freckled with a dollop of red hair. The queen was trying to get everyone's attention. But Bea couldn't hear what she was saying.

"Where's the volume on this thing?" Bea spoke aloud. All of a sudden, the music was blaring and the queen was shouting above the din in a regal, melodic voice, "Heysay, Heysay!" The music was as loud as the TV turned up full volume. Her hands reacted to the sudden noise before her brain and sent the device sailing. Immediately the noise stopped and the screen went black as it shifted back to its original size.

She waited a moment, listening for Uncle Pete. After a moment of silence, she approached the viewer—that's what she'd decided to call it.

What was she supposed to do with this thing? Across the room its dark surface begged for her to pick it back up. At the same time a little flinch in her belly was flashing a warning. There was something very strange about how it felt in her hands, about the promise it made, about the mystery of it. But why would someone send her a high-tech device to watch movies? What did any of this have to do with her past? Didn't matter—she heard the minivan pull up in the driveway. She tucked the viewer under her pillow and lay back down on her bed.

There was a clatter in the foyer, then thundering footfalls on the steps, and finally the somewhat restrained knock on her door. Teddy.

Bea could hear her aunt calling up to him softly from downstairs, "Teddy, leave her be. She might still be sleeping."

"It's okay, Aunt Lucy, I'm awake," Bea called back.

Teddy burst into the room and ran to give Bea a hug. His backpack and teddy bear slid forward and thumped Bea in the shoulder. "Are you better, Beasey? Can I fluff your pillow or somethin'?" He was so sincere.

"Yes, I'm better. And I think my pillow really could use some fluffing." She leaned forward to release the pillow before she remembered the viewer. As Teddy reached, Bea quickly slipped her hand under the pillow and slid the device down next to her body just he pulled the pillow from behind her. This secret thing was harder than she'd thought it would be.

Teddy made extravagant arm motions, complete with "fluffing noises." When everything was to his liking he said, "That's better, I think."

"Oh, that is much better. Thanks," Bea said, trying not to laugh. She settled back into the pillow and gave a satisfied look, the viewer safely tucked up next to her hip. Teddy puffed up almost as much as the pillow. "How was your day?" she asked.

"Good. We had a birthday party for Sister Marie and she gave us all butterscotches and we got to eat them right then. We didn't even have to wait," Teddy said, with the excitement only a six-year-old can feel for candy. Bea wished that a butterscotch could still do that for her. How had everything gotten so complicated?

"Wow, that's great—" Bea was cut off as Patty stormed in.

"Teddy, mom told you to leave Bea alone." Patty threw her backpack on her bed, put her hand on her hip, and stared at him. "You'd better beat it or I'm gonna tell."

"Awww," Teddy said, and stared back. Patty stomped her foot. "I'm goin', I'm goin'," he sulked. He started to leave, stopped at the doorway, and looked back. "Are you still gonna read to me tonight?"

"Nooo, she's sick, remember?" Patty said.

"I'm a lot better. I can still read to you," Bea said, smiling at Teddy. He stuck his tongue out at Patty and ran into the hall.

"Whatever, just go, toad," Patty said and swiped the door closed behind him. Patty spoke to Bea as she took off her school uniform. "You know, I was just trying to help you out. You never say 'no' to him. I thought maybe you'd want to rest." Patty always did that, stepped in and "took care" of Bea, always assuming she knew what was best for her. It had never really bothered Bea before. She had never thought about doing things her own way; it hadn't occurred to her that she had a "way." Now that the thought had come to her it made her mad, but she couldn't exactly figure out what she was mad at.

"I like having him around," Bea said, with a hard edge to her voice. But she immediately felt bad. Lately, controlling her emotions was going about as smoothly as watching P.J. learn to drive—start, stop, go really fast, then squeal the brakes.

"You know, Bea, ever since you found that stuff in mom's closet..." Patty spoke like she was looking for the right words. "I don't know. I mean, I'm just saying it's not a big deal. Nothing's different."

Bea was surprised at how hot the anger burned in her chest. How could Patty say that? If Patty weren't so busy trying to manage other people's lives and stopped to think about what Bea really needed, maybe she'd know how big a deal it really was. "Errrg," Bea huffed. Patty would *never* understand. Bea rolled over and pulled the blankets up over her head. She knew Patty was standing there staring at her, waiting for an answer.

"Bea, nothing else has changed," Patty said. "Just you."

She heard Patty let out an exaggerated exhale and then stomp out of the room.

She stayed in her room just long enough to avoid dinner prep duties. Tigger followed her as she came downstairs slowly, trying not to limp because of the pain in her foot and knee—probably added a nice sick effect. The whole family was around the table just starting to dig into their dinners. P.J. sat at the far end with ear buds in, eating to the beat. Patty sat next to him, spoon in one hand, texting with the other, purposefully not looking at Bea.

Teddy waved. "I saved your seat." He motioned to the seat next to him, across from Patty. The seat she always sat in. She rubbed the top of Teddy's head as she sat down. At least it still felt normal with him.

Uncle Pete tossed a napkin at P.J. "No electronics at the table." P.J. pulled the ear buds out and set his MP3 player on the table. "That goes for you, too, miss with thumbs-faster-than-light," he said, looking at Patty. Bea couldn't help but wonder if Patty was texting mean things about her, telling the whole world they weren't really related.

"Hey, hon, you feel like eating? I could make you some chicken soup," Aunt Lucy said, starting to get up.

It was the smell of Aunt Lucy's chili that had brought Bea downstairs. Until she had caught its scent she'd forgotten that she hadn't eaten anything all day.

"Oh, you don't have to make anything special for me. I'll just eat whatever you've made."

"That's sweet, honey, but if you're not feeling well—"

"I'm feeling better," Bea interrupted her. "I don't know what it was but I think it's gone. I'm just tired."

Uncle Pete looked at her skeptically. "You sure? You looked awful this afternoon."

"Really, I'm fine." Bea heaped chili into a bowl. It smelled so good.

"I guess your appetite is back, at least," Aunt Lucy said, sitting back down and smiling.

As Bea picked up her spoon, getting ready to dig in, she had a pang of regret. Her fake sick day had caused her to miss helping her aunt make the chili. And that was one of her favorite things to do, a special thing she and her aunt did alone. They never used a recipe. Aunt Lucy liked to just "feel it."

This kitchen, with its honey-colored cabinets and baker-print wallpaper, had so many memories. Aunt Lucy teaching Patty and her how to use the cookie press at Christmas—what weird-shaped tree cookies they'd had that year. Patty and her at the sink putting temporary tattoos on every visible inch of Teddy's skin—Uncle Pete nearly swallowed his tongue when he saw that. And last summer, handing water balloons out the window to P.J. only to have Aunt Lucy throw one at her right there in the middle of the kitchen! Bea had never laughed so hard. Tears welled up but she swallowed them; she didn't even know why she felt like crying. She was mad at herself for feeling this way and scared that maybe things would never feel normal again. All these stupid emotions made Bea's stomach churn. She pushed the bowl of chili away from her.

"Maybe your stomach's not quite as ready as your appetite," Aunt Lucy said, reaching for the bowl. "I'll fix you some chicken soup."

Chapter 3: The Waiting

As Vaslow walked through the market the twin suns were sinking onto the horizon, casting a deep gold light. The sounds of the colorful t'ouhk flags snapping in the breeze blended with animal bleats and water vendors urging him to buy today before the price went up tomorrow—making a frenetic symphony. Because there were mandated Allegiance Celebrations tomorrow, the market was more crowded than usual. A sea of faces passed, some Dillag, with their deep red skin and broad yellow eyes, and some Z'rhed, the color of water flowing over sand, with eyes so pale as to have no color at all, their facial markings barely visible. There were almost no Cass, like Vaslow himself, with his cream-colored skin with brown facial and body marking. For the most part it was Sloan faces that filled the market, with their wiry black hair and tawny unmarked skin. Even though Vaslow had lived on the market's edge for nearly two years, the sight of all the different races still seemed foreign to him. A few of the vendors nodded to him as he passed, and as slight as the gestures were, that small connection was something he had thought would forever be out of his reach when he'd first arrived here.

Vaslow stopped at his favorite meat vendor's stall. He nodded at Shashi, a middle-aged man with a crooked shoulder, who sat in the shade of the tent corner. The Sloan man didn't rise to hawk his wares when he noticed who his customer was. Vaslow always bought his meat here, though Shashi continued to treat him as if they'd never met. Braided meats hung three rows deep from the tent supports, an uncommonly good supply today. Vaslow knew he should buy while the stock was so plentiful. He fingered a twisted rope of particularly plump aul beast. But he couldn't force his mind to concentrate on such mundane tasks as buying groceries.

It had been two days since he'd delivered the cantomount, wrapped like a present, and still no response from Bayatrice. *Why hadn't the girl contacted him? Had something gone wrong?* He had designed the program on the cantomount to make the instruction key the first symbol she would press. He must have miscalculated. If she didn't make contact soon, he'd have to figure out how to make another jump. Her life depended on it. Someone in this Jaru-forsaken district would have to help him—he'd find a way to convince them.

He could sense her, feel that she was still safe—for the moment. He'd been able to sense her all these years, the same as if she were blood of his own line. He couldn't explain that—by genetics it shouldn't be happening—but it was. Perhaps it was a bond that had been forged when he was with her on Earth. He didn't know, but he accepted that fact as a responsibility. One he wouldn't shirk, no matter his status, age, or reputation in the court. It was what kept him honing his fighting skills, kept him sparring with imagined enemies, kept his senses always on the ready. He wouldn't walk away from her. He hadn't abandoned her all those years ago when the coup had occurred, and he wouldn't now, as tensions rose again.

He released the rope and left the meat swinging—an insult he'd normally be more careful about—and walked on down the row of vendors.

He'd been able to make the jump to deliver the cantomount to Bayatrice because he'd finally convinced one of the market vendors to put him in touch with a Sloan techie. As if by smoke and mirrors, the meeting was arranged and the techie had scrambled his craft's energy signature, enabling him to jump offworld and get to Earth without detection. It was risky jumping offworld without proper authorization, and the penalty for getting caught was labor camps. But there were no Sloan detained in those labor camps for jumping, and yet they always managed to have a supply of goods from forbidden offworld. No one had to tell him that they knew a thing or two about the shadier side of technology. And as he'd suspected, they were masters at scrambling any craft's energy signature, making it virtually undetectable to Protectorate scanners. But if he was going to make another unauthorized jump he would need his ship rescrambled, which meant asking for another favor. That would take time—time Bayatrice didn't have.

Vaslow stepped off the path at the market's largest intersection, where the wide gap allowed him a view past the marketplace, past low sand-colored buildings, and out over the band of stiff gnarled trees that rimmed the coastline beyond. From where he stood, looking east, he couldn't see the towering buildings of Verlona, the capital city that loomed beyond the edges of Sloantown. For a moment he could let himself think that he'd never have to leave this place, with its exotic faces, pungent foods, and thrum of foreign languages. That these streets teeming with the few minorities left on Vedra were his home. That no weight of responsibility pulled him back to the other side of the city's pristine walls. That time wasn't running out for Bayatrice. But with that final thought, Vaslow's moment of imagined peace was gone, evaporated like steam off a pot of Li. And reality was back, sharp as a killing knife.

Stepping onto the path, back in pace with the fray of other shoppers, Vaslow thought he'd happily risk any torture if he could just go and rescue the girl and bring her back. But if he tried to leave without having his craft rescrambled, he'd be arrested before he even left Vedra's atmosphere, left to rot in some prison cell. And Bayatrice would surely not survive her patou. A spike of fear shot through him at the thought of what would happen to her if she underwent the coming of age transformation while still on Earth. He'd buy time by placating the Protectorate—it was the only way to keep them at bay. Even though the thought of it turned his stomach sour, he'd have to play politics.

The Protectorate had been hounding him to deliver a sound bite for the news feeds. They wanted to show the citizens of Vedra once and for all that the loyalist resistance was dead. The Allegiance vows made at the Celebrations every six years were meant to be a voluntary vote of confidence. Even the most respected royals of the past had received, at most, a three-quarters pledge from those in the government and the military. The Protectorate, however, had their sights set on being the first rulers with one hundred percent commitment. And they knew Vaslow's pledge still carried weight; his years in retirement hadn't changed that. The words he spoke tomorrow would crush any last bits of hope in anyone foolish enough to dream of a world without the Protectorate.

Once he said what they wanted him to say for the news feeds, they would let him be. It would betray everything he'd fought for, every rule he'd lived by, but Vaslow would make this one false vow to uphold the vow he'd made as a leader of the Royal Guard all those long years ago. He cursed the Protectorate and the workings of this world.

He lived in this rather undesirable district of Pleet—more commonly known as Sloantown—partly because it was densely populated with Sloan and partly because it was the furthest borough from the palace, government buildings and all the political things he so longed to separate himself from. Sloantown was one of the last havens for Loyalists and those that wanted to live without their every move being catalogued by the Protectorate.

Here, beyond the brush that painted the rest of Vedra, people lived the way their ancestors had. They did just enough to maintain a tentative peace with the Protectorate and its Guard—obeyed mandatory observance of Vedrian holidays, taught their children Vedri in schools—so that it was a district forgotten, or at least ignored, by the Protectorate. The businesses here closed their doors at sundown as had been the custom before Vedrian society had been mechanized. They hung meats in the traditional twists, honoring the mind, body, and spirit of the animal, and ate only food harvested on land within a day's walk. In the eyes of "civil society" these people were the naïve, unclean masses. Vaslow was happy to get lost in this throng.

But getting lost wasn't easy. The Sloan kept their interactions—and their coveted technical skills—within their securely woven community. It shouldn't have surprised him. They were a leery people—a millennia of persecution had carved that into their nature. They weren't the only minority without Cass marking on their faces and necks, but they valued the absence of this trait more than any other. His fingers found their way to the beard he had grown to hide the markings during the time he had spent on Earth. He never could bring himself to shave it, always keeping himself on the ready should he need to return. He guessed that decision served him well in this part of town, making the differences between him and those he desperately wanted to befriend less pronounced.

His pace waned and he meandered through the crowded market, forcing the foot traffic to split around him as if he were a rock in the stream.

When Vaslow had moved into his rented rooms overlooking the market, he'd kept to himself, sensing that being too eager would make his task harder. Feigning no interest in those around him, it took all his will power to wait them out. He knew they wondered about him. Why would a pocked, as the Sloan referred to those with Cass markings, want to live among the "unclean?" A delicate dance of curiosity and protection had been played out until about a year ago when one Sloan, Wharton, had befriended him. Well, friend might be a bit of an overstatement.

Vaslow recalled the day it happened. It was nothing he had planned. Nothing he could have planned. He had been shopping in the market when a vendor manning a booth he typically shopped at called to him, "No krint today, buddy-buddy. You try tomorrow."

Vaslow was irked; he hadn't had a ripe krint in weeks. It was a simple thing, just a sweet, protein-rich fruit, but it was the one constant he had come to expect in his nomadic existence: a couple of krint for breakfast. It was true that since the Protectorate had taken over food wasn't as plentiful as it had been under the royals' reign, but a krint was, after all, considered a poor man's food. He should be able to find a decent one in this of all places.

Just as he was about to give up and do without breakfast, he heard a small cry. It could have been the yelp of a dog underfoot, just an inconsequential complaint of something small, but the way it ended piqued Vaslow's ever-alert senses. He left the canvas tents of the market and turned down a small alley. He saw the back of two enormous black-cloaked Protectorate guards and a small crumpled figure in a dusty robe. The words the guards spoke were partially lost in the flurry of blows they were delivering: "...tell your father every action has a consequence..." He pulled the hood of his cloak up over his face and walked toward them.

"Keep walking," the first guard said upon noticing him. "This doesn't concern you."

Vaslow didn't slow his pace.

"This is a military matter," the other guard said. "Go back the way you came." Vaslow maintained his approach.

"Are you deaf?" The first guard spoke again, obviously used to being obeyed. Vaslow looked past the guard to the heap on the ground. He saw, between the folds of the dirty robe, the face of a Sloan child not more than nine or ten. Rivers of clean skin marked the tear tracks on the dust-covered cheeks. Vaslow continued to move toward the guards.

"Leave now or you become our next task." The guards turned from the child and faced him.

"I'm interested in your current task." Vaslow spoke in an even-pitched tone. "The fight seems a bit unfair, doesn't it? Maybe I can even the odds."

"You had your warning," the first guard said, motioning for his partner to take care of this new problem.

The second guard pulled a small club from his hip belt and approached Vaslow. Rather than backing off, Vaslow walked right into him, forcing the man to bend his arm as he swung at Vaslow's shoulder. Vaslow absorbed the full force of the blow without flinching. Before the guard had a chance to pull back the club, Vaslow shoved the larger man's chest in a quick sudden motion. It caught the soldier by surprise and he stumbled backwards into his partner. Then, in an a flash, Vaslow leapt up and spun with amazing speed, the crisp edge of his hand connecting with the first guard's throat, then the second, rendering them both unconscious. In an instant it was over. The child stood, shaking. Vaslow dropped his hood and knelt. The familiarity of the small face made his breath catch in his chest. The boy reminded him of a promising student from years ago who'd nearly broken his heart when he pledged to the Protectorate. The resemblance was so strong he almost said the name Islook aloud.

The realization of his own foolish emotions broke his reverie. "Are you hurt? Can you move?" Vaslow asked.

The child stared up at Vaslow with wild eyes, and then, without warning, began to run.

"Well, I guess you're not hurt," he said to the back of the retreating boy.

The next morning he opened his front door to find a small basket of beautifully ripe krint on his stoop. And he had remained in good supply since.

It was Wharton's son he had rescued that day. By everything he'd seen, Wharton led the marketplace contingent—and most likely the entire Sloan community. Vaslow no longer found shops inexplicably lacking what he needed or closing for lunch as he approached. Over this past year, at chance meetings over a cup of Li or buying meat in the market, Wharton had casually thrown him tips on how to avoid Protectorate detection. But he needed more than a comforting breakfast, happenstance meetings, or illicit advice. Bayatrice's fate—and possibly the fate of all Vedra—rested solely on his ability to get Wharton to help him again.

The sounds of vendors pulling down their wares and dropping the flaps over their stalls for the evening brought Vaslow back to the present. He couldn't avoid the unpleasantness that lay ahead of him any longer; it was time to go home and begin preparations for the Allegiance Celebration he must attend tomorrow. He made his way out of the chaos of the closing market and back towards the rooms he called home.

Chapter 4: A Quiet Place

Bea woke up early on Saturday morning; the sun was just cresting the horizon. That dang dream with its suffocating darkness and eerie voice had come again. Her subconscious was not doing a very good job of working things out. The dream left her feeling even more unsettled. Her stomach hurt, she guessed because she'd barely eaten any of the chicken soup her aunt had made for her. Maybe a pastry and some fresh air would help her shake this queasy feeling before she started in on the viewer again. She threw on a sweater and her favorite pair of Mudd jeans, and pulled a stocking cap over her bed-tangled red hair.

Quietly sneaking down the stairs, she put on her baby-blue parka with the white faux fur trim and tucked the device in the deep side pocket. She went out the back door and through the Perkins' yard to Elm Street, cutting through backyards until she got to Maple. Normally going to Hal's Grocery was part of her Saturday morning routine with Patty. She wondered what Patty would say when she woke up and saw that Bea had gone without her.

She followed Maple to the corner of 49th. As she walked the quiet streets, watching the few winter birds that were brave enough to stick around peck at the snow, she thought about how many times she'd done this walk with 'her cousin.' They had the routine down. It was Patty who'd come up with the idea of sticking the pastry bags in their coats to keep them warm on the walk home. Bea thought it was brilliant, hating the way the microwave made the flakey texture of the pastries mushy when you tried to reheat them.

All her best memories were with Patty. In her bones she knew Patty was right—it was only Bea who was different. It was unfair to Patty, but at the same time Bea couldn't be Patty's shadow anymore. The pieces didn't quite fit together in her head. It wasn't Patty's fault, but it couldn't be the same. As weird as it felt to be doing this alone, it also felt right. Maybe if she just found out what the viewer was all about, maybe if she just got some answers to the questions about her past, maybe then she could make everything right again.

As she rounded the corner, it was so quiet she could hear the buzz of the store sign—Hal's Grocery—that had hung above the store since Uncle Pete was a kid. Bea loved that old sign.

The thickly painted door opened with the sound of the chimes that dangled from the hinge. "Be with you in a minute," Hal's deep, gravelly voice called out from the back.

Hal Beech came out through the heavy curtain that separated the backroom from the store area. "Well, well, Miss Bea." He shook his head and smiled, his white teeth contrasting with his umber skin as he spoke. "Patty sick this morning?"

"No. I just wanted to get going early." It felt like a lie and she wasn't sure why. Bea went right to the pastry case, pulled out a still-warm cinnamon roll and dropped it into a wax paper sack with the metal tongs, making sure it was a clean drop. She didn't want any of the frosting getting on the outside of the bag. She neatly folded the top down and creased the edge.

"Hmm. How 'bout a hot cocoa to go with that?" He pulled at his grey-streaked mustache in a knowing way.

"How 'bout make it a mocha."

"You kids are too young for coffee. But far be it from me to get in the way of a sale."

Bea smiled as Hal turned to make the drink. The curtains at the back of the store ruffled and Calvin Beech, school geek, came out carrying a box of canned peas. Nearly her height, he was a skinny dark-skinned African-American boy with braces. He looked like such a nerd, especially when he smiled, which he rarely ever did. It was a common belief that Calvin was the smartest kid in the entire school.

"I didn't know you worked here," Bea said. She'd never noticed that he and Hal shared the same last name before. Hal seemed too old to be his father. Maybe Hal was his grandfather.

"Well, I guess you don't know much then, do you," he said in typical Calvin fashion as he walked past her without slowing.

"Well..." was all she could get out before he retreated to the back room. *What a jerk*, she thought. But then she thought maybe he was tired of living life on the outside too. He'd been an outsider longer than she had; maybe that's just what it did to you. Hal handed her the mocha. She thanked him, paid, and thought it was too bad for a nice man like Hal, having such a pain for a grandson.

"Tell your family I said hello," Hal said, giving her a corny little salute as she left. Bea winced a bit at the word family, but it was it her family, wasn't it?

She tucked the wax paper bag into the top part of her jacket and zipped it up. It felt warm against her chest as she set off in search of someplace she could just sit and look at the viewer undisturbed.

She wasn't used to trying to think of a place to be alone, someplace Patty wouldn't want to go. Of course, the roof. Patty hated it out there, especially when it was cold.

She got home and ran right upstairs. She opened her bedroom door as quietly as she could, though she knew that Patty could sleep through bombs dropping. She crawled out the bedroom window and pulled the curtains shut as best she could from the outside, and then tucked her Pink Pearl eraser on the sill to keep the window from shutting all the way. No way she wanted a repeat of the other night. Getting settled on the orange crate, she pulled the pastry out of her jacket, tore open the sack, and took a huge bite. It was warm and buttery, practically melting in her mouth, but when it hit her stomach she felt like it might not stay there. Bea took a few smaller bites and swallowed a sip of the mocha. It took a minute for her stomach to come to a tentative peace with the food. She dug the viewer from her pocket, the thought of what she might find making her stomach lurch again.

The viewer settled in her hands, tingled and expanded. The image of the stone wall moved in front of her, the soft music growing louder.

The moment was shattered when Patty bellowed from her bed, "Bea, what the hell are you doing out on the roof?" Patty was sitting up just enough to be sure she'd be heard through the cracked window.

"Nothing. Just sitting. Go back to sleep."

"Like, duh, it's cold. It feels cold enough to snow in here now." Patty curled up and pulled the covers over her head. "Just close the window. Gah, Bea, what are you thinking?"

Even half-asleep, Patty could muster a condescending tone that shot right through you. Patty had used it on others over the years, but Bea wasn't usually on the receiving end of it. "Whatever." Heat rose in Bea's ears. Maybe she shouldn't have left the window open, maybe Patty was right, but that didn't seem to matter. The fire spread across her face and made her mouth dry. Ordinarily, she'd apologize—even if she hadn't done something wrong—just to keep the peace. But whatever burning emotion that had hold of her wouldn't let that happen today. And maybe it was for the best—it wouldn't look so odd now if Bea wanted to go off by herself, but where else could she go?

She went back through the window, downstairs, into the kitchen, and out through the mudroom into the garage, making sure to shut the door tight to muffle any unexpected noise. Ignoring all the stacked boxes and the faint smell of motor oil, she crossed to the back of the garage and sat on an aluminum trashcan, the viewer already in her hand. No one would look for her here.

The now-familiar tingle, then the shape-shifting and the *bwoom-bwoom*, came as expected. It instantly took her to the last place she had been—moving along the wall, getting closer to the party. As the wall ended and people came into view, the music was rocking-loud.

"Quiet!" she shouted, and it was immediately muted. "Louder." The sound came on, barely audible. "Louder," she tried again. The sound level came up a notch. She could hear, but it was no longer blaring. "Back up." Nothing happened. "Rewind." Still nothing. "Repeat." The image on the screen changed to the stone wall she had seen earlier. She concentrated on every inch of that wall, the sound getting louder as she moved along. Determined to pay attention to every detail this time, looking for some sort of clue to help this all make sense, she forced her focus to be sharp. The harder she stared, the more real it became.

Then, suddenly, she wasn't staring at a flat, small screen. The world inside the viewer wrapped itself around her. Every way she turned the illusion surrounded her. She was no longer looking *at* the room, she was *in it*. She was standing at the edge of the great ballroom next to a woman who seemed as real as the trash can she was sitting on.

The woman stared forward with rapt attention, gown glowing, her hair done up in elaborate tiny twists, revealing strange dark marks along either side of her long neck and up the sides of her face. Bea wondered if perhaps it was some sort of animal pattern makeup.

Looking ahead, Bea began to move forward, walking but not walking at the same time. Partygoers surrounded her and she could smell the women's perfume and the spicy scent of foreign-smelling foods wafting throughout the hall. This new world became real so fast it was almost as if she'd been transported right out of her garage and into some other dimension. As she looked on, seemingly unnoticed, she saw that everyone in the room had some variation of the same animal-like markings on their necks and faces. This wasn't visible the day before when the picture was at the smaller size. Some of the spots were darker or lighter, smaller, clustered, or more spread out, but all shades of the same brown. No, this wasn't makeup.

She had been so engrossed she hadn't noticed how crowded the room was. Something was happening at the front, but she couldn't see over the bobbing heads before her. The volume of the murmurs was increasing, but still she couldn't quite make out what was being said. The music, a constant electronic pulse, filled her ears. The crowd began to push closer together, taking her involuntarily with them. She looked for a gap in the horde, but saw none. The people pushing together were tugging her forward with the motion of the throng. Bea's breathing became shallow in her chest. The thought came to her, *Could I get out of here if I wanted to?* "Stop," she called rather loudly. It dissolved instantly and the trashcan was still firmly beneath her in the empty garage.

The door from the kitchen, in desperate need of WD-40, creaked open. It was Teddy.

"Whadder you doin'?" he asked, smiling.

"Huh?" Bea was not fully back yet.

"Would you make me breakfast? Mom doesn't want to get up yet."

"Oh, sure," Bea said, shaking off the odd feeling. "You got it, Tedmeister." Well, that was all she could handle of that crazy thing for now anyway.

Teddy looked at the garage and back at Bea. "What heck were you doing out here anyway?"

Chapter 5: Gone Awry

The suns' dimming light cast long shadows in Vaslow's nearly empty living room. It was time to head to the palace. It was expected that he'd be there for the opening ceremonies of the Allegiance Pageant, which would happen just after sunsdown. He checked his uniform in the interface glass one last time, pulled at his cuffs, and straightened the sash. After such long disuse, the material felt heavy and stiff—just like the rest of him. Having spent the night tossing, turning, and obsessively checking the cantomount for messages, he was feeling his age more than he had in a long while.

Three days and no contact. Time was making the decision for him. The familiar sensation washed over him, the tangible connection that time and distance did not weaken. Bea was on the cusp of beginning her change, probably barely noticeable to her, but with each passing hour the likelihood that he'd have to make another jump increased. Only one hurdle could be leapt at a time. Tonight, it was the Protectorate. Tomorrow, after they left him alone to wallow in his shame, he would concentrate on Bayatrice.

Vaslow glanced at the cantomount sitting lifelessly on the shelf. It hadn't been out of his sight since he'd delivered its mate to Bayatrice, but tonight he'd leave it behind rather than risk any message from her being intercepted. He left it sitting where he'd propped it up, next to the ornate flask the men and women of the Royal Guard had given to him as a retirement gift. Picking up the leather-bound flask, he remembered the strong bond of loyalty he had felt from his soldiers that day. The meaning behind it radiated from their faces. Though he wasn't much of a drinker, he'd kept it all these years. Just the weight of it in his hand brought the feeling back. He would take it with him as a reminder of where his loyalties truly lived.

He walked into the living room and picked up his overcloak from the spindly chair. Outside the window the market was even busier today than it had been yesterday. He was fairly certain that these Sloantown shoppers were about as eager as he was to commence this evening's celebrations. But celebrate they would. While the streets of Vedra would be full of commoners going through the motions mandated by law, he would be behind the palace walls with those who ruled the planet, making a claim of loyalty that would be a lie. A festive night, indeed.

***

Vaslow left Sloantown riding a small, beat-up personal hovercraft—his sled—with his sand-encrusted overcloak covering his military dress uniform. The weight of the flask deep in the folds of his garments was a subtle reminder of its presence. Maybe a drink would steel him for the distasteful task ahead. He had gone west, leaving the low saffron buildings behind, into the sea of towering glass high rises of the Tanloo district.

As suddenly as if a line had been drawn, the desert disappeared and the soil sprouted glass buildings of varying heights, artfully nuzzled against one another. Every meter architected and executed, no detail left to chance. At first glance, the effect was pleasing. Greenery cascaded down from the lofty elevations, wrapping the edges of the sterile buildings, softening them. Rooftop gardens burst with blooms. Manicured parks were dappled throughout the city construct at regular intervals.

Perhaps it was beautiful and Vaslow was just too old and stuck in his ways to see it. But the fact that the mask of lushness was fed by the dwindling water reserve tarnished the experience for him. And he missed the food carts on the corners selling Z'rhed lunches, the birds that used to roost in the mismatched awnings, and the beast-drawn carriages. All flaws that had been rectified, if he were to buy into the Protectorate propaganda. But mostly he missed the heart of Tanloo.

At the district's center there had been a tree stump, nearly ten meters across. It wasn't a formal memorial, but the people knew what it stood for—a requiem for the fallen. Not a somber death marker, but rather the reminder of greatness that had been. The sight of it harkened back to days, even before Vaslow's time, when the planet had supported the growth of these enormous trees in great clusters. Whenever he saw it, he thought of one of the queen's favorite sayings: "What has been can be again."

Now a stark metal monument to the Protectorate stood in its place. As Vaslow drove, he went the extra six blocks out of his way to make sure he avoided it.

He maneuvered the sled through the rush of hoverdomes, glidecrafts, and other sleds to make his way to the hospitality strip. Hotels, bars, and restaurants lined both sides of the street as far as the eye could see. When Vaslow was in the Guard, he and the other officers had come here on occasion to blow off steam. Everything had been tidied and automated since those days. Gleaming brass entrances with video greeters had replaced the hawkers and mismatched colored flags of days gone by.

Vaslow let that thought go and concentrated on the task at hand. The Louxant had the largest number of glidecrafts for hire out front, so Vaslow stashed his sled and cloak between buildings and went in to make a deal. He rejected three vehicles before settling on a late model gleaming glidecraft with a well-appointed driver. Though it cost him a month's rent, he wanted to go beyond expectations, to make sure the Protectorate accepted his lie without question.

The driver nodded respectfully to Vaslow, or to his uniform, as he opened the door. Vaslow settled in the back seat as the glidecraft rose up alongside the hanging gardens. He wondered how much longer there would be water to maintain the artificial lushness. Once at go-height, the driver accelerated and the craft sped above the bustle of the city, heading to the last place in the world Vaslow wanted to go: the palace.

Traffic knotted and slowed as they approached the gateway to Verlona City. The waning light of the suns lit up its surface in brilliant golds, and the flecks of metal in the stone shimmered and danced, making this massive arch seem almost translucent. As one of her first acts after she took the throne, Queen Gwynlott had the gates rebuilt as a symbol of what she saw for Vedra's future. She'd christened them with her oft-said phrase: "What has been can be again. Even greater." It served as a symbol that the citizens of Vedra were on the cusp of an evolution that would make poverty, race wars, and even a ruling class obsolete. The gates were wide at the base, tapering to a slim graceful arch at the top, seeming to defy gravity as they reached for the heavens. Even now the sight of them took his breath away.

He yearned for those better times, days of glory and honor. In the years since he'd been back from Earth, he'd watched as everything was made less great, as all the progress the queen and king had made eroded. He'd watched as the Protectorate had dismantled every institution and decree Queen Gwynlott and King Solhan had established to usher in a new era for Vedra. From the moment they usurped the throne, they worked tirelessly to ensure every aspect of the government was under their control.

The Lifework Ministry had lasted longest of all the royal institutions because the people had clung to it so fiercely. Using ancient teachings, Gwynlott and Solhan had established the Ministry to discover a person's true profession. Sahtars, those with the gift to see into others' hearts, were appointed to enable people to see their true calling, their life's work. Energy Guides were commissioned to help people work together to make the most of their talents. Unemployment had virtually disappeared, job satisfaction was the norm, and, most important, everyone felt the interconnected energy among Vedrians. The people felt empowered. Though there was obvious dissent among the Cenates about how the people's trajectory would effect the government, the royals had assumed that time and knowledge would heal that rift. How wrong they'd been.

By the time the Protectorate had closed the doors of the last Lifework Ministry five years ago and decommissioned the institution itself, people had become too disheartened to band together. Minority leaders and their followers retreated to the outskirts of the city in self-imposed exile, Vaslow guessed to bide their time and see what the Protectorate government had in store.

With no one to guide the energy of the people, to make connections tangible, the population had started to fracture into the clans they had been generations earlier. "One Vedra" was no longer held together by common bonds, but by the strong arm of the Protectorate.

Vaslow could see the crowds below getting denser the closer they got to their destination. Millions of people in this city, yet he felt utterly alone.

During all the years of his active duty in the Guard, news feeds always featured one soldier or another regaling the audience with a story of his feats. As hard as Vaslow tried to avoid that kind of publicity, the public loved a hero.

It was Vaslow's gift that put him in the public eye. He recalled the day he'd discovered his ability in his first foray into combat so many years ago. Separated from his column, he was alone in enemy territory. There were seven men between him and safety. At that time he had only completed basic training in hand-to-hand combat. His options were death as a prisoner or death as a warrior. It took him no time to decide to move on the men. Faced with certain death, he moved forward not as a wild man, but as a soldier, concentrating every effort on using what he'd learned in basic training.

As his moves became a dance of precision and blood, his mind let go. At first he thought he was dreaming, that time had stopped, but only for him. He could see where a punch was going to land as it was being thrown and he moved between time to dodge oncoming blows. He could see the trajectory of a laser and drop his body before it seared his flesh. Much to his surprise, he had bested those seven men in that battle. He understood that day that he wasn't like other warriors.

Over the years he found that he could use his skill on a larger scale as well, saving whole columns of soldiers with his ability to move between time. He could predict the enemy's strategy by watching their formation, accurately predicting the method, timing, and placement of an attack because he could actually see it play out before it happened. He was dubbed a tactical genius and rose through the ranks quickly. But he did not rely on mind tricks alone; he studied tactics more thoroughly than anyone else in the legion. He knew the strengths and weaknesses of every military leader in Vedra's history—not just the glories of the Cass leaders that had been approved for the history books. It had been a tumultuous ascent to his final rank as Commander of the Royal Guard. He had often bucked authority along the way, overriding orders from superiors that he knew would have deadly consequences. The only thing that had saved him was he was always right—and the thousands of guards who owed their lives to him were undyingly loyal.

Vaslow was sure the public had found another soldier to lavish their praise on during his years of retirement. He was never recognized in a restaurant or stopped for a blessing as he was walking down the street in Sloantown. He wondered if he would still be remembered in the walled city.

They made halting progress as they approached the gates. The driver was sharp, maneuvering into the fastest lane at each opportunity. Once through the gates, they picked up speed again. Ever closer to the Protectorate and their mock court.

Vaslow could hardly stomach to be in their presence. He'd lived the last fourteen years with the knowledge—with hard evidence burning in his hand—that the Protectorate had been behind the coup. But there was no one to hand that evidence over to. No one alone could bring justice. He could no longer be certain who the loyalist Cenates were. Vaslow knew the Protectorate suspected he had managed to take Bayatrice offworld, but being unable to find the girl, they had no proof. So for years they had been in a silent standoff, each side with their own secrets, biding their time. Only now, with the Protectorate fist clamping down on the free will of the people, had Vaslow begun to fear for his own life, not because he feared death but because if he died there would be no one to rescue the child. The evidence that could turn the tide on this cold war sat moldering in a lockbox on the other side of Vedra, useless. And the Cenate who had given his life to make sure that proof was documented lay rotting in an early grave.

Vaslow had spent his life speaking the unadulterated truth and suffering the consequences as they came. It was the only way he knew how to live. He was ill-suited to this role of biding his time and letting the truth sit and wait for better timing. But if he had any hopes of staying alive to rescue Bayatrice, he knew he had no other choice but to pledge the loyalty they wanted. Saying those words tonight would burn his lips, but his heart would beat stronger knowing it brought him one day closer to righting this injustice.

The glidecraft eased to a stop in front of the palace. The square was full of thousands of revelers and hundreds of horn players who lined the gateway to the entrance; staccato bursts of sound were building excitement. The ground vibrated with the low steady rhythm of the Cicant drums. Enormous videos were projected into the air above the people; images floated in front of the palace so the common folk outside could catch glimpses of the happenings inside. Iridescent gowns and luxurious jewels, all the finery Vedra had to offer, was on display.

A video swipe came across the screens. Large fields of brown, dying crops; dejected farmers and townspeople in leaderless energy circles willing the rivers to flow down from the mountains. Cut to water drills and tankers of water, then lush green fields with Trone Knowledge Industries hovercrafts irrigating the fields from above. The tagline read, "You don't have to wait on the rivers. TKI — bringing water to you." Behind the words, images of healthy green crops swayed in the sunslight, and then the swipe faded again, revealing the lovely gowns and glowing jewels inside the palace. Of course, nothing was mentioned about how ineffective people had become since losing their energy guides. But that was the way of the Protectorate. The propaganda was obvious to Vaslow. He wondered if people were simply too worn down to care, or if they even remembered how it had been anymore.

The onlookers pressed forward, hoping to get a glimpse of those entering the palace. Excitement was an electric current lighting the faces it touched. Vendors trolled the crowd selling commemorative trinkets. Jugglers and fire-eaters stood on crates, entertaining the groups of people their magic could reach. All over the city, in every district, even in Sloantown, there were celebrations. Once these celebrations truly had meaning, but now people joined in just for the spectacle and because it was an excuse for a day off.

Vaslow straightened to his full height as he got out of the glidecraft.

"Vaslow, it's Vaslow!" a voice rose above the din. His name echoed through the dense mass of people like a ball bouncing off a wall. He was surprised to be recognized so quickly. He was sure he looked much older, and he hadn't had the beard when he was a regular feature on the news feeds. He looked down, not wanting to meet the expectant gaze of the crowd. He hurried down the narrow swath that cut through the sea of bodies. There was a commotion just ahead of him and he looked up. An old woman in tattered Sahtar robes reached through the crowd and grabbed his arm with a steel grip. She gazed solemnly into his face. He wanted to pull away, afraid she would see his impending blasphemy. She gave him a small, sad smile.

"Bless you, Vaslow." Was she praying for his damned soul or wishing him well? "I know you still fight for the true Vedra."

A guard disentangled him and shepherded him past the crowd and up the stairs to the entrance. He could still feel the weight of the woman's hand on his wrist and her words on his heart as he prepared to cross the threshold.

Chapter 6: Pledging Allegiance

At first glance, this celebration had the same appointments as all the others he'd attended in years past. The guests in their finery, new sculptures displayed, copious mounds of delicacies, and, he suspected, the most talented musicians debuting great new works, though he no longer kept track of such things. But it didn't take a Sahtar to see into the heart of this event and know that it was hollow.

He tried not to think of the many pageants he had attended with a glad heart. Flashes of those days filled his head anyway. Days when the queen and king had used their powers to enable the people to feel their energetic connections—to each other, to their planet, and to their life's purpose. Together the royals, touching a river of collective hope, had used their abilities to guide the energy generated by the people to steer the very forces of the planet: oceans, crops, winds, hope. He wondered if little Bayatrice would grow up with any of her parents' gifts.

A man dressed in all white extended a tray with vine fruit and crisp breads. Vaslow waved him on; to him the delicacies offered here were beyond tainted.

Vaslow kept to himself, enduring the occasional small talk with an old acquaintance, for that's all he had left now—acquaintances. From across the room he saw his former student, Islook, looking proud and eager in his crisp black uniform. Islook was now First Rank in the Young Guard. In the fall he would join the Protectorate Guard proper. Vaslow shuddered at that thought. As he watched the young man's stride, he could still see greatness in him, agility, wit.

Vaslow remembered the day he met Islook during intake at the Young Guard assembly. There were dozens of boys, just barely beyond their patou, seemingly not a standout among them. As he sparred with each one in turn he could feel dark eyes studying him, the gaze intense, as if each move was being cataloged. The earnest boy, younger than most, having gone through his patou at thirteen, was Islook. By the time Vaslow began his foray with him, he knew this boy had the gift. He could, like Vaslow, move between time, step between the passing seconds, and move away from punches, deflecting impending danger.

In all his years he'd never met another who possessed such ability. He vowed to give this student all the benefit of his discoveries, perhaps instill a sense of true valor while he was at it. Having no other draws on his attention, Vaslow had given the boy all of his free time. They practiced during off hours. Islook had willingly read every book Vaslow even casually mentioned. The boy was a sponge, yet not a blank slate. In the evenings when they had taken meals together, Islook questioned Vaslow's tactics, respectfully but thoroughly. His mind was hungry, looking for his own path, his own answers, and Vaslow had felt the boy's spirit was true. He had even begun to think of the young man as a son he might have had if his life had called him in a different direction.

Even now, after he knew the truth about Islook, the pain of the loss was like a hole in his center. Vaslow turned to avoid an encounter, but it was too late. Islook had seen him.

"Old man, I am surprised to see you here," Islook scoffed. "I would have thought you'd be too feeble to come to such a function." Though Vaslow was a tall man, Islook towered over him.

"Sorry to disappoint," Vaslow said in an even tone. A spark of light shone in the young man's eyes, just as it had when Vaslow had first met him. In their years of training, Vaslow had thought the young man understood that often a battle avoided was a battle won. Apparently that was not the case.

"You should be used to disappointing others by now." Islook slapped Vaslow on the shoulder in a playful manner, but with the force of a more serious intent.

Vaslow's disappointment was threatening to turn to rage when the horns called for Proclamations. Islook headed toward the front of the room to take his rightful place.

The five members of the Protectorate stood on the stage, their faces barely visible, dappled in shadows from the hoods of their matching deep purple robes. They moved together, yet separately, like sand between fingers. They bowed deeply in unison, righted themselves, and looked out over the crowd with bottomless expressions. The one in the center spoke. "Heysay, Heysay!" The horns called and answered once again and a hush fell over the crowd.

The member just left of center spoke next. Vaslow hadn't seen them in years, and he was reminded now of how strong the illusion of unity was. One would speak and then another would continue, in no particular order, without pause, back and forth as if they were one mind speaking. Vaslow was certain it was this hive-mind behavior that kept the people at bay, believing that they, like the royals, had the true power to rule.

This parlor trick had worked to their advantage, as it had convinced the unwitting population that the Protectorate, like the lineage of royal predecessors they'd overthrown, had a connection to the interconnected energy of Vedra and the source of greater knowledge.

"We who are here
to serve you,
are in your
presence to be judged.
We who are here
to serve you,
accept your will
whether it be

yea or nay."

They spoke fluidly from one to another, saying the familiar words. "We who are here

to serve you,

only have the power

you give to us." They paused.

"Will you give

us that power?

Who will be

the first among you

to speak your will?"

"I will!" Vaslow bellowed from the back of the room. He felt the weight of the gazes of all those around him. The Protectorate would get what they wanted and he'd get out of there.

The crowd gave a collective gasp as he moved toward the front of the hall. A taut silence fell on the room, ready to snap. The last time he'd stood before them, he had come perilously close to the edge of denouncing them outright. He had been the first on that occasion as well, and though none stood with him, he knew there had been like-minded people in the crowd too cowed by fear to join him.

"Who stands

before us?"

"I, Vaslow, son of Aramede, former Commander of the Royal Guard, stand before you." The words were clear and loud enough for all to hear. Vaslow genuflected in the customary manner, touching the back of his hand briefly to his forehead. He then knelt on one knee, bowing his head.

"Stand, Vaslow, son of Aramede, and speak your will." The Protectorate spoke unflinchingly, without anticipation.

Vaslow stood slowly and swallowed hard. "I, Vaslow—" His traitorous voice broke. He cleared his throat and continued. "I, Vaslow, recognize your authority to rule. I pledge my allegiance to the Protectorate. I hereby vow that I dedicate my deeds to serve your will."

The silent room was now frozen.

"We hear

your pledge

and humbly accept

your vow."

Vaslow genuflected again, then turned and faced the bewildered crowd. Behind him a long line of noteworthy people stood ready to pledge, and yet none of them met his gaze. As he moved back down the line the spell was broken, the room began to stir, and the people quickly engaged in the next speaker.

Vaslow's shaky legs carried him to the front exit. He could see the night sky and he longed for escape. Once outside, he made his way alongside the building where he could be alone with his thoughts. In his youth, during the Bradour Wars, Vaslow had spent countless nights sleeping on the desert sand, braving blistering heat, only to be cloaked by the invading cold in his sweat-drenched clothes. He had owned nothing save the pack on his back and the pride in defending a just nation, an honorable queen, a lineage of truth. He had come to understand that was all he needed.

Now, though that queen, Gwynlott's mother, was long buried, and Gwynlott most likely dead as well, he still fought for what he now felt convinced was his destiny—to bring Bayatrice back and restore the rightful order of things. He understood what those who lived so carelessly today did not: that there was more to this world than win or lose by one's own hand, that there was a river of truth greater than ourselves, and a purpose more noble than an individual's own glory.

Fingers on his flask, he was about to take his first drink when a hand landed heavily on his shoulder and spun him around. Vaslow was staring into Islook's black eyes. The young man's gaze was sharp and fiery, full of emotion. They were alone in a vast, open space between buildings. It was not unlike the practice rooms the two had sparred in together during better times. Islook held Vaslow's shoulder in a crushing grip for a moment and then turned back the way he had come.

Vaslow wasn't sure what he had seen in Islook's face. It didn't look like the glow of victory he would have anticipated coming from Islook. Was it disappointment, sadness? He didn't know; he just knew the emotion coming from the younger man intensified his own shame.

Vaslow put the flask to his lips and turned it up, letting the pleasant burn of the thick liquid warm his throat as he swallowed.

Chapter 7: Piano Practice

The rest of the weekend limped by and Bea hadn't made any more progress with the viewer. She'd tried looking at it after everyone went to bed at night, knowing she'd never wake Patty. But Uncle Pete, with his cat-like hearing, had come in a few times and told her to "turn off the radio and go to sleep." Not wanting to risk him seeing it, she put it away until she could think of a way to find time to herself.

Finally, Monday morning came and, with it, the regular school routine. Bea and an unusually silent Patty making lunches, P.J. feeding the cats, Teddy trying to find both his shoes. Bea tried to get into the rhythm of the familiar tasks, but even this felt different. There was only one thing she could think about: getting answers.

The perfect plan to get time alone formed in her head. The one bad thing was it required her to "borrow" P.J.'s MP3 player-recorder. If she asked him, he'd say no—he refused to let anyone "touch his stuff." Just this once, maybe she could use it and get it back to him before he ever found out it was missing.

As everyone was filing out the door, Bea called out that she'd forgotten her geometry homework and ran back inside. Up the stairs and into P.J.'s stinky closet. He was a slob, but when it came to his electronics he always put them in their cases. She reached into his top drawer and took out the small gray case. Bea felt a pang of guilt as she dropped it into her backpack. He would be so pissed if he found out she was in his closet, much less that she'd touched his precious elec-tronics drawer. And this was his newest toy—he'd used three months of allowance and all his birthday money to buy it. But she needed this; there wasn't any other way to make this idea work, she told herself as she hurried back downstairs and out to the car.

In the car on the way to school, Bea laid the groundwork for her plan to explore the viewer. "Aunt Lucy, I'm going to catch the bus home tonight if that's okay. I want to stay after school and practice piano." Ordinarily, Aunt Lucy would push for Patty to stay with her, not liking the kids to ride the bus home alone, but the extra space her aunt and uncle had been giving her since her "discovery" was changing their approach to rules.

"I thought you were through with the piano?" Aunt Lucy asked, clearly pleased, but not wanting to push it.

"Yeah, me too. But I guess I miss it."

"And those keys are still sticking on ours?"

"Yeah, kind of annoying. And hard to play when it's like that," Bea said. At least one part of her story was true.

"Okay, honey, just be home before dinner." Aunt Lucy beamed. She had always made it clear she thought Bea had a gift, but she was also so desperate for one of the Parker kids to follow in her classical piano footsteps that it made Bea feel anxious to play in front of her. "And I'll get Uncle Pete to call the piano tuner."

Well, at least she'd have a week or so. She wouldn't worry about actually having to practice piano at home until she had to.

***

The final bell couldn't have come soon enough. Each class seemed longer than the one before. Mr. Belk had called on her three times in physical science, and caught her not paying attention each time. She'd pay for that, she was sure.

Before the *brrng* of the bell had faded, Bea was out of her classroom and racing down the hall. Her feet automatically led her right to Patty's locker, because that was their after-school routine. She was about to turn away when Patty saw her. "Hey, Bea," Patty said, with an awkward forced effervescence.

"Uh, hi." Bea hated this feeling of not knowing what to say. It was Patty. Patty who'd been by her side her whole life. "I, ah, just came to say bye."

"Oh, great." Patty smiled. "Well, I hope you have a good practice."

"Thanks," Bea said as she turned and headed for the music building.

Patty called out from behind her. "I'll make sure P.J. doesn't bogart your dessert!"

The brief conversation was clumsy and not how they usually talked to one another, but it gave Bea hope. Maybe there was a chance things would be normal between them again.

By the time she made it across the courtyard there were only two practice rooms left. She signed up for the one on the far end, thinking the sound would carry less from there.

When she reached the door, Calvin Beech stepped in front of her.

"Um, Calvin, I...I signed up for this room," Bea stammered.

"Um, whatever-your-name-is, check the schedule again. You signed up for that room." He pointed to his left, stepped inside, and closed the door, leaving Bea standing in the hall.

Though a middle room was not ideal, Bea had no time to argue.

The tiny space was all beige linoleum and cream paint dotted with chips and smeared ballpoint scribbles that Mrs. Hallowell had diligently tried to scrub off, with no success. An upright piano, which had surprisingly good sound, and a somewhat dependable bench, were all that occupied the room. Everything was doused in the harsh green-white being thrown off from the fluorescent lights above. Bea closed the door, making the room fairly soundproof.

She took P.J.'s MP3 device out of her bag and out of its case—praying he didn't look for it before she got home—and set it up to record. She began with an elaborate warm-up by Brahms. It had been nearly four months since she had played but the notes flew effortlessly from her fingers. Maybe she really did miss it.

Bea propped her backpack against the door. She tested the recording and then propped the MP3 player on her pack, set it to repeat, and let it play at full volume, which was just loud enough to pass as a real piano, Bea thought.

Viewer in hand, crouched in the corner, she braced herself for, well, whatever. The same tingle, grow, and *bwoom-bwoom* routine happened and she found herself smack-dab in the middle of the crowd. This time she let herself be pulled along. She remembered to breathe. The great hall was alive with color and sounds and joyous voices. Everyone was moving toward the front. Bea was able to move from side to side until she got a view of the platform at the front, which was just a few feet in front of her. At the front of the room, the king and queen were requesting everyone's attention. They both had long purple cloaks that cascaded down their backs and pooled onto the ground. As they turned, laughing or talking, Bea could see some kind of metallic insignia woven into the back of the fabric. The woman was unusually tall and slender. Though, as she looked around, it seemed that everyone in this room was unusually tall and slender. Up close Bea could see the crown on the woman's head, encrusted with tiny jewels; silky strands of cinnamon hair were woven in and out of the intricate filigree.

A plain girl with brown hair and no facial marking swished across the stage and handed the queen a baby before disappearing again. It was the same baby she'd seen before; she was rosy-cheeked, laughing, with light red-gold tufts of hair, a lighter version of the queen's. The baby's long iridescent silvery gown matched that of the queen. Though the baby didn't have the same facial markings, she had to be a young princess. The baby reached for the tasseled clasp at the queen's neck and pulled. The queen said something Bea couldn't make out and the whole room let out a peal of laughter.

The music changed, the pulse faded away, and some sort of ethereal trumpet made long sonorous call. Another answered. The room began to still. The queen absent-mindedly shook the tassel for the baby as she spoke. "Heysay, heysay!" The trumpets called and answered again. The baby let out a little squeal as she finally caught the tassel. Laughter rippled through the crowd, breaking the quiet.

The king began speaking in a deep, booming voice. She could hear him clearly, but she couldn't understand him. "Repeat," Bea said aloud. The whole room froze and jiggled around her for a split second, and then began at the king's first words. She tried again to understand. Listening to the words made Bea's head hurt. She could almost grasp what he was saying but not quite, something about allegiance. "Repeat," she said again. By the fourth or fifth time repeating, her head was really pounding but she was beginning to decipher what he was saying. Then the queen spoke these words: "We, who are here to serve you, only have the power you give to us." The queen paused and took the king's hand. "Will you give us that power? Who will be the first among you to speak your will?"

She was about to say "repeat" again when she heard a pounding on the door. "Stop," Bea said, and the projected world dissolved around her.

The MP3 player had stopped. The pounding on the door had not. Bea scurried to the door, a bit wobbly. The backpack had gotten stuck under the door, which was the only reason Mrs. Hallowell was not already inside the practice room. Bea moved the pack and freed the door.

Mrs. Hallowell was glaring at Bea over the top of her reading glasses. "What on earth are you doing in here?"

Bea started, "I was just—" and Ms. Hallowell cut her off.

"Don't try to tell me practicing. Calvin said the piano stopped forty minutes ago." Mrs. Hallowell was not a pleasant woman when she was upset.

Thanks a lot, Calvin, Bea thought as she tried to explain. "Well, I was practicing—"

Mrs. Hallowell cut her off again. "I heard the noise. This is no place for videogames. If your parents won't let you play at home, too bad."

"I wasn't—"

Bea couldn't get a word in edgewise. Mrs. Hallowell continued, "And you of all people, Bea. You have such talent and you're wasting it on…on mind-rotting videogames."

"But I wasn't—" Bea protested.

"Save it. I'm closing up now. You'd better get going or you'll miss the last bus." Mrs. Hallowell shook her head. "And the next time you come in to one of my practice rooms you'd better practice, got it?"

Last bus? "Yes, Mrs. Hallowell." Bea made no attempt to smooth things over. She shoved everything in her bag and raced out of the music building toward the bus stop. The sun had set, and the street lights were burning bright. Dry snow whipped through the cold air. She ran all the way and just caught the driver before he closed the doors. Last bus meant 6:45. Last bus meant Bea had missed dinner. She checked her phone—she'd missed two calls from home and a text from Patty saying, "where r u? u r gonna b so grounded." She wasn't used to being scolded, and more was waiting for her at home. And what if Ms. Hallowell called Aunt Lucy? All because of this dang thing. She had half a mind to throw it into the next trashcan she passed. It was the other half of her mind that wouldn't let her think of anything else but it.

***

Grounded. *So this is what it feels like,* Bea thought. She sat leaning against her headboard in the dark bedroom, twirling her hair. Two weeks. Aunt Lucy and Uncle Pete had only given her one week, but then P.J. made a big deal about his MP3 player. Not only was she no closer to getting things back to normal, now everybody was mad at her. Of course, she'd expected her aunt and uncle to be angry. She just hadn't expected that everybody else would be too. P.J. went ballistic about Bea going through his things—okay, she could have predicted that. Patty was pissed all over again. And worst of all, little Teddy looked at her like he didn't know who she was anymore.

Ugh. Bea had never felt so alone in her entire life—and at the same time so crowded. Her face was still hot and puffy from crying. She was never going to get any time to look at the viewer. Worse than that, she was beginning to wonder if it was dangerous. Not only had she lost track of time, it was as if she had been in some kind of trance. She'd been completely taken over by that thing, obsessed about figuring it out. Her head still pounded. She couldn't do this alone, but there was nobody else.

Aunt Lucy had given her the whole trust speech routine that P.J. got regularly. But to Bea, it really meant something. She felt like she had betrayed her aunt and uncle. Part of her wanted to tell them everything right then, but she knew that having kept the secret this long would just make matters worse. And the thought of them making her get rid of the viewer was unbearable. She didn't know what to do. She could no longer hear that little voice inside her that usually told her right from wrong. At the moment, she hated that thing that sat like a red-hot coal in the bottom of her backpack. No matter what she did with it, it would burn her. And she could tell by the look in her aunt's and uncle's eyes they were not only mad but worried—like they had more to say but were afraid. There was a gap growing between her and her family that felt like it could grow into the Grand Canyon if she didn't find a way to stop it.

***

Patty stomped into the room, turned on the light, and got out her pajamas. She pointedly did not look in Bea's direction. Bea wanted to say sorry, something to make it better, but she didn't know how to explain and still keep her secret. Patty finished getting into her pajamas, got into bed, and shut the light off with a loud harrumph. As she pulled the covers over her head, Patty said, "Just want you to know, I ate your dessert."

Bea scooched down to put her head on her pillow, letting the hot tears roll down her cheeks and soak into the soft cloth. For the first time, Bea missed Patty's motherish advice about what she should do.

Bea drifted off into an uneasy sleep. Her mind traveled the familiar path to her recurring dream: It's pitch black. Across the room from her is the strange face that melts from one shape to another, dappled with an eerie greenish hue. He...she...whatever this morph-man thing is... raises its hand as if reaching for her. But this time she can hear what it is saying.

"We

are

getting

close."

Bea sat up with a scream caught in her throat. Her body was trembling all over. It felt so real she almost checked her room to make sure they weren't really here. Terror had her limbs quivering; she'd never get back to sleep now. She put her aching head back on the pillow and stared into the darkness.

Chapter 8: The Morning After

Vaslow's mouth was dry and his head throbbed. He felt a pat, pat, pat on his leg. He opened his eyes and winced, the early morning light searing into his brain. He was vaguely aware he was lying on the ground, and his last memory was closing time at a bar in the Tanloo district. He tried to let his mind settle for a moment, but it wouldn't focus. There was a child staring down at him with black, familiar eyes. Islook? No. Wharton's son.

"Come on, mister-mister," the child pleaded in the Sloan sing-song accent, tugging on Vaslow's cloak. "You gotta move now."

In some still-functioning part of his brain he knew the boy was right, he should move, but his head hurt so much. He pulled his cloak from the child's hands and shut his eyes. The boy let out a frustrated breath and padded off down the street.

He wasn't sure how much time had passed when he felt the pat-pat again. And then a not-so-gentle large foot in his back. He sat up and felt for his flask, but it was gone. Vaslow didn't want to take in his surroundings, but his trained mind couldn't help it. He was on the ground, in the hard-packed yellow dust of an alley, surrounded by overturned crates and market waste, the smell of old garbage and his own breath threatening to turn his stomach. His sled was in a mangled heap against the building. He looked up; it was the boy again, but this time he was with his father. Vaslow rubbed his eyes and covered his face with his hand. Drink hadn't made him brave; it had made him numb. Numb and stupid.

"Yes, shame can come later," Wharton said matter-of-factly. "Right now we need to get you off the street before these vultures wake up." He motioned to the rundown housing buildings that surrounded them, and then pointed to Vaslow's cloak, twisted and riding up his leg. It revealed the now soiled cloth of his military uniform. "And they would do more than pick the meat off your bones if they saw that."

Vaslow made a weak attempt to cover his uniform, not meeting the man's gaze. What had he done? The last thing he wanted was to be seen parading around Sloantown in his military dress uniform. His aging face, scruffy beard, and civilian dress had kept the people of Sloantown from connecting him to his military past. He had hoped the Sloans' notorious aversion to Protectorate news feeds would keep his false vow from being public knowledge here, but now this one wrong move threatened to shatter that thin façade.

Vaslow tried to make his mind come up with an explanation, some excuse to give the man, something to keep Wharton from shutting him out now when he needed him the most. How could he find something to say? There was no excuse for this behavior.

Vaslow moved his stiff muscles, Cicant drums banging in his head as he swayed under the weight of his conscience, struggling to stand fully upright. Wharton stood with his arms crossed and watched.

"The sled, is it registered to you?" Wharton asked, pointing at the twisted pile of metal.

"It was an accident. I swerved and ran into the building."

"Yes, an accident, buddy-buddy. I can smell the accident on your breath." Sarcasm dripped from Wharton's tongue. "Is it registered to you or not?"

Vaslow shook his head. Wharton continued, "Leave it then. I don't know what your story is, but I will keep your secret. And now, Gray Beard, you and I are all evens." He turned to his son. "Si," he ordered, "make sure he gets home." As he walked out of the alley he called over his shoulder with a dark chuckle, "And, Si, make sure he don't yack on you."

Vaslow stood for a long moment trying to get his bearings. He believed the man's words; Wharton wouldn't say anything. But would all the progress he'd made with the Sloan now evaporate? Would this kill his chances of getting his craft rescrambled?

The child was looking up at him, nervous and too still. "It's okay, boy. Run along." Vaslow waved his hand, dismissing the child. How could he have been so stupid? What if Bayatrice had tried to make contact while he'd been passed out? He brushed the dust from his cloak with unnecessary force.

The boy shook his head. "Popi say make sure you gets home."

"I'm fine. I'll get home," Vaslow said, more gruffly than he intended. He was impatient to check his cantomount, which he'd programmed to receive any messages, intentional or inadvertent, from Bayatrice. He stared at the boy for a long moment. The boy did not move. "Okay, then, let's get me home."

They walked in a heavy silence along the covered market tents. An occasional squeak of a shutter opening or the twisted squawk of a desert bird was all they heard as they shuffled through the still-sleeping streets. Vaslow could feel the weight of the boy's gaze on his back. Would it hold disgust? Pity? He wouldn't turn and find out. Instead he sped up his pace, but the injuries he'd sustained in his collision wouldn't allow him to sustain it.

"You limp, mister-mister," the boy said, more as an observation than out of concern.

Vaslow grunted, hoping they could make it to his door without having to engage in conversation. No such luck.

"You a soldier? Is that how you put the big hurt on those two in the alley, that day you fought for me? But you too old to be a soldier," the boy said.

"Yes, I am too old to be a soldier."

"So, why you wear the black-black, under you cloak?" The boy narrowed his gaze. "You a spy?"

Vaslow wasn't going to be able to let this go. If he didn't answer correctly, the whole district would hear whatever version of the story the boy would conjure up, and his two years of trying to make inroads into this community would have been wasted. He cursed himself again—how could he have risked his mission and dishonored the memory of those he served? He wouldn't have to wait until later for the shame to come.

His instincts told him to tell the boy the truth—or some version of it that wouldn't jeopardize the plans to save Bayatrice. His head hurt and his thoughts seemed to have to walk through cobwebs before they could get to his mouth. But he couldn't just ignore the boy's curiosity.

"Si, that's your name, right? Si?" The boy nodded. "Is it short for Simoud?" The boy nodded again. "You bear the name of a great warrior."

"How come a pocked like you knows of our great hero-hero?"

"I know more than you'd think, Simoud. I know Simoud led the Sloan in many great battles. I know that even when the odds were against him he found a way to win. I know he built tunnels to protect your people when they were being hunted." They were nearing Vaslow's rented rooms. He stopped and put his hand on the boy's shoulder, and looked him in the eyes for a long moment. "The way you held yourself when the soldiers attacked. The way you stayed to help me. I can see there is a lot of that great warrior in you, boy. I can see the way you watch things, know things by looking. Do you think you can trust me?"

The boy looked at Vaslow's face with wary, thinking eyes, but didn't answer.

Vaslow continued, "I need you to reach down inside yourself and call upon that warrior part and answer that question. Do you sense danger from me?"

The boy stood, twisting his face as he thought. Finally he spoke. "No."

Vaslow nodded in agreement. "Then, Simoud, I am going to tell you the most important secret you will probably hear in your entire life. But before I do, I need for you to swear to me that you will not share it with anyone…not even your father. Can you promise that?"

It was clear the boy was taking this seriously, was contemplating his answer before he gave it. "Yes, Mister-Mister, I will keep your secret."

Vaslow accepted the boy's solemn answer. "I am here to bring the royal bloodline back to the throne."

"What, you can bring them back from the dead?" The boy looked confused.

"No, the Princess Bayatrice still lives. And I will not rest until she is sitting on her throne."

The boy's eyes grew wide as he heard the words and let the implications of this secret sink in. Vaslow watched the importance of it settle into the boy's body, saw the way he shifted his balance to take on the weight of this new responsibility. Though he couldn't be certain, Vaslow sensed he had a new ally in Si.

Chapter 9: Grounded

Bea sat by herself at a lunch table for rejects. Patty and her crowd were across the cafeteria, laughing and flirting as usual. Bea's seat was empty. Her cell phone vibrated as a text message came in. She pulled the phone from the front zip pocket of her backpack. It was from Patty. "Like r u a loozr now?" Bea slammed the phone shut and dumped it back into her bag. Was that was Patty's way of trying to make up or was she highlighting how far Bea had fallen?

Bea chewed at the corner of her peanut butter sandwich. Being grounded was bad enough, but the way things were between her and Patty was twisting her whole world. It was like all the things she feared the most—that she wasn't really one of the crowd, that she was just Patty's shadow, that she didn't belong—were really true. How could it ever be the same?

Geeks and nerds. And her. Her new station in life. She was about to get seriously depressed when she suddenly realized that this could be the answer to solving her problems and get her back to a normal life! She took a monster bite out of her sandwich, shoved it back into her lunch bag, and crumpled it along with the remains of her chips. The mouthful landed in her stomach like a bowling ball.

So what if Calvin was a complete jerk? He was insanely smart. And she bet double her Christmas money that he'd be interested in the viewer. She tossed her lunch bag toward the garbage can across the table without thinking. Swoosh. It landed right in the center—why couldn't that ever happen when anybody else was watching?

Bea gathered her books and headed right toward Calvin.

She slowed as she got close to the table—how could she possibly explain this? She didn't have to think about it long. Before she even arrived at the table Calvin began to speak.

"No," he said without looking up.

"Excuse me?" Bea was bewildered.

"I really don't care that you got busted for playing videogames at the practice rooms." He managed to speak and ignore her at the same time.

"But I wasn't going to—" Bea tried to get a word in.

"Still no." He reached into his canvas lunch bag, a clear sign of an outcast. "No, I don't sell reports. No, I won't do your homework for you. No, I don't know what will be on the next quiz. Whatever your question, the answer is no."

"But I wasn't going to ask you about—"

He cut her off. "It doesn't matter, no." He looked up. She just stood there, mouth hanging open. "Now, either you can go back over there or I will. Your choice." Bea was stuck. She hadn't gotten past the "no" yet.

"Okay, fine," Calvin said, and he picked up his lunch and moved to the other end of the table, leaving Bea standing dumbstruck.

What a complete and total jerk. She didn't need his freaking help. She flung her hair over her shoulder and walked out of the cafeteria without looking back.

Nothing was worth dealing with a clumpnugget like that. Her brain spun, trying to think of other options, but every revolution kept landing on the same fact—Calvin was her only solution. She did want to talk to him; she *needed* to. As unpleasant as it was, he was the only person on Earth that could help her.

If she could just show him, he would beg to help her. Geek that he was, that was a sure thing. Calvin was in physical science with her second period after lunch. Between now and then she *would* figure out a plan.

***

It wasn't perfect, but it was a plan. She would write a note, sneak it to him in class, get him to meet her in the only place she could think of where no one would be watching, and she would show him the viewer. Done deal. She'd have him hooked. But what could she possibly say that would make him want to meet her? The truth.

Despite the fact that science class lasted about twelve hours after she dropped the note on Calvin's desk, Bea was in a good mood. She finally saw a chance to figure out the stupid viewer and find something out about her past, and then maybe start to repair some things at home. The bell rang and she didn't even look at Calvin. She sprinted for Patty's locker to tell her she'd be home late. She knew the bit about "cutting-edge technology she wasn't supposed to know about" would at least get him to show up.

She saw the gang—Christy, Angie, and Marie—hanging out by Patty's locker. She broke through the human barrier and walked up to Patty. "I've got something to do for science class. I'm taking the next bus. Let Aunt Lucy know, okay?"

"Sure, I'll let my mom know," Patty said. Had she heard her right? Did she just say "*my* mom?" Maybe Bea was being paranoid? Or maybe they really were in their own personal cold war. Maybe Patty was waiting for Bea to apologize? Before piano practice they seemed to be on the verge of going back to normal. And now you could play full court basketball between them. Bea just stood there and said nothing. Christy and Angie exchanged a confused look. As she headed back out toward the football field, she figured there'd be time to think about all that later.

Around back behind the gym, Bea weaved her way underneath the visitors' side bleachers. Despite the cold, she passed three couples from the upper grades making out along the way. They wouldn't care what she was doing with Calvin—that's what made this spot so great.

Hopping from foot to foot, she tried to keep the blood flowing to her now frozen toes. She looked at her watch. 3:15. *Dang it. Maybe he didn't even read the note?* She was just about to head for the bus stop when she saw his red down jacket coming around the corner.

"This had better be for real. If you pull some Dora Leap Pad out of your bag, I promise you'll live to regret it." He let his book-laden backpack fall with a thump onto the frozen ground.

"Fine, just take a look at—"

"All right! All you lovebirds! Follow me!" Coach Walker's voice cut her off, impatient and loud. "You heard me. Under the bleachers is clearly marked as off limits. This is not a joking matter. All of you. Detention Hall."

"You think this is funny? Payback for piano or something?" Calvin shouted at her with a murderous look in his eyes. "Some joke. You get detention, too, you know."

Bea was speechless. Detention. That meant that she wouldn't be on the next bus. That meant the coach would call her aunt and uncle. That meant she would be grounded until June.

Chapter 10: The Scientific Method

Okay, life was seriously twisted. Aunt Lucy and Uncle Pete were past worried and onto panic. They were now looking for an appropriate therapist to help keep Bea from completely going off the edge into darkness. Her "lying, stealing, and boy-crazy antics" were apparently a cry for help. Oh, please, if it were only that simple. Bea had a perfectly logical explanation...and she couldn't tell anybody.

"Bea, you know how much we love you, don't you?" Uncle Pete had asked.

Aunt Lucy, in tears, had said, "I couldn't love you any more if I *had* given birth to you. *You're my daughter.*"

Bea had just stood there. She wanted to hug them back and tell them she knew. She wanted to melt into their arms and rewind time to before she'd discovered those papers, but she couldn't. The secrets she was keeping and the need to know about her past were like a barbed wire fence that was tightly wrapped around her. If she let them any closer it would hurt them all. So she just stood there, watching her aunt cry.

Between the guilt, this obsession with getting the viewer to explain her past, and the dark dreams that haunted her, her stomach was constantly upset. She had to crack this thing or life as she knew it would be over forever. And leaving it alone now simply wasn't an option.

She was grounded until next Christmas. Well, it was actually only for a month, but it might as well be a year. Even if she could convince Calvin to help, she wouldn't be able to get out to see him. And she refused to risk getting caught again. She couldn't bear seeing her aunt cry anymore.

Bea had voluntarily skipped dinner and had spent the evening in her bedroom stewing instead.

Hearing Patty clomping up the stairs, Bea quickly rolled over and pretended to sleep.

"Nice try, delinquent," Patty said as she walked into the room. "I heard the sheets rustle. No way you're asleep."

"So, you're a psychic now. Good for you."

"Were you really making out with a boy?"

"No, I really wasn't." Bea continued to face the opposite wall.

"I promise not to say anything. Just tell me." Patty was talking to her like she used to. "I mean, what was it like?"

"I swear to you, Patty, that is not what I was doing."

"Yeah, right, whatever." Patty's climate chilled in an instant.

Bea rolled over and faced Patty. "I would tell you. Really, I would if that's what it was. It was about science. Honestly."

Patty stood for a moment, at a loss. Bea watched her anger turn to frustration. "I don't know what would be more pathetic, if that's the truth or if that's the story you made up."

"Okay, this is the deal. I went there to meet Calvin Beech. *About science.* I didn't want anyone to see me talking with such a pathetic nerd in public. I didn't explain that part because I knew that would make things worse."

Patty stared at Bea, blinked, and shook her head. "You just got grounded over a science project. And *you* didn't want to be seen with a geek." Patty stood for a moment staring at her with her one hand on her hip before shaking her head and turning away. "You're wrong, by the way." Patty paused. "Nothing could make things worse."

***

Bea had cried herself to sleep, which was getting to be a regular routine these days, only to be greeted in dreamland by dark-gray morph-man. The dream started the same way it always did, the green light just barely enough to make out the hooded, liquid play-dough gray face in the shadows. It began to speak.

"I think

she is

sensing us."

And then, poof, it was gone as quickly as it started, leaving behind the familiar unsettling feeling. When she woke up, the sun was shining. She could see the drip, drip, drip from the icicles outside her window. Patty was already dressed and downstairs; once again she hadn't bothered to wake Bea up. Bea rushed through her already brief morning routine and made it to the car in time, but had skipped breakfast to do so.

She was like a ghost. One day floated into the next in a strange gray mist of existence. She was invisible. Nobody talked to her. Even her teachers didn't call on her anymore. She guessed that word was out. Fragile Bea. Handle with care. Might crack. She imagined standing up on top of a lunchroom table, stamping her feet and screaming at the top of her lungs: "I'm still here. Talk to me!!!!" But she didn't imagine that would have the desired effect.

This situation was seriously gnarly. But she was stuck. She had to find out what the viewer was trying to tell her. As a matter of fact, she had a deep yearning—yes, yearning, she now knew what the word really meant—to study it. To hold it in her hands. To get lost in it. About once an hour she had an uncontrollable urge she had to obey. She stuck her hand deep down to the bottom of her backpack where she kept it hidden and just touched it. To make sure it was still there. To make sure it was really real.

She sat through all her classes just waiting for the lunch bell. When it rang, Bea walked through the courtyard and into the caf. She went directly to the outcasts' table, walking the long way around the room to avoid walking past Patty's table. She was about to take her now usual spot when she noticed Calvin getting his lunch out of his worn canvas sack.

What was left to lose? She walked up to him. "Calvin—"

"You have some nerve to even talk to me. Do you know how much trouble I got in?" He was speaking quietly, but his voice was sharp.

"Calvin—" Bea started again, but he cut her off.

"No." He was firm, but Bea remained standing in front of him for a long time. Some kids from the table behind Bea saw them together.

"Look at the geeks!" a boy in an A&F sweatshirt cackled.

And then, as if on cue, two girls started singing, "K-I-S-S-I-N-G." The whole table burst out in laughter.

Calvin looked Bea directly in the eye. "I wouldn't care if you told me you had proof of life on another planet. I wouldn't go anywhere with you."

Well, that didn't go as well as she'd hoped, Bea thought. Bea walked right past "her" seat and left the caf, dumping her lunch in the trash on the way out the door.

***

Bea's stomach grumbled all through algebra but she ignored it. She was afraid anything she put in it would just come back up. The bell rang, time for Physical Science. Great. Like that would settle her stomach.

She walked into the class just as the second bell rang. Mr. Belk, a young southern man who was usually quite serious, was sitting on the edge of his desk holding a letter on his lap and smiling. He looked like a kid on Christmas. "Okay everybody, take your seats. Quickly. I've got a surprise for you." This couldn't be good. He waited for all the kids to get into their desks and stop shuffling around. "I received this letter from the Board of Education. Our request to enter the All City Science Fair has been granted!" A couple of kids actually were excited.

But mostly it was just grunts and groans. "Hey, we are the first private school to be eligible. And winning it could mean grants, science scholarships." He saw he was alone in his glee. "...an all-expense-paid trip to New York City for the group of finalists." The room was quiet.

"Cool," said Brook Pierce, the most popular kid in the entire freshman class.

That did it. The kids all started talking at once.

"Do our parents have to go?" Billy Mert asked.

"Is it in spring? New York is really best in the springtime," Tammy Claussen added knowingly.

"How long do we have to get our projects ready? What do you have to do to win?" All the questions were coming at once.

"All right, all right. Let me explain how it works." Mr. Belk motioned with his hands for the kids to settle down.

It would count for twenty-five percent of their grade for the year. Extra credit for teams that reached the city finals. Teams. They had to work with a partner. He would hang the class roster on the wall and everyone was to sign up before they left class today. If you didn't sign up, he would assign you. Once you were signed up there was no changing. No exceptions. Great. Just when she'd turned into a social pariah, she needed a partner.

Wait a minute, this *was* great! She waited until Mr. Belk stopped flapping his jaws and then she rushed to the sign-up sheet with her black sharpie. She edged past the real science geeks to get there first. On the top blank she wrote her full name, Beatrice Parker. Followed by CALVIN BEECH, in big block letters. Ha, now he had to talk to her. Right?

Okay, so Calvin wasn't pleased, to put it mildly. And by the time he realized that she'd chosen him as a partner, it was too late to do anything about it. Mr. Belk actually was sympathetic toward him, which made Bea feel like a total loser, but said he couldn't change the rules. And even if he could, everyone else was already paired. To make things even better, Mr. Belk wanted a word with Bea after class.

After sign-ups, Calvin had gone into an eerie, quiet-boiling state and had not said a word the rest of class. He just sat there, fuming. Well, it had to be done. He might feel bad now, but he'd understand later, Bea reasoned.

Bea was still queasy. Lately, anything she felt certain about was completely the wrong thing to do. And ended up adding more weeks to her in-home incarceration. Maybe the viewer wouldn't be that interesting to anybody else? Maybe it was just her own personal obsession? She wondered if she'd ever be able to trust her gut again.

When class ended, Bea waited for everyone to leave and then did the death march up to Mr. Belk's desk. She would have to lie—again. She stopped in front of his desk and stared at a small hole in her slip-on Vans.

"Bea, I gotta tell you. I really think it was an unfortunate choice to force Calvin to be your partner. You can't make someone like you. It just doesn't work that way," he began in a patient teacher-knows-best voice. "You are on a slippery slope. I know you've made some other poor choices lately. I hate to see a girl as bright as you lose your way. Is there something going on at home?"

AHHHHHHH! Bea screamed in her head. She pushed her toe up through the hole in her shoe, wriggling it with all her might, trying to keep her body still.

Mr. Belk continued, "Is it something you want to talk to the school counselor about? You know, Ms. Paterson really might be able to help you out."

Just let it end. Please, God, let him just stop talking. He thinks I'm a total freak.

"You know, Bea, you could talk to me. I don't have a degree in that or anything, but I was a teenager myself not that long ago. I bet I could relate to whatever you're going through."

Not likely, Bea wanted to say. Okay, she had to say something or this would never stop. Mr. Belk just kept on talking.

"I would really like to help you—"

Bea looked up at him and jumped in. "Thanks. I mean, it's nice of you. I just think I was being dumb. It's not that big a deal. We'll finish the project and it'll be over. I promise to think more about my choices next time."

Mr. Belk crossed his arms and nodded slowly, clearly aware he was being shut down. "All right, Bea. But just remember, you don't have to go it alone, okay?"

When he finally let her leave, Bea shot out of the classroom like a human bullet. Patty was already gone. She headed toward the buses. This had to end. She couldn't take being the class freak. Mr. Belk's words rang in her ears, "You can't make someone like you." Ugh, everybody thought she was pathetic.

She made it to the edge of the courtyard in time to see Calvin, complete with hostile body language, boarding the number 55 bus. The doors closed and it merged back in with traffic. The 56 was right behind it. Bea jumped on and showed her bus pass. The two buses traveled the same route for the first couple of miles or so. If she was lucky she could see where Calvin got off and follow him home. Hey, if she was going to be a freak she might as well add stalker to complete the picture, right?

The buses weaved in and out of traffic. At the first few stops, she watched passengers getting off, none of them Calvin. When the two buses were close enough, Bea thought she could see Calvin in the back of the bus, leaning against the window. Not sitting like his stop was coming up any time soon.

At the next stop, she watched Calvin's shape in the back of the preceding bus, still not moving. Her bus stopped as well, and as it pulled away from the curb, she saw Calvin crossing 49th. She had been watching the wrong boy.

Bea reached up and pulled the cord for the bus to stop at the next street. She tried to keep her eye on Calvin as she made her way down the aisle and off the bus. He was about a block ahead of her. She shifted the weight of higher learning in her backpack and rushed to catch him.

As soon as he crossed Maple he started heading off at an angle. Behind Hal's Grocery. Maybe he worked after school. She jogged a little, the weight of her books threatening her balance. She got to the alley behind Hal's and nothing. Calvin was gone. The loading door was down and she would have heard if he had pulled it open to enter that way. Well, he couldn't just disappear. She looked back at Hal's. There was a door next to the loading area, neatly painted in a hopeful green with a small empty planter beside it. Next to the door was a bell and a small sign that read: "The Beeches." The Beeches. Bea had never connected the two. Hal didn't just own the grocery store—he lived there. And apparently Calvin did too. She couldn't help wondering what the story was.

Through the small window on the door she could see a tiny landing with coat hooks and a staircase leading to the second floor. Bea took off her glove and pressed the small, black doorbell with a shaky finger. She heard someone moving about, followed by footsteps on the stairs, and Calvin's gray socks appeared as he made his way down. Then she could see all of him. His face went ashy when he saw her. *Too late to run,* Bea thought. He opened the door, clearly in shock.

"Hi," Bea said, raising her arm in a dorky little wave.

"I can't believe you! You really are some kind of freak. You need to leave, now!" Calvin was really shouting at her.

"Okay, Okay. I know you're mad." Bea was fumbling through her pack, digging around at the bottom.

"No, if you knew how mad I was you wouldn't be standing here. You'd be very, very far away. Are you trying to ruin my life? Is that it?" Calvin was still shouting. And the stupid viewer was like an eel slipping through her fingers. Calvin went to slam the door, but Bea stuck her foot in it just as she caught the viewer. Calvin looked at her with crazy mad eyes. She reached through the gap and placed the viewer in his hand. As Calvin looked down, he let go of the door. Bea pulled her throbbing foot back. Thank God her Vans had thick soles.

He turned the viewer over in his hands. Bea watched his face as he looked at the edges, felt the material. It landed in the same comfortable position Bea held it in. He stared at the surface. She saw his eyes widen as he felt it tingle, and when it started to grow his mouth dropped open. He was hooked. She heard the *bwoom-bwoom*. The screen glowed. And then it turned red, buzzed, and shrank again.

"What is it?" he asked, all the anger forgotten. He was mesmerized.

"I don't know exactly. That's why I've been wanting your help." She reached to take the viewer back and found it firmly gripped in Calvin's hand. With a tug she retrieved it and put it in her pack. She wanted to make him work for it now. "But if you don't want to, that's cool." She turned to leave and got about four feet from the door.

"Okay, I'm sorry." She kept walking, a sly smile forming on her lips. "Really, really sorry, okay?" he said as he chased after her in his stocking feet.

Chapter 11: A Hot Cup of Li

"I can't smell any 'accident' on your breath," Wharton said as he passed Vaslow, already seated with a Li pot in front of him, and took a seat at the next table over. "I think today will be a better day for you." He chuckled to himself.

"I think I've got a pretty good shot at that," Vaslow replied. "Any day would be a better day than that one."

Vaslow sat at his usual table in the Li room, back to the side wall, next to the handwritten sign with the new prices. Apparently water costs had gone up again. He was going through the motions of taking independent news from the circuit on the hovering translucent screen of the personal viewer installed at the table. The room was dark and rugged, no touch of a woman's hand in this place. Dust danced in shafts of sunslight that filtered in through the half-shaded windows. The floors and walls were lined with traditional Sloan mats woven in dark colors; the thick dense weave had the additional benefit of absorbing sound. A few of the other tables were occupied by lone men sipping Li and reading by the beam of the kane light, which produced golden pools of light just large enough to illuminate a single table.

Steam from a traditional carved-stone pot wafted up, brushing the edges of the moving images of the circuit Vaslow was pretending to read. He had chosen this table because it was directly across from Wharton's usual spot.

The Sloan rituals had been a mystery to him when he began trying to break into their circles. Vaslow had thought that a Li room would be the best spot for making connections. He hadn't understood that after drinking Li on a regular basis you no longer experienced the light-headed giddiness. The more habitually you drank it, the clearer your thoughts became. He had been counting on loose lips and back-slapping camaraderie. Instead, he found a bunch of men who preferred to read Sloan doctrine or take news from the independent circuits. He also found that he enjoyed the Li ritual so much he continued coming despite his lack of progress.

A thin boy put a Li setup on Wharton's table and went back to the kitchen. Wharton lifted the cage of dry Li berries and put it at the center of the steam chamber, hit the release, and pulled it out again.

It had been more than a week since Vaslow had left the cantomount with Bea. He could sense her lifeforce shifting, waning even, and still she had made no connection. Jaru forbid if her transition should hit before she contacted him. Bayatrice needed him. He had to get his craft rescrambled, now.

"We could get you a bone player accompanist and hire you out for weddings," Wharton joked, not really sounding amused.

Vaslow looked at his hand. The edge of his nerves had apparently found its way to his center; he'd been rhythmically tapping his crest ring on the stone pot without realizing it. Wrapping his hand around his Li glass, he decided to make a move. He had seen men in the market defer to Wharton, had witnessed fights dissipate simply because Wharton shook his head. Vaslow no longer had the luxury of time to wait the man out. He moved, uninvited, to Wharton's table.

"I think you and I have some common interests," Vaslow said as he sat down.

"Really? I could hardly imagine that being true," Wharton responded. If he was unnerved by Vaslow's proximity, he didn't show it.

"I know the Protectorate is no friend of the Sloan." Vaslow worked at keeping his rattled nerves from affecting his voice. "Just like you, I can't stand to see these hundreds of young men and women rattling around the markets with no work, empty shelves at every market, soldiers on every street corner."

"Ah, you're a humanitarian," Wharton answered. "But our situation is no worse than any other water-poor district on Vedra. I hardly think those feelings on the matter are unique."

"I was just thinking about the old days, perhaps when you were young and the sovereigns ruled. They wouldn't have let it come to this."

"A nice stroll down my childhood's path, but it is irrelevant."

Vaslow leaned forward, "What if it's not irrelevant? What if I am talking future rather than past?"

"Then you are talking to the wrong man," Wharton said, impatience seeping into his voice. "I am a simple merchant. Such ideas are beyond me."

"If I believed that I'd be a fool." Vaslow looked into the man's eyes. "There isn't much time. I need to jump. And I need help."

Wharton reached into his cloak and pulled out a handful of coins, tossing them on the table. "I'm afraid my Li has soured." With that, Wharton stood and left.

Vaslow wanted to run after the man and shake him, make him listen, but he knew that would only push him farther away from his goal. Wharton was the key—that much felt clear. He'd only made his last connection after Wharton had "opened the market" to him. But now the man was no longer in his debt. Vaslow dropped his own payment on the table and left the Li room.

He felt like a caged aul beast, wild and ready to strike, yet trapped. He cursed under his breath and kicked at the sandy soil, sending yet another plume of dust across his outercloak.

"Popi. He make me mad like that, too," a small voice said to him from behind.

Vaslow turned and saw Si leaning against the Li room's alley wall. "Hello, Simoud," Vaslow answered, and continued to walk. He had no time to entertain a child.

"I saw you talking to Popi. You ask him for somethings, right?"

"He and I were just talking, nothing more." Vaslow wanted to dismiss the boy and get back to his planning.

"Mister-mister, you know, whatever you ask from Popi, I can get you," the boy said with the utmost seriousness.

Vaslow stopped and let a small chuckle escape before he answered. "I'm sure you could. But there is nothing I need today."

If the boy noticed Vaslow wasn't taking him seriously, he didn't show it. "I am biggie-biggie, like Popi. Popi say you and he are all evens. But it wasn't his chit, it was mine. I owe you, Mister-Mister." The boy stood and stepped toward Vaslow. "What you need? Who you want to talk to?"

The moment hung suspended, the prospect almost too great to resist. He bet this boy, as small as he was, could put him in contact with a techie. Vaslow knew if he took the boy up on his offer there would be no guarantee the techie would cooperate without Wharton's approval. And if he got the boy to do something his father had already refused, Vaslow would be shut out of Sloantown for good.

The boy stood there, ready to pay his debt, no matter the price. Vaslow had to admire that. There were, indeed, qualities of the great Simoud in this little one.

"Thank you, but there is nothing I need," Vaslow repeated, and with that he turned and continued walking before he changed his mind.

Chapter 12: Best Laid Plans

Well, Bea had been right about one thing, Calvin was dying to help her out now that he had seen the viewer. She had shown it to him, but only in an ever-so-brief glimpse because she had to rush home so she didn't get more grounded—or would that be groundeder? She wasn't used to the grammar of a juvenile delinquent. Hopefully, now that she had help, she wouldn't have to be.

Mr. Belk had called Aunt Lucy, "just to express his concern." Did teachers have any idea what a stupid move that was? Well, at least it didn't make matters worse. In fact, in made them better. Now everybody believed that her antics were about a science project. Which in turn made them all worry again. But at least drugs and teenage sex were out of the picture. Bea could feel it. She was slowly regaining ground. Her aunt and uncle said she could work with Calvin from after school to dinner every weeknight to work on the science project.

For the first night in weeks, Bea slept like a log, without crying her way into it, and, thank God, for once she didn't have that awful dream. In the morning, Patty woke her up instead of going down to eat breakfast without her.

Patty gave Bea's shoulder a little shake and Bea's eyes flipped open.

"Whoa, that was a little freaky," Patty said. "You're an eager beaver this morning."

"Yup, I start work on the science project today," Bea said, feeling an odd sense of relief that she could at least sort of tell Patty what she was doing. Being able to tell the truth was a step on the path back to being normal, back to having Patty and the rest of her family in her life again. Well, maybe it wasn't the truth exactly, but finding out what the viewer did was kind of like a science project, right?

Patty was already dressed. "Want me to get your lunch for you?"

Yes! Life as she knew it was not over. "Yeah, that would be great," Bea said, as if it were no big deal. Patty nodded and headed downstairs. Before Bea got out of bed, she dragged her backpack over and for once didn't reach for the viewer. She pulled her phone out of the outside pocket and texted, "hope u have a gr8 day ," and sent it to Patty with a smile on her face.

And Patty was correct, Bea was excited. No, that didn't even come close to describing how she felt. Bursting? Closer. She felt like soda in a can that someone had given a good shake.

Today—finally—she and Calvin were going to his house to look at the viewer! It hadn't been easy, but when Calvin wasn't being a jerk he managed to be amazingly persuasive. Together they had gotten the parents to agree to let them do the science project at the Beeches'. It was a tough sell at first because one of Hal's rules was no friends over without an adult home, and Hal worked until 8 PM. But because Calvin had all his research books, science kits, and the better computer at his house, Hal had agreed. Which was perfect.

Hal was very strict with his grandson. Bea had no idea why Calvin lived with him instead of his parents, or where his parents were. Just knowing he had holes in his family too made her think they had more in common than she first thought, that maybe whatever family wrinkles life had drawn inside her had also been drawn inside of Calvin.

***

At last bell, Bea got up and went to Calvin's desk. She could feel Mr. Belk watching her. "Wanna ride the bus together?" Bea asked Calvin.

"Sure. I can't wait to get started," Calvin said with more of a smile than even Bea expected.

Mr. Belk watched, eyebrows raised. He'd see, Bea thought. She didn't have to try to make someone like her. In truth, it didn't matter if Calvin liked her or not, but it would feel a lot better if Mr. Belk thought he did.

They walked to the bus stop together. "So, where did you get it exactly?" Calvin asked.

"Not here." Bea said in a hushed voice. "I'll tell you everything at your house."

"Wow, is it like some spy gadget or something?" Calvin said mockingly. "Is your uncle in the CIA?"

"I'm serious. Do you want to help me or not?"

With that Calvin shut his mouth and the two of them rode the bus in silence all the way Calvin's stop.

Calvin unlocked the alley door with a key he kept on a long string tied to a loop in his backpack. He asked Bea to take off her shoes and he did the same. They hung their coats on the coat hooks on the wall and went stocking-footed up the old painted stairs.

The top of the stairs opened onto the living room. The first thing Bea noticed was that everything was neat. Not just neat, but clean, like no dust was ever allowed to fall here. And that must have been some trick, considering the dozens of small frames with family photos that stared back at her from around the room. The second thing Bea noticed was that nothing looked new. Nothing was worn or bent or dented, it just didn't look as if it had come from this decade.

"Wait here while I get some stuff from my room," Calvin said, dropping his backpack with a thump at the end of the desk that was tucked into one corner. "So, secret spy girl, I can talk about it now, right?"

"Yes," she said, rolling her eyes. Her hands were clammy and it felt like a case of the fidgets had been let loose in her limbs. Now that she was here, she didn't exactly know what to do.

Calvin came back in wheeling a small gray task chair with a couple of three-ring notebooks on the seat. He was yapping the whole
way, going on about his theories. Funny, once you got him talking,
you couldn't shut him up. "It must be some covert government dev
project. I mean, they're the only ones who could fund something this
complex." He stopped pushing the chair for a moment. "How the heck
did you get it? Or maybe I don't want to know."

"A couple of weeks ago somebody left it on my bed in the middle
of the night. It was weird. I don't know how they got in or anything."

"Right. I'll take that as an 'I don't want to know' then," Calvin
said, looking at her skeptically. "You have to promise me that whatever you did to get it, if we ever get caught, you'll swear I had nothing to
do with that part."

"What?" Bea asked.

"I need you to promise me that you've got my back if we get
arrested or something. Otherwise, I won't help." Calvin was firm.

"I'm not joking. It came with a card with my name on it. Well,
pretty much my name." Bea began to dig in her backpack for the card.

"Yeah, right. Like someone would give a highly specialized
bleeding-edge prototype to a kid." Calvin was not convinced.

Bea found the card and shoved it at him. He read the words. "Like
this proves anything. Is your name really Bayatrice?"

"No, but that's not the point. Somebody meant me to have it,"
Bea's volume inched up.

"All right, whatever. But when they come looking for it, and they
will come looking for it, I am making note of when I am starting in on
this project and that the viewer was already in your possession. I'll
want you to initial it."

Bea rolled her eyes again. "Fine."

Calvin pulled one of the notebooks off the seat and scribbled in it. Then he handed the notebook and pen to Bea. She
scribbled her initials and handed it back. "Perfect. We're good
now," he said, and his brow relaxed. He handed her the other

notebook and pushed the second chair up to the desk. "I got us each our own notebook for recording protocols and results. I think I should record while you are driving the device and you'll record while I'm driving."

"Wow. You've really thought this out." Bea looked at the red vinyl notebook Calvin handed her. "Okay, you want to 'drive' first?"

"No, I think you should. Show me where you get stuck, and I'll see if I can take it farther."

Bea dug the viewer out of her pack and they both sat down. She was facing the desk and Calvin was watching her from the side, leaning on his open notebook ready to record.

Bea went through her regular motions to get it to play.

"Wait." Calvin stopped her. "Tell me exactly what you do as you do it." His pencil was poised.

Bea looked at him cock-eyed. "I pick it up and hold it like this."

"Like what?" Calvin asked.

"I don't know. Like this. Just like this." Bea showed him her grip.

"I need to know precise details," Calvin said with his pencil at the ready.

"Uh, like, well, my hands are um, here and here," Bea said with as much detail as she had in her.

"Okay." Calvin exhaled. "I'll just have to draw a diagram of it later. Keep going. What do you do to get to the next phase?"

Bea had held this thing dozens of times, had wondered about it for hundreds of hours, but she had never thought about what she did. "I don't do anything. I just look at it."

"You have to do something," Calvin countered.

"Well," Bea thought for a moment, "I just *really* look at it. If I'm not totally concentrating on it, nothing happens."

"Unbelievable," Calvin said, writing furiously. "Wow. I wonder if it uses retinal scans or brainwaves? It could be thought-induced actions! Show me."

As Calvin watched, the device grew in Bea's hands. She flicked her thumb, as she had done in the past, and the great room appeared on the screen, then rose up around her. "See? Isn't it amazing?"

"I can't see it. It just looks like you're in a haze of blue light." Before he got too disappointed he added, "Which is pretty amazing by itself."

"Stop," Bea said, and the haze faded. "You try. That's about as far as I've gotten anyway." She handed Calvin the viewer. He took it, wide-eyed and grinning, a grin that could have powered a city grid. He held it in his hands as if he were holding an entomological example of a rare butterfly. "I've dropped it a couple of times. It won't break," Bea told him. "It won't even dent." Calvin's face scrunched in horror for a moment, but then snapped back to rapt focus.

The viewer seated itself in Calvin's anxious hands. He focused with such intent that his brows furrowed and a vein in his neck throbbed. Bea watched as he felt the tingle and the growing and heard the *bwoom-bwoom*. The viewer glowed blue, and then it turned red and buzzed.

"That's weird," Bea said. "That's never happened to me. Try again."

Calvin tried three more times. And on the third time the buzz was accompanied by a rather large shock. "Ow," Calvin yelped, more in surprise than in pain, and involuntarily flung the viewer. It skittered across the floor and stopped as it connected with a couch leg.

He looked at Bea and she looked at him. Bea slumped. Calvin raced across the room and gingerly picked it up, examining its still pristine surface.

"It's user-protected," Calvin said solemnly. "It won't let me in."

It was almost five o'clock. Bea would have to leave soon. And nothing new had happened except that Calvin had a weird tingle in his fingers and refused to touch the viewer again. Bea's emotions were on Space Mountain. This morning she couldn't have been happier. Now she couldn't be more the opposite.

"Our outline for our project is due Monday," Calvin reminded Bea, as if she hadn't been depressed enough. Bea thought she might cry.

"Don't worry," Calvin continued, "I'll just write something up over the weekend. How about we build a Layden jar capacitor?" Bea looked at him, totally blank. "You know," he said, "like electricity in a jar. I already made one for the heck of it over the summer."

"Whatever."

"It's not totally original, but it has some pretty flashy applications," Calvin said hopefully.

"Fine."

"I'm sorry, Bea." That didn't make her feel any better. "I can still help you. You can just describe what's happening as you experience things."

"We already saw how well I did at that." She started to pack her things up. She felt the all-too-familiar hot sting in the corners of her eyes.

Just as her tears were about to fall, Calvin shouted, "I've got it!" He was looking energized again. "It could just be a proximity thing. If I could just have my line of sight in your field of vision I would piggy-back on your experience!"

He seemed so excited. But Bea had no idea what he was talking about. "Huh?" she uttered as intelligently as she could.

"I just have to sit really, really close to you." Calvin said, looking at the floor.

"You're not just trying to get back at me for the under-the-bleach-ers thing, are you? Which was totally not my fault, by the way."

"Nah-oh," Calvin said, a little embarrassed. "Believe me, if I thought there was another way..."

They got set up by sitting together on the same chair, Bea in front and Calvin in the back. Bea moved all the way forward with just the tiniest bit of her butt hanging onto the edge of the seat. Sitting so close to him, a boy she wasn't related to, felt odd. Even if it was Calvin Beech. It was beyond uncomfortable for so many reasons. She pulled her elbows against her own boy-shaped body in hopes of being as small as possible, but still she felt Calvin's chest up against her back.

No way around it, they'd have to be touching each other to make this work. And she had to make this work.

She held the viewer in one hand and took a deep breath.

"Come on already, you need to get home on time or we won't be able to meet anymore," Calvin said impatiently.

"Okay." Bea tried to make herself begin, but she just couldn't. This was really her last hope. What if it didn't work? What would she do then?

At first he was so rigid, leaning up against him was like leaning up against a statue at the Museum of Science and Industry. Then she heard him take a quiet slow breath, like he was smelling her, leaning in toward her ever so slightly. Then he snapped back to his statue-state.

"Well?" Calvin nudged.

What was that about? Bea wondered. "Okay, okay." Bea grabbed the other edge of the viewer with her left hand. She looked down at its surface and...they heard Hal open the downstairs door.

Calvin was so surprised he stood up, which pushed Bea right off the front of the chair. She landed squarely on her butt.

Hal crested the top of the stairs and saw the two of them, each seated properly in their own chairs. "How's it going?" Hal asked.

Calvin hesitated and Bea jumped in. "Oh, just great. We're building lightning in a jar. Your grandson is so smart."

"Uh, electricity in a jar, actually," Calvin corrected, looking as if he was trying not to wince.

"Well, that sounds like a fine experiment. Maybe you could build enough so we don't have to pay Mutual Power and Light anymore." Hal chuckled. He put the mail in a bin on the desk corner.

"Who's watching the store?" Calvin asked.

"Your cousin Lem offered to close up for me. The Parkers have invited us to dinner." Hal looked at his watch. "And it's just about time we were leaving."

***

Dinner was a pleasant surprise. The only kind of bad part was that Patty was eating dinner over at Nell's. Bea wasn't used to them each doing their own thing, but at least it wasn't because they were mad at each other. P.J., Calvin, and Teddy ganged up and were making fun of Bea. Never before had being teased felt so good. They didn't treat her like a glass doll, or worse yet, a ticking bomb. And everybody laughed. The kind of laugh that melts the distance between people. Bea was warm and safe. For the first time in a long while she felt like she belonged. Here in this house, with her family around her, she felt like hot buttered toast on a cold night. She realized that it had been like this most of her life, but it took almost losing it to really appreciate it. Maybe her life wasn't permanently messed up.

Though the laughter and teasing made her feel almost normal, there was still a tiny niggle in the back of her head that kept her from fully absorbing the warmth around her. She knew it wouldn't go away until she found out who she really was. That small part of her made her fingers twitch, longing to pull out the viewer and make it do whatever it had come here to do. She hoped that figuring out this stupid device would be like a scavenger hunt, that she would go through everything on the list and it would end and she would be done with it. She sat on her hands and waited for everyone else to finish dinner.

The kids cleared the table. She and Calvin had eaten the last of Aunt Lucy's biscuits while loading the dishwasher. Bea had eaten more than she had all week, and the nausea was only background noise at the moment. Maybe her stomach would finally go back to normal once she and Calvin cracked the viewer's message.

"It was so good to see you actually eat something," Aunt Lucy said as she came into the kitchen through the swinging door, with the saltshakers and the salad dressing. "You're so thin. I was starting to worry." Aunt Lucy had a contented smile on her face.

Bea just nodded. She finished putting detergent in the dishwasher and set it to run.

"It was a really great dinner, Mrs. Parker," Calvin said, rubbing his stomach. "My G-pops can't cook like that."

"I'm glad you liked it. Hope you saved room for dessert," she said, pulling a cheesecake from the fridge.

"Uh, Calvin and I were gonna go upstairs and work a little more on our outline," Bea said, testing the waters. She'd never had a boy over and wasn't sure what the rules were about having him in her room.

"Okay, maybe later on the dessert?" Aunt Lucy asked. Calvin's gaze lingered on the cheesecake, but he followed Bea out of the room.

They both sat on her bed. Bea was on the edge with her feet on the floor, so she could simply stand up if they heard someone on the stairs. Calvin was pressed up behind her, more willingly than he had earlier. Somehow she felt a little more comfortable doing this in her own room. She started showing Calvin the buttons she had pressed so far. He was geeking out as she described the way she could feel the buttons that were only made of light. To him it seemed to make sense. He called a row of colored dots around the edge of her thumbs that she hadn't even noticed before the navigation. To him, there was a pattern, hierarchy, order. Somehow Bea had started out midway through the levels.

"This is...this is...well, it's unbelievable. It's so advanced. I never thought we would get to this in my lifetime. I just wish we could understand what they were saying." Calvin was actually breathless.

"What do you mean? It sounds okay to me," Bea said, puzzled.

"Yeah, but it's not English."

"What do you mean 'not English?' I understood them fine. I think the queen, or that's what I call her, is really kind of funny." Bea laughed, remembering a bit of the speech they had just heard.

Calvin leaned around and stared at her with his mouth gaping open.

"What?" Bea asked, clueless. Calvin just stared. "What?"

"Uh, I speak three languages and have basic syntax knowledge of about fourteen others. This isn't like any language I have ever heard before."

Bea stood up and looked at the viewer in her hands. She looked back at Calvin. "This is creeping me out. How can I know a language you've never heard of? And how come I didn't know it was another language?"

Bea thought back to the day at the practice hall. She remembered not understanding things at first. She told Calvin about repeating and repeating. And then how her head had pounded for two days afterwards.

"Bea, I think this thing taught you another language," Calvin said quietly.

"Okay, now this thing is really weirding me out. Like it was inside my brain or something." Bea tossed the viewer across to her bed as if it were burning her fingers.

"This thing is even more advanced than anything I could have dreamed of. You can't stop now." Seeing Bea was not convinced, Calvin continued, "Hey, it taught you another language. It didn't damage you."

"How do you know that? It wasn't in your brain." Bea was hot and trembling. "Maybe it's dangerous."

"Why would they send it to you? It's not like a fourteen-year-old kid could do much in a plot to take over the country or anything," Calvin said. He seemed so calm.

"This is all wrong," Bea said, feeling more confused than ever. "This thing…it's just supposed to tell me about my real parents. What does another language have to do with that?"

"I don't know." Calvin shrugged. "I guess you'll have to dive back in to figure it out."

"Yeah? If it's such a great idea, you do it then."

"Bea, I wish I could." The wistful look in his eyes left no doubt in Bea's mind that he would trade places with her in a second. "This is by far the most technologically advanced device I have ever seen, read about, or dreamt of in my whole life—and believe me, I've been to just about every site that exists on this kind of stuff." He looked at the viewer on the bed next to him, but didn't reach to touch it. "For some reason it was given to you. I don't know why, but I know whatever the reason, it must be pretty important."

"Important doesn't necessarily mean safe. I think maybe it's time to tell my aunt and uncle."

"You're kidding, right?"

Maybe Calvin was right. Maybe her birth family had been from a different country—she hadn't ever thought about that before. After a bit more assurance from Calvin that he didn't think her brain would melt, Bea decided to explore it a little more.

Calvin asked her to touch an iridescent green dot that was blinking. Bea moved her thumb ever so slightly and touched the dot. She felt an odd wave of energy, yet another new sensation from this crazy device, and then everything shifted.

Chapter 13: Home to Roost

Vaslow woke when the North Moon was high. Out his bedroom window, the stars were vivid white and expansive in the abyss of the sky, more visible here in this low-tech district which shut down when the workday ended. He thought of the night on Earth so many years ago when he had awoken, sensing the Protectorate guards had found them. This night vibrated with the same sense of danger.

He looked out his window to the ground below and saw nothing. But in the distance, he could see two Protectorate hovercraft invading the otherwise peaceful night sky. *Just like the Protectorate,* Vaslow thought. *Now that they got what they wanted, they want me dead.* He should have anticipated this, should have counted on their inability to keep a promise.

He quickly threw on his cloak and shoes. If he was to be taken, it wouldn't be in his skivvies. He was sitting on the edge of his bed, considering going out the window, when the door to his bedroom opened. He didn't move. It was too soon for the Guard to have landed and made their way into his building.

"Ever prepared, eh, Vaslow?" It was Islook who stood before him.

He hadn't been prepared for this. Islook standing there, dressed in a full Protectorate Guard uniform. He must have received his commission early. Vaslow knew the young man had rejected his teachings, knew they were at odds, but never once had he thought Islook to be capable of going so far as to volunteer to be the one to bring him in.

"They've issued a decree of arrest for you," Islook said. "Did you really think pledging allegiance would protect you?" He was clearly disgusted. "Next time try not getting shitty drunk and spouting your mouth off in an officers' bar in Tanloo."

No words could have cut him more. Vaslow's own weakness had led him to this moment.

"They are on their way to take you in right now," Islook said, slowly and clearly.

"So you thought you'd get a jump on them and take me in yourself? Earn chits for your new posting in the Guard?" The pain of this betrayal was compounded by the fact that he was failing Bayatrice. If he were taken in now, she would be lost forever. His petty weakness, his vile pride, his simple stupidity, had threatened the last hope for his people. He wiped his sweating brow with a steady hand. The feeling of failure threatened to crash down on him, a suffocating wave. He hated to raise a hand to this boy, even after all that he'd done.

Vaslow's move was swift. He sprang up and spun around behind Islook, and connected a solid punch in the young man's right kidney. Islook hunched forward and gasped in surprise or pain, Vaslow wasn't sure which.

"No," Islook said, struggling to take in more air. Maybe this path was more distasteful than he had anticipated. But Vaslow couldn't leave it now. He had to get out of this building and not have Islook on his trail. Vaslow landed another blow on the young man's hunched body. Islook rose and brought his elbow up, connecting with Vaslow's chin, sending the older man reeling into the e-wardrobe behind him.

Vaslow feigned being stunned and slid down the wall. The younger man began to speak, "Listen, I came here tonight—" Vaslow took advantage of the respite in attack and cantilevered himself off the ground, landing both feet on Islook's chest. The young man was forced back with such intensity he made a torso-shaped depression in the wall, dazed but still moving.

Islook shook his head, trying to get his bearings, and then they heard a high-pitched scream. In all the commotion Vaslow had missed the cantomount's quiet vibration, the message receipt chime, and the opening of the connection window.

Both men froze. All the fight in Vaslow disappeared. He ran to the cantomount. The image was projected from the viewer, a window across the expanse of space into another galaxy. A young redheaded girl with her hand over her mouth sat with a dark-skinned boy behind her; both wore shocked expressions.

Vaslow could only utter one word, "Bayatrice."

Chapter 14: The Bat Phone

The 3-D world the viewer was projecting around her fell away. It shimmered, then shrank and settled back flat on the viewer's surface before fading entirely. There was a brief pause, as if the machine was thinking, and then a projection rose up in front of them. It wasn't like before; it wasn't a room projected around her, but rather a window suspended in mid-air. Formed with four sides, the image inside the window was as clear and real as if she were looking outside her bedroom window. It was large enough for Bea to see everything in it clearly. There were two men—one old, one young—fighting, trashing the room they were in. They were both wearing robes. They were moving in ways Bea hadn't thought humanly possible. When the older one kicked the other guy into a wall so hard it broke the plaster, Bea let out a yelp. And then they both stopped and looked right at Calvin and her, as if the men could see them.

The older one stepped toward her, looking as shocked as she was, and then said her name. It came out sounding odd, more like "Bay-a-trees," with the r rolling like Mrs. D. did in Spanish class. He reached his hand toward her, through the projected window and right out into the room. She leaned back into Calvin to avoid his grasp and lost hold of the viewer. It fell to the floor, and the screen went black.

"He said your name," Calvin said in disbelief.

"Wow, that seemed *so* real," Bea said, standing up and forcing a nervous laugh.

"Ah, Bea, I think that *was* real," Calvin said. "They could see us."

"You're crazy. It was just a video or recording or something," Bea said a little too quickly, unable to squelch a nervous giggle.

"Bea, I thought we were messing around with some high-tech equipment. I thought this was some kind of black-ops instrument or something—which was intense enough. But that's not what it is." Calvin paused. "Most definitely not. Remember when I made that joke about proof of life on another planet?" He said, "Well, I think we found it."

"Come on. You are such a drama queen." Bea was almost angry. "Just 'cause they have weird spots on their faces? That's not proof."

"No, not the spots. Did you see out that guy's window?" Bea shook her head. "There were two moons."

"Holy shit." The word just tumbled out of her mouth, unplanned. It was not part of her usual vocabulary and felt foreign on her tongue, but no other response seemed to fit. She slumped onto Patty's bed. She couldn't make her mind wrap around this. She had no idea how to handle it. Why would anyone, scratch that—any *alien*—want to communicate with her? She thought this was about her birth family, about her past. Why would someone from another planet know her birth name? She was just about to ask Calvin when Patty opened the bedroom door.

"Yo, science geeks," Patty said playfully, sweeping into the room with her backpack over her shoulder and an armload of clean folded clothes. "Whoa, what happened to you guys? Somebody steal your Bunsen burners?" She laughed. Neither of them even looked at her. Patty dropped her backpack on the bed. "Really, guys, what's goin' on? Somebody die or something?" Patty was still trying to force a laugh.

Hal called from downstairs, "Hey, Calvin, time to go, buddy."

"Uh, coming, G-pops," Calvin yelled back down. He looked at Bea, who felt almost catatonic. "It'll be okay. We'll figure it out, I swear. Just don't turn it on without me, okay?" Bea couldn't respond. Calvin bent down to get eye-to-eye with Bea. "Promise me." Bea nodded.

"Hey guys, it's a science fair. It's not the cure for cancer." Patty looked a little confused. "And there's always next year, right?" When neither answered, she rolled her eyes and turned to put her clean clothes away.

**

Bea had somehow managed to brush her teeth, put on pajamas and get into bed. Patty was making the soft sounds of an easy sleep. Bea couldn't close her eyes—meeting morph-man in dreamland wouldn't be any escape. She didn't toss and turn. She just lay there, barely blinking. This couldn't be happening. The last two weeks she'd thought she'd been playing with an elaborate toy, but it was really some kind of alien device. What if they were trying to brainwash her or give her some alien disease? Her head ached and her stomach churned. Maybe they already had. Calvin hadn't needed to make her promise to leave it alone. The last thing she wanted to do was get near that thing. Her mind spun on this same little loop over and over, taking no thought any further.

Then, from her closet, she heard a faint vibration. Bea froze. Then she heard a soft *bwoom-bwoom*. Holy crap! The sound was getting louder. And louder. Patty rolled over. Bea scrambled out of bed, threw herself into the closet and shut the door behind her. She unzipped her pack and dug the viewer out of the bag. As soon as her hands touched it, the viewer grew and the window formed.

It was the old man again. He was standing in the dark, outside some old building. He had dried blood on the side of his head. He looked intense and nervous. "Thank Jaru, Bayatrice. I don't have much time–"

"Stop!" Bea tried not to yell it. The image faded. She dropped the viewer in her pack, but as soon as she did it began to vibrate again. It began the soft *bwoom-bwoom*. No, no, no! Bea picked it up and again the window formed.

"Bayatrice, don't disengage." The old man was impatient and demanding. "Please! Didn't you go through the instructions? We need—"

"Stop!" Where was the "off" switch on this thing? The viewer vibrated in her hand and immediately the window opened up. This time the old man didn't say a word. He just reached forward.

Bea saw his arm come toward her. It extended right out of the window. And then she felt his hand on her wrist, grabbing her hard, tugging her. "Stop!" Bea shouted, and the window closed and the man's hand disappeared. She was shaking, silent tears were running down her face. What was happening? She dropped the viewer back in her pack, put on her froggy slippers, and opened the closet doors.

"Bea, what are you doing?" Patty mumbled groggily.

"Nothing. I had a nightmare. Go back to sleep." Her voice trembled.

"Could you dream a little quieter then?" Patty said and rolled back over.

God, how Bea wished this was a dream. She started down the stairs, feeling the viewer vibrating again. It began its *bwoom-bwoom* as she darted across the family room to the patio doors.

The volume increased and she fumbled with the lock and pushed the doors open. She darted across the yard, the thin, icy snow cracking beneath her slippered feet. Tiny chips of ice hit her ankles and ran down into her slippers. The noise coming from her pack was getting louder.

The garden shed door was unlocked. Thankfully P.J. hadn't remembered to put the lock back on after the season's last mowing. She reached the shed and pulled at the metal latch, flung the door open, and looked around. Stacked pots, coiled hoses, rakes, shovels, and a whole lot of potting soil.

She sandwiched her pack between two twenty-pound bags of potting soil and put a third one on top for good measure. The noise was muffled. She stacked bags of vermiculite and violet food all around for extra insulation. Feeling along the dirt-covered shelves, she found the lock and key to the shed.

She stepped outside, shut the latch, and fastened the lock. She dropped the key into her robe pocket, turned, and leaned back the on the shed door, noticing a tiny trickle of blood from a scratch on her wrist where the man had grabbed her. She felt like a character in one of P.J.'s horror movies, locking up the evil, thinking it was safe, not knowing what would happen in the next scene.

Chapter 15: Shut Down

Vaslow stood in the dead end of an alley on the other side of Sloantown. It was dark and still, save for the faint sound of rodents scurrying through piles of trash. He held the cantomount in his bloody, aching hand, using all his will to keep from smashing it up against the building. Islook lay in a heap on the floor back in his rented rooms. Vaslow had done what he needed to do to get the cantomount and get out of the building before the Protectorate Guard arrived. He hoped the young man would survive, but he couldn't worry about that now. He'd gone out his second-story window and used the awnings to make it to the ground without breaking his neck. Heading away through back alleys, he heard the commotion in the distance as the Guard stormed his building. Though more Protectorate Guard hovercraft combed the skies, he'd somehow managed to make it across the market down to the other side of the district without being spotted.

Lungs burning, he hunched over with his hands on his knees to try to catch his breath. He had made it worse—the girl was terrified of him. She had no idea who he was. He assessed his situation: the programming had failed; she hadn't learned the truth about who she was; she didn't know what was coming or why she needed him. And on top of it, he was now probably the most wanted man on all of Vedra.

He kicked at a rock in the yellow dirt, sending it up against a trash heap. In the dark, he could see several small mangy gurdrus run out into the open, their pointed snouts snapping and their slimy tails dragging behind them as they circled in panic. He watched them scatter, seeking refuge, and then heard another soft shuffling—too much sound for a gurdru.

He pressed himself up against the wall, calmed his nerves, and tried to sense the numbers approaching. Just one. Light of foot, small. He cursed his lack of weapons. He tucked the cantomount into his pocket, reached down for a small piece of broken board from a trash heap at his feet and readied for a swing. The shuffle came closer, accompanied by a hushed voice calling into the night, "Old man? Hey, Mister-Mister?"

Vaslow dropped the board and waited for an instant. Just as the shuffle approached, he reached his arm out and caught the slight, cloaked shoulder and swung it toward him. He used enough force to lift the small body off the ground. Vaslow set him down gently and said in an angry whisper, "Hello, Simoud."

"Don't do that, mister-mister," the boy replied, struggling to keep his volume down. He dropped his hood. "You gonna make me wet myself."

"Go home, Simoud. And pretend you never saw me."

"Never saw you? I been tracking you for an hour, Mister-Mister. You gotta come with me," the boy said firmly.

"Si, I don't want you to get hurt. You need to go home." Vaslow saw that same fierce look in the boy's eyes he'd seen the morning after he'd crashed his sled. "Not this time, Simoud. You are in danger just by being near me. I can't risk that."

"Mister-Mister, you come with me or Popi will not let me back in the house." The boy put his small fingers around the old man's wrist and tugged. Si was here at Wharton's request?

Together Vaslow and Si walked through the shadows in the sleeping streets. Vaslow was amazed the boy had found him. Maybe that myth about the Sloans having a tracking gene was actually true. Si led at the quick, steady pace of a boy on a mission. They cut kitty-corner through the alley and around the side of the adjacent building. Then Si took Vaslow down a musty crooked staircase. The boy knocked just once on the door at the base of the stairs and waited. Vaslow tried to speak, but Si put up his hand to stop him.

After several minutes the door was opened by an armed man who simply nodded and stepped aside to let the pair in. They entered a long dark tunnel carved out of the soil of Vedra itself. The sand and clay had obviously been treated with a hardening agent. Metal supports dotted the path ahead, fitted with large kane lights, illuminating golden pools for them to follow. Si led them forward without saying a word.

Vaslow followed as the boy made twists and turns, passing other paths without hesitating. He'd read of a tunnel system and chalked it up to lore. Never had he imagined a complex network as intricate as this existed beneath Sloantown. He wondered if the Protectorate knew about it.

"Okay, we almost at my house now," Si said, making one last turn. They went down a short tunnel, ending at packed clay steps leading to a fortified door. Vaslow had seen Wharton's house, a simple well-maintained home surrounded by a thick wall of the same material, all the color of sand. It was just like all the other houses on the block, not the larger more elegant house one would have expected of the Sloan leader Vaslow knew Wharton to be.

Just as he'd done at the entrance to the tunnel, Si gave a single knock on the door and waited. This door was opened by another armed man who gave Si a gap-tooth smile and ruffled his hair before admitting them. They went up a staircase that opened onto a large room. It was not remotely like the dingy basement Vaslow had expected.

Instead, it was a dimly lit, high-tech nerve center. There were a dozen manned jump-terminals lining the walls, monitoring numerous off-world jumps simultaneously. Armed guards were moving with precision through the space and onto their next assignment. In the center of the space was a monitoring system. Dozens of semi-transparent views were projected into the air, not just views of the house but of various districts throughout the city, and throughout this elaborate underground network.

A tall Cass woman in pants, an oddity here in Sloantown, was flipping through the projections like turning pages in a book. There were layers upon layers of views, even views from inside the palace. Vaslow turned slowly, trying to take it all in. He had known Wharton was more than a simple vendor, but never had he imagined this.

"Gray beard, we are no longer evens," Wharton said as he came through a doorway on the far wall.

"I didn't ask you to bring me here." Vaslow's response was more of a reflex than an answer.

"It's not the bringing you here. It's keeping the guards off your scent since you leapt from the window. You're good, old man, but not that good." Wharton chuckled. As he came closer he noticed the dried blood on Vaslow's forehead and cheek and the wound still open. He turned to Si and barked an order in Sloan. The boy ran off. "I had to wake half of my men in this district to cover your tracks."

Did Wharton have an entire rebel militia?

Wharton continued. "Yes, we are a very efficient cadre," he said, apparently in response to Vaslow's surprised look. "And no one in the Protectorate Guard even suspects we exist. Well, practically no one." He smiled slyly at Vaslow.

"Your reach is far beyond my meager expectations. Thank you. But I am afraid I have nothing to give you to make us 'evens' again."

"Old man, you underestimate yourself."

"If I am, that'll be a first," Vaslow said matter-of-factly.

Si and a dark-haired girl, a taller female version of Si, descended the stairs and approached Vaslow. Si carried a tray of cut vegetables and rolled meats and the girl had a small basin of water, cloth, and a traditional Sloan medical roll. "I'm fine," Vaslow said, waving the children off.

"Don't be foolish. You can't be running through the galaxy with a gaping wound. You and I may have different strategies, but we want the same end." Wharton still sported a smile suggesting he knew more than he was saying. "And I need to protect my investment."

Was Wharton really willing to break the law for him and arrange another jump? Had Si told him about Bayatrice? They were now both dancing on the edge of the knife, death the penalty for a wrong step. Vaslow would let Wharton show his hand first. He leaned against the wall, bending slightly to let the girl begin cleaning the wound, which was no small feat considering the amount of grit in it. She worked with deft fingers, rinsing and dabbing. Wharton sat at a small table in front of Vaslow, picking at the food, watching, occasionally nodding in approval.

The girl's medical roll reminded him of something a painter would store his brushes in. She also had a small container that looked like it had been carved from an animal horn. She opened the lid and scooped a bitter-smelling salve onto a flat wooden stick and then onto her finger. He could feel a healing warmth as she dabbed it on his wound. She pulled paper-thin material from a pocket in the roll, rubbed it with the same ointment, and stretched it over the wound. Vaslow wondered if it was the skin of an animal. He didn't like the idea of these native healing practices, but refusing treatment wasn't an option. As she smoothed the skin bandage on his wound he felt it tighten against his skin, sealing his wound as it did so. Then she switched her focus and began to dab at the torn flesh on his fingers. When she was satisfied it was clean, she used the ointment on the skin around the knuckles and applied more skin bandages. Vaslow flexed his fingers and was amazed at how well the dressings held. After she'd finished, she packed up her instruments. Taking one final look she stood back and said, "Alhura, mod dunny-dunny." Then she smiled and went back up the stairs.

"That's my sister, Alhura. She won't speak anything but Sloantalk," Si said, shrugging.

Vaslow let his fingers explore the bandage. It was completely flat; he could barely distinguish it from his own skin. "Please tell Alhura thank you. She did a fine job."

"She knows," Si said.

Wharton, seeming satisfied with the bandaging, moved on to the next topic. "Si, you have done well tonight. You have made me proud." Si beamed. "It's time for you to leave us now."

"But Popi, I can help," Si protested.

"You are becoming more of a man every day, but you are not ready for this," Wharton replied firmly.

"I owe gray-beard a chit. I choose to stay to repay him," the boy said, standing as tall as his frame would let him.

"You already have, by bringing him here. Go on now." Wharton pointed towards the exit.

"No." Si stomped the ground as he spoke. "I brought him here 'cause you say so. It's not same-same."

"Maybe I've taught you too well." Wharton stretched back in his chair and looked at his son. "Okay, you can stay." He turned toward Vaslow and pointed at the projections above the monitoring station. "So, you like our tunnels?"

"I have to admit I am a bit surprised by their existence," Vaslow answered, remaining standing.

"You might be more surprised to know they are not just under Sloantown. There is a maze of them that runs under the entire city, built before the sovereigns even took power. Only the Sloan know of their existence—until tonight, that is." Vaslow could see Wharton studying his face. "Yes," the Sloan leader said, "I think we have plenty to talk about."

Wharton smiled again, put his foot on the rung of the chair next to him, and slid it toward Vaslow. "We may as well take nourishment while we plan to overthrow the government."

Chapter 16: Being the Mouse

Bea had gone back inside and crawled into bed. Every time she started to doze, she imagined she could hear the viewer calling to her. She noticed every twitch of her muscles, felt each ragged breath. Her eyes were hot and dry, her head throbbed, and her limbs were made of lead.

When she finally did drift off to sleep the dream had come, worse than ever. A chill went down her spine as the familiar voices began to speak.

"We

have

found

her."

One long, cloaked arm reached for her. This time it touched her with a single icy finger. The cold oozed up her arm, cutting through the skin, moving like it was alive. Gasping for breath, she sat up, cold but sweating.

The sun was rising. She could hear the next-door neighbors getting in their car. People just beginning an ordinary Saturday. Then she remembered the scratch on her arm, probably the reason for this version of the nightmare.

The fear from last night's alien encounter reignited. What if she got some sort of alien infection?

Bea got out of bed on shaky legs and walked to the bathroom. She pulled out the antibacterial liquid, put her arm over the sink, and poured it on the small scratch. She kept squeezing the bottle until it released nothing but air.

"Hey, Howard Hughes." The sound of Patty's voice made her jump. "You trying to drown that or what?"

"Oh, I guess I just wasn't paying attention." Bea put the empty bottle back in the medicine cabinet.

"I'm pretty sure nobody ever died from a paper cut," Patty said, making her way past Bea and into the bathroom.

"Ha, yeah." Bea forced a weak laugh.

"What are you doing up so early on a Saturday anyway?" Patty asked, yawning.

"Oh, I'm going over to Calvin's. You know, more stuff on the project."

"Geez, Bea, it's like your brain has been taken over by science or something," Patty said.

"That is totally not funny!" Bea snapped.

"Gah, it was just a joke…" Patty looked at Bea. "… or maybe not." All of Patty's humor evaporated. She gave Bea a little shove out into the hall and closed the door in Bea's face.

The whole time she was dressing, Bea was on the verge of hyperventilating. She pulled on the same jeans as yesterday and an old school sweatshirt. She let her sleep-twisted hair fall where it might. She didn't grab her hat or her gloves. She couldn't even manage to zip her parka.

The whole way to Calvin's, she kept pushing up the jacket sleeve to check the scratch. It was redder, wasn't it? Maybe it was beginning to swell? How would she explain this at the emergency room?

As Bea reached the store, she could see Hal through the display window, stocking cans of peaches neatly in a pyramid shape. She went around back and pressed her palm to the doorbell with continuous pressure.

She hadn't heard the footsteps, hadn't seen Calvin approach the door, so it was a surprise when Calvin was staring her in the face.

He was groggy and rumpled, wearing a t-shirt and flannel pajama bottoms.

"Ah, usually people stop ringing the bell once the door is answered." He looked at Bea, more curious than annoyed.

"Oh, yeah." Bea pulled her hand off the doorbell. "Calvin, it's bad. It's really bad." She pulled up her sleeve and showed him her wound. She turned her head as if she couldn't bear his reaction.

"What am I looking at?" Calvin asked.

"Are you blind? Can't you see the cut?"

"Oh, you mean that little scratch? You came here to show me a scratch?" Calvin shook his head. "Well, I'm not a doctor, but I think you'll live. Can I go back to bed now?"

Bea stepped into the foyer and pulled Calvin in behind her by his shirt. He closed the door.

"He scratched me. The old guy from the viewer."

"He came here?" A look of concern crossed Calvin's face.

"No, he reached *through* the window."

"Bea, you promised not to look at it without me," Calvin said, as if it were her fault this happened.

"I didn't! He called me!" Bea shouted.

Calvin started to protest, but Bea guessed the tears she couldn't keep in ended the argument before it could even start. Calvin took her upstairs and made her a cup of tea, saying it was always what his Gran used to do for him. Bea explained how the alien had tried to tug her through the window and how she had safely gotten rid of the viewer... at least until spring. Usually Bea's problems felt smaller in the light of day. Not this one. One look at Calvin's face and she knew he was worried too. But he swallowed and composed himself.

"Okay. So, you did the right thing. I don't think we should get anywhere near the viewer." He looked down at her arm. "And the likelihood of any sort of infection is infinitesimal. It's a tiny scratch, Bea. And it's far away from any major blood supply."

Bea looked down at the limb that was attached to her body, but which now felt foreign and disowned.

"Your arm is fine." Calvin's mind worked in logical equations and probabilities. He didn't know how to handle Bea when she was emotionally distraught. Bea could see the disconnect in his eyes. But then, as if he was reading her mind, he reached out and gave her a hug. It was stiff and awkward, but it worked just the same. "See," he continued, "I wouldn't get this close to anyone I thought had alien cooties."

Bea punched him lightly in the ribs. He laughed and pulled back. "Okay, that's more like the Bea I know."

"You know, Calvin, you're really not a total jerk after all."

"Yeah, well, just don't tell anybody else. I've got a reputation to maintain."

***

Calvin convinced Bea to go home, brush her hair, change, and come back at eleven to play free pinball in the store. "I've got connections," he joked. He'd meet her down there and they could just cut up and not think about anything. Not even the science fair.

That sounded so good to Bea. Not thinking. That would be a good trick.

Bea got back to Hal's about ten minutes early. Donny and Ross Peters were on the pinball machines in the back of the store. Bea decided to just hang out on the bus stop bench out front until Calvin came down.

She was sitting, leaning against the ad for Elmhurst's number one real estate agent, swinging her feet, when she noticed someone crossing the street out of the corner of her eye. She looked up and saw an older man in jeans, his coat collar turned up against the cold. He was looking down at the pavement and all she could see was the top of his head and his thick gray hair. Something in the way he moved, sure and strong, gave her the willies. He moved too young to be so gray. He lifted his head and smiled at her from behind his gray beard, a sad slow smile—his blue eyes begging something.

It was him. *He was here.* She took off as fast as she could, racing around the corner. She could hear him calling after her, saying her name in that weird way, "Bayatrice, wait, please." He said something else, but she was too far away to hear.

She reached the back door just as Calvin was coming out. "Hey, Bea, I was just—" Bea cut him off. She grabbed his arm and kept running, with Calvin reluctantly in tow.

"He's here," Bea said between ragged breaths. "The old man." They started to cut through the Griesmer's yard and both looked back. The old man was just rounding the corner, running faster than she'd ever imagined an old man could. He stopped behind the grocery, looking disgusted or disappointed, Bea couldn't tell. She let go of Calvin's arm and ran faster.

"Geez, that was really him!" Calvin said in disbelief. He sped up to match her pace.

They cut up Maple, past the neighbors, past her front yard and around her house. They entered the garage through the side door and Bea locked it behind her. They were both panting.

"Bea, this is the first place—" he took several gulps of air, "—he'll come looking for...us."

"I don't know where else to go!" Bea's thoughts were spinning so fast she couldn't make logical connections. Her lungs were fighting for more air, making it even harder to think.

Too late. The old man's face appeared in the window on the other side of the door they had come through.

"Wait, please. I won't hurt you." He raised his hands as if in surrender. "I won't even open the door. I just want to talk to you."

Bea and Calvin stood there, stunned. Bea grabbed Calvin's hand and tugged at him.

"Bea, we've got nowhere to go," Calvin said, breaking his arm away from Bea.

"Please, Bayatrice." The old man's voice broke. "Please."

Bea turned to face their pursuer, but kept her distance and a line of sight to the door to the kitchen.

"I left you the cantomount." At their blank stares, he continued, "The device which you called me on."

"I didn't call you." Bea's voice shook.

"Okay, the device..." he acquiesced. "It didn't function as I had planned. I designed it to explain who you were, where you came from." He paused. "So you would know me, your guardian. I will protect you with my life. My name is Vaslow."

"If that's all you wanted, why didn't you just knock on the front door? Why didn't you talk to my parents?" Bea was scared and wanted this creepy guy to leave. As much as she wanted some answers about her past, this was wrong—all wrong. He was an alien, and that couldn't have anything to do with her. "You need to leave me alone. I don't want to know anything you have to tell me. And take that canta-thing with you."

"Bayatrice, I can't leave without you. There are things you *need* to know about your past." The patience in his voice was melting into urgency. "Your patou is coming fast. I can see it in your eyes. *I can feel it.* You don't have much longer."

"I don't have any idea what you're talking about, but you'd better leave before I call the cops." Bea tried to sound solid but inside she was dissolving, because as crazy as he sounded, part of her felt like she needed to listen to him.

There was a double flash of blue light from behind the old man and the ground beneath them vibrated. "Damn it, they're here." Vaslow spun around. There was a whizzing and the sound of splintering wood. A streak of burning light cut through the garage door just over Vaslow's head.

"I'm sorry. I don't have time to convince you." He leaned in with his shoulder and in a fluid move broke open the door. As soon as he stepped through, another blast hit the metal ceiling rack, dislodging the front end and sending a cascade of ski gear and sparks raining down on them. "If you two want to live, you'll have to trust me."

Chapter 17: Mind Over Stomach

Bea lurched toward the door to the kitchen and in her over-reach she lost her balance and fell on the step. The trashcan next to her exploded and bits of trash, plastic, and metal rained down on her. A thick scream was stuck in her throat. She wasn't remembering to breathe.

"Not that way." She heard Vaslow's voice, felt his strong hands on her, lifting her to her feet like she was a paper doll. She turned and looked at him. He was holding a viewer, a window that opened into some kind of vehicle. "Climb through," Vaslow shouted at Calvin, who didn't climb as much as he succumbed to Vaslow's shove. The window shimmered as a blast from a laser passed dangerously close to it. Bea was frozen. Vaslow lifted Bea, and with his arms wrapped around her, dove up and into the window. As soon as they were through, Vaslow slammed his fist down on a button, closing the window. Just as the view of the garage began to fade, she saw the kitchen door open and Teddy's startled face appear.

"Nooooo!" The scream that had been stuck dislodged with amazing force. She saw Calvin wince. She could hear Vaslow pleading with her to be quiet. But she couldn't shut her mouth. The sound kept pouring out of her, bouncing off the walls of the tight quarters.

She didn't see it coming; she just felt the flat of Vaslow's palm connect sharply with her cheek. She involuntarily sucked air in, cutting off her yell. The fear became anger.

"You hit me. You actually hit me!" Bea screamed at Vaslow.

"It was for your own good. You were hysterical," Vaslow said, as if it were all perfectly logical. He turned his focus on the vehicle's instrument panel.

Bea cupped her burning check. She was fuming, and trapped.

"Bea, you were losing it. He had to do it," Calvin said, sounding like he was trying to be a mediator.

Calvin's words made her lose all sense of reason. Why wasn't he on her side? Why was he so ready to be kidnapped by this maniac? "Let us go. Let us out of here right now!" Bea shouted. "I've got to help Teddy!" She reached for what looked like a door handle and tugged. It didn't budge. It was then that she looked out the small, tinted window. They were moving.

Straight up.

Bea's stomach jumped. The vehicle seemed to pause mid-air and then jolt. Not exactly forward, not exactly up. Everything outside the window blurred and then she felt the vehicle pause again. If there had been breakfast in her stomach, it would be in her lap right about now.

Outside the window was blackness. She saw a brilliant blue and green ball floating beneath them—Earth. She took a deep breath and promptly fainted.

Bea felt consciousness call to her, felt her stinging cheek, could hear talking, but couldn't open her eyes.

"What's happened to her?" Calvin voice was shaky.

"She's fainted. The rest will do her good," Vaslow said. She could hear him pushing buttons.

"You should take us home." Calvin was sounding more determined than before. "We have to call the police."

"Calvin, those soldiers that were after you, they're dangerous. Your police won't be able to protect you from them. And they don't want to see Bayatrice live to her next birthday."

"What? Why would anybody want to hurt Bea?"

"Not hurt her, kill her." At Vaslow's words, Bea was out again.

⋆⋆⋆

When Bea awoke, she had no idea how long she had been out. Even though she knew they were floating in space, gravity felt normal. She looked around without moving. The vehicle—*the spaceship*—was about the size and shape of her Aunt Lucy's minivan. It had small shallow windows on both sides and a deeper window in the front. Below all the windows, on every wall, were instrument panels, blinking lights, and gauges with funky symbols.

They were in a freaking spaceship! They were here because armed aliens had come *hunting her!* No, she couldn't deal with this. This wasn't real. She just had to get home. It would all be okay once she got home. This crazy man was going to take her home, she'd make him. Her thoughts whirled as she tried to force a plan to form in her head.

She, Vaslow, and Calvin occupied three of the five form-fitting seats, which seemed to conform to the passengers' shape and size. There was a low hum of what she guessed was the engine, but it was a soft, rolling kind of sound. She could see Calvin's face, glowing with a dumb giddy expression. He was asking question after question.

"So, the cantomount actually bends space?" Calvin asked incredulously.

"More like slices it. If there is an open receiver on the other end, it cuts out the matter in between. Almost like a magnetic attraction between the two windows." Vaslow managed to answer each question patiently as he worked feverishly at some task on the instrument panel.

"So it only works between two linked devices. I see. And you use 'jumping' for travel when there is no second device?"

Vaslow nodded and then addressed Bea. "Good, you're awake," he said without turning to look at her. "As soon as I finish the diversion scatter we can jump. It will send buoys in a dozen different directions. They won't know which to follow. But we still can't go directly back to Vedra. We'll have to jump to another off-world location, maybe Tentra

6, until I am sure they've lost our trail." Vaslow finished his calculations and turned to look at Bea. "If you're going to be sick, there is a container in that panel."

"I'm not going to throw up." Bea spat the words at him, as if saying it could make it true. She pressed the panel she thought Vaslow was referring to, looking for some sort of handle. As soon as she touched it, it automatically slid open, revealing an intricate weave of multicolored wires.

"The panel below that one," Vaslow directed.

Bea looked at him, then pressed the panel above. More wires and a smooth surface panel with rows of buttons. Vaslow said nothing. She continued to press until the whole wall beside her was open, all the wires, buttons, and instrument panels exposed.

"I feel your head is aching. You've been having a hard time eating lately, and your limbs are feeling very heavy." He looked at her closely. "Maybe your eyes have been burning? Tingling in your fingers?" Bea stared daggers through him. "It's all normal. It's all part of your patou. The human equivalent would be puberty, but for us it happens all at once. You might not want to admit it, but your body is changing. I know you feel it, and it will get worse before it gets better."

"Us? Human equivalent? I don't understand and I don't want to. You need to take us home." Bea couldn't think. Puberty! Why did he bring that up in front of Calvin? Nothing could have embarrassed her more. Two weeks ago she wanted nothing more than to have puberty hit her. Now it hardly seemed to matter. She needed to make him take them home.

"Bea, I think you need to listen to him," Calvin said tentatively.

Bea glared at Calvin, letting his words bounce right off her. She kept picturing the flash of Teddy's face. Vaslow's words made her head hurt worse. "I saw Teddy as they were shooting into our garage. We don't even know if he's okay." She had to get home. She had to. "I need to go home—now."

"Teddy is fine. But Bayatrice, I can't take you home. It isn't safe for you."

"You don't know that. You can't know that it's not safe for me. And there's no way you can know if Teddy is okay!" Bea's voice was shaking and thin, and she knew she was sounding frantic and unreasonable. Calm was a train that had left the station and she couldn't call it back. "You need to take us home now!" Bea had balled up her fists and was pounding them on the armrests, punctuating her words.

"Bayatrice, I can't take you home—"

Bea cut him off. "Yes, you can, and you better or we'll all be sorry!" She reached up and started pushing buttons, flipping switches, and pulling wires. The lights flickered and a high-pitched alarm sounded.

"Stop!" Vaslow tried to spring out of his seat but the safety straps held him in place. She figured she'd have enough time to do some serious damage before he could release his straps and make it back to stop her.

Bea spoke evenly as she punctuated each word with a push of a button. "My. Guardian. Wouldn't. Kidnap. Me."

"Okay, okay." He relaxed back in his seat, raised his hands, and motioned for her to be calm.

"You'll take us home?" She held still, holding another set of wires in her hand. "Now?" She could feel the weight of Calvin's gaze burning into her, but she didn't look at him.

Vaslow exhaled, long and slow. "Yes. Yes, I'll take you home right now if you promise to meet with me tomorrow after school. Give me a chance to explain. Will you promise that?" Bea nodded. His face softened as he looked at her—pleading and patient at the same time, as if she were a wall he couldn't scale. "Bayatrice, there are so many things that I need to explain to you," he began in a slow, gentle voice. "I know that your body is about to go through a big change and you'll need help. I know that you have a calling, a responsibility you can't walk away from," Vaslow looked into her eyes with an unflinching intensity. "I know you aren't human. You are Vedrian."

Chapter 18: Letting Go

Vaslow looked at her. He could see past this shroud of childish frustration to the part of her that reminded him so much of her mother. But it was like a gem lost in the fog; he couldn't quite get a bearing to reach it. He would have to wait for the weather to pass; he had no more control over this situation than he did the forces of nature. He could take her back to Vedra kicking, screaming, and ripping the vessel apart, but that would only make matters worse. The fight for her trust couldn't be won by force, and he didn't have the time wait her out. Vaslow took a deep breath and tried to get an accurate handle on her physical state, letting the connection wash over him. She had a day, maybe two, before her transition. Because he knew how much easier it would be on her if she went with him by her own choice, he'd give her that long to try to understand. After that, the timing of her patou would make the choice for them both.

"I can send out a diversion buoy. It will mimic this ship's energy signature and make them think we've gone back to Vedra. I've got people on the ground that can help with the charade. But they will figure it out and come back. Your home won't be safe for long." Vaslow turned off the last squawking alarm. "Perhaps when we meet again I will be able to convince you of your destiny. There are a lot of people counting on you, Bayatrice."

The girl glared at him with hot angry eyes.

"You and I have made a bargain," he said, sensing she had no intention of meeting him. "I am upholding my end. You need to do the same. If you don't, you know I will find you anyway. And you should pray I find you before the others do." He wanted her to be frightened of the guard, to let her know how serious the danger was. But even as he spoke these grave words, he could see they weren't sinking in.

"I said I'd meet you," Bea said, sullen and stubborn. She was more of an angry child than he'd expected.

"You need to know what I have to say, not just for yourself, or me, but for the thousands upon thousands who wait for you back home."

"Home? This is my home. I've lived here my entire life. I don't know what a 'Vedrian' is, but whatever it is, I am certain I am not one. I think you are seriously confused." Bea looked at him with hate in her eyes. "Just take us home."

Vaslow recalibrated his instruments, pushed a button, and sent a small drum with a great burst of white light flying out into space at amazing speed. "The diversion buoy and the people on the ground will give us three days at the most before the Guards come back to Earth looking for us." Feeling the pain in Bea's head, he added, "But I don't think your patou will hold off even that long."

Vaslow maneuvered the ship, beginning a slow steady descent. "We'll have to use crawl speeds instead of jumping to get back into the atmosphere, otherwise they'll track us."

Once they landed, he'd keep up his end of the bargain. He'd let them go, but he'd never let Bayatrice out of his sight.

***

Bea closed her eyes and leaned her head against the padded wall, pretending to sleep. Calvin was "uh-huhing" everything Vaslow said as if he were following it all. His even-headed logical acceptance of Vaslow's explanation made Bea's blood boil. It felt to her as though

Calvin had crossed into traitor's territory, wooed by shiny objects and the promise of unfathomable knowledge.

Vaslow had said that at this slower speed, it would take them hours to retrace the distance they had traveled in seconds. Bea thought her head might explode before they got there, not just from the pain, but from how Calvin was acting.

He and Vaslow talked about something called Particle Theory, magnetic wormholes, and a dozen other things Bea couldn't understand. Then Vaslow switched from the scientific to the personal.

"I remember my own patou. It was so violent they didn't think I would live through it. And I was so cantankerous, I wasn't sure my parents wanted me to." Vaslow told the story to Calvin as if they were old friends. It was making her crazy.

"You're kidding, right? About the not living through it part? I mean, who ever died from puberty?" Calvin asked, hooked on this man's tale.

"I said it was *like* puberty. But for us it's much more serious. With good nutrition and proper medical intervention, it's almost never a problem. But if Bayatrice starts to go through it alone..." His voice trailed off and she hoped he'd just be quiet for the rest of the trip back.

"I know this is hard for you to understand," Vaslow said, speaking directly to Calvin, "but I need you to know the danger is real, and very close. It's not just the forces that have been sent against her. Her own body will be the enemy. But you and I are going to save her." It was all Bea could do not to shout at them. He was a stranger. Calvin had no business talking to him about her.

"I'm just a science geek. I can't protect her," Calvin said quietly. "I can't save anybody."

"Where I come from we have a saying: From the many, the brave are called," Vaslow said. "I am not sure why, but I know you have been called. And I know that you can, and will, rise to the need."

At last the vehicle landed lightly on solid ground. Vaslow had found an empty street near Bea's house. Bea sat up as soon as they stopped moving, ready to jump out when the doors opened.

"So what happens if someone sees you jump?" Calvin asked. Bea rolled her eyes.

"On your planet they don't see what they don't want to see. The craft has been designed to look like one of your automobiles on the outside. If it is not there one minute and appears the next, people just assume their minds are playing tricks on them."

"Really, people don't ask questions?" Calvin looked disbelieving.

"Calvin, we're home. Let's go." Bea cut them off.

"Yeah. Right. Okay," Calvin said, shifting toward the door reluctantly.

With the sound of an airlock release, the door beside Bea opened. She jumped out and impatiently waited on Calvin to climb out. Calvin faced Vaslow and gave him a sympathetic shrug. She tapped her foot impatiently.

"Remember the symptoms I've explained to you," Vaslow said. "If Bayatrice shows any signs, any at all, call me right away. You'll be tempted to call her parents or a doctor, but you can't. She wouldn't survive if you do." Vaslow paused. "I've reprogrammed Bayatrice's cantomount remotely. You'll be able to use it now. I am counting on you. Bayatrice doesn't know it, but her fate is now in your hands."

That was the final straw. They were talking about her as if she weren't even there! Bea stomped across the cold pavement, not waiting for Calvin. Her fate was in no one's hands but her own. All she had ever wanted was to know who her parents were, to know about her real past. This alien, sci-fi stuff had nothing to do with her. She didn't know what this crazy Vaslow guy was trying to pull, but she was sure Calvin was being stupid by believing him.

She hadn't gotten far when she heard Calvin call after her. She didn't slow her pace. "Bea, wait up." He jogged up alongside her.

"So, is he your new best friend now?" Bea asked, unable check her anger.

"No," Calvin snapped back.

"You know he kidnapped us. I don't get why you were all friendly with him," Bea said, walking faster, swinging her arms with her hands curled into fists. "For all we know he was trying to kill us."

Calvin stopped. "Bea, if he was trying to kill us, we'd already be dead. Remember those other guys? The ones with guns? Vaslow saved our lives."

Bea stopped and gave him a loud harrumph, rolled her eyes, and marched on in her own little cloud of anger.

"I think you should listen to him at least," Calvin yelled after her as she stomped toward her house. "He used to work for your parents. He says he has lots to tell you about them. I thought that was what you wanted?"

Her parents? Vaslow used to work for her parents? Had he really known them? What if it was just a trick? But how would he know she wanted information about her past? Tomorrow. Vaslow was right, she hadn't been planning on getting anywhere near him again, but now maybe she would show up and just see if he was telling Calvin the truth.

They were one street over from the Parkers' house. She felt Calvin's gaze on her as she cut across the Joneses' front lawn and disappeared behind the house.

***

Calvin watched as Bea trudged off. He looked back down the street and saw Vaslow hadn't taken off yet. He could still see the ship, looking exactly like a burgundy Dodge Caravan on the outside, right down to the smallest detail. The windows were dark-tinted and it was too far away to tell if Vaslow was still watching them. Calvin turned back around just in time to see Bea disappear behind the gray-green of winter-infused shrubs. She was such a pain. Totally illogical. He stared at the trail Bea had left in the crusty, half-melted, ashy snow. Vaslow wasn't kidding when he said Bea would be moody and easily angered. The old man had not talked to him like a child, but as an equal. It reminded Calvin of how his G-Pops used to talk with his father. Something in his tone made Calvin want to carry whatever weight Vaslow set upon him. He'd said her fate was in his hands now, so it looked like he'd have to be logical enough for both of them. And he wanted to do it for her. He followed Bea's path, though he didn't call after her, knowing that would only make her madder. Instead, he quietly went around the back of the Parker house and to their garden shed.

***

Bea crossed the patio, her Vans pounding against the concrete. She flung open the door and sensed the commotion, men's deep booming voices, doors opening and closing, red lights flashing. She had totally forgotten about the garage. Teddy, she needed to find Teddy.

She ran across the family room. Outside the window she could see a fire truck in the driveway, idling with all its lights on. She powered through the swinging door into the kitchen. She stopped in her tracks when she saw Teddy come into the kitchen from the garage entrance. He was smiling, without a scratch on him. She didn't say anything, just rushed across the room, sank to her knees, and gave him a bear hug.

"I can't breathe," Teddy croaked out.

"Oh, sorry. I'm just glad to see you," Bea said, letting him go.

"Did you hear? We have barking!"

"That would be 'arcing,'" Aunt Lucy corrected as she came in from behind Teddy. "It was lucky Teddy found it when he did or the whole house could have burned down." She patted Teddy's shoulder and he smiled proudly. "The firemen have been here for hours. They are just leaving now."

"What?" Bea managed.

"Earlier this morning, the ceiling rack your uncle hung came loose. It slammed into the pegboard near the electrical panel. They say a nail from the pegboard punctured some live wires and sent the whole panel arcing. It's a mess. I think our ski gear is melted. Thank God no one was in there."

"No one was in there?" Teddy must have come in after they were through the window; the soldiers must have never gone into the garage. Bea thought that maybe it was time to tell the whole story, as weird and impossible as it would sound.

"Yeah, you should look. It's a mess. Totally cool," Teddy added.

Bea stood up to follow, head pounding. Arcing, right. At least Teddy was okay. She was woozy and her legs didn't want to move the way she was telling them to. "I think I'll look later." She turned and headed out of the kitchen.

"Bea, honey, are you feeling all right? You look so pale." Bea could hear the concern in Aunt Lucy's voice. "You have dark circles under your eyes. I'm worried that you're getting sick again."

"I just think I got up too early."

"Okay, sleep. We'll call you down for dinner. I made your favorite, chili."

"Great," Bea eked out, though the mere thought of it made her want to hurl. She needed to lie down. After a nap in her own warm bed she'd feel better and she'd be able to focus. Yeah, she'd think about everything after she slept. She'd know the right thing to do. Somehow it would all make sense then.

Chapter 19: Out Cold

Aunt Lucy stood in the middle of the kitchen with her hands on her hips, using her this-is-final tone. "Bea, you look like something the cat dragged in. There's no way you are going to school today." Bea watched her aunt, her stomach roiling. She had gotten out of bed briefly last night and tried to eat dinner, but just couldn't force herself to actually put food in her mouth. Aunt Lucy had been concerned, but didn't push it. But now, she was way past concerned and almost into call-the-doctor mode. Bea couldn't let that happen.

Bea faced her aunt, dressed and ready for school, with backpack slung over her right shoulder. "I'm fine, really. And you saw for yourself, I don't even have a fever." Bea's voice came out high-pitched and squeaky-pleading. She had to go today, just had to. She would meet with Vaslow, get answers, and leave all of this craziness behind.

"You know, I think she's wacky," Patty interjected. "But, Mom, she's begging to go *to* school. How can you argue with that?" With that, Patty went back to making lunches.

Aunt Lucy looked at Bea and then seemed to resign herself to losing this battle. "Okay, but if you're going to school I want to see you eat some breakfast." She pushed a bowl of oatmeal toward Bea.

Bea felt the hot bile in her throat, felt saliva pooling under her tongue. And now she had the added fear of the men with guns returning. Nothing was making any sense, but she couldn't make things better by staying home. She had to meet with Vaslow.

"Fine," Bea said, dropping her backpack and sitting down. She picked up the spoon and dug out a clump of oatmeal. The oatmeal was plain and had been sitting a while, giving it a firm, gelatinous consistency. Bea opened her mouth and let the lump land on her tongue. She held back the forces that wanted to spew it all over the kitchen and swallowed. It was all she could do to keep it down. "See, no problem." And she dropped the spoon.

"Oh no, you're not getting in the car until that bowl is empty. I haven't seen you eat in days." Aunt Lucy stood watching Bea.

"Ga-ross." Patty shuddered as she passed by, grabbing her backpack. "Mom's oatmeal is bad enough with a ton of sugar. But plain, gag me."

"Okay, we'll add sugar," Aunt Lucy reached for the container, flipped up the lid and turned the jar to pour it into Bea's bowl. Bea reached up and put her hand over the spout.

"Ah, no thanks. I'm trying to cut down." Bea smiled weakly and took another bite. "Mmmmm."

Bea managed to get all the oatmeal down and keep it there through first period. But now she felt worse than ever. Sweat was bleeding from her pores and soaking into her uniform, but she was cold all over. The headache had grown into a pounding in her ears that made it hard to hear. Her arms and legs felt rubbery and tingled at the same time. Maybe she was getting sick—what if Calvin was wrong and she really had gotten an alien infection from that scratch? The mere thought of that sent shivers down her spine. Or worse yet, what if she really wasn't human? Oh God, she couldn't even go there. She tried to concentrate on Mrs. Eisner, who was happily in the heated throes of diagramming a sentence. No use. The oatmeal was rising. And this time Bea knew she couldn't beat it back. She raced to the front of the room, holding her mouth and her stomach. Mrs. Eisner wisely waved her on without asking any questions.

Bea flung open the bathroom door and rushed into a stall. She fell to her knees and let the undulating waves of heaving begin. She threw up until all the oatmeal was out of her system, but it didn't stop there. The staccato urges kept coming until she thought her insides were coming out. The sweat beads pooled on her hairline and fell into her eyes each time she lurched forward. She was dizzy and her sides ached. Then with a swirl of vision, her world went dark.

**

Calvin paced in front of the door to Mrs. Eisner's classroom. He had ducked out of world history early to check on Bea. The bell rang and the kids began to file out into the hall. No Bea.

"Yo, Beech, you looking for your *girlfriend*?" Russ Beacon asked, laughing. Calvin nodded. "She ran out of the room ready to hurl." The group of kids around him laughed along with him as they passed Calvin on the way to their next period.

Calvin scanned the hall. The girls' bathroom was down on the right. He slowly inched closer, watching as girls went in and out. Never had he even looked in the direction of the girls' bathroom before. He felt a little creepy staring at it so intently now. The hall was starting to empty. The bell rang again, signaling the start of third period, prompting a flurry of activity as kids slid into their respective classes just under the wire. Still no Bea—he was sure he couldn't have missed her. Classroom doors swung shut on their squeaky hinges, leaving Calvin alone in the deserted, locker-lined corridor.

Calvin raised his hand and knocked lightly on the door, just below the picture of the stick figure wearing a skirt. "Hello?" he called out weakly. He looked left, then right, swallowed the lump in his throat and pushed the door open. Bea was his responsibility. "Bea?" No reply.

His G-Pops would be crazy-mad if he saw him now. Calvin shook his head; he had to do this for Bea. The bathroom looked familiar but different at the same time. It had the same cracked tile walls and thick creamy oil paint on the window frames as the boys' room. It was just a lot cleaner, it didn't smell like pee, and there were only stalls, no urinals. Two of the ten stall doors were closed. He pushed on the first one. It was just stuck; it swung free under the weight of his hand, revealing a lone commode. He walked to the end and pushed on the second closed door. It didn't budge. He bent down and saw the bottoms of Bea's Vans—and her puddled in a heap behind them.

"Bea!" Calvin shouted. She didn't move. "Bea, let me in!" He got down on the floor and pulled on her foot. "Bea!" For a split second he thought about running into the hall and screaming for someone to call an ambulance. But the weight of Vaslow's words clung to him: She wouldn't survive.

Calvin dropped his pack. He steeled himself against the vile odor and slid on his belly until he was inside the stall next to Bea's sprawled body.

"Bea?" Calvin gently shook her lifeless shoulder. "Bea?" Calvin pleaded, on the verge of tears. She looked even worse up close. She was pasty and her eyes seemed to have sunk back in their sockets. He unlocked the stall door and reached for his backpack. By the time he turned back around, Bea was shaking. Not shaking, seizing. Was he doing the wrong thing? She needed a doctor. But Vaslow said she wouldn't live if she went to an emergency room here. Calvin wished someone else were here with her instead of him. He was a master at Euclidean geometry, could spell any word in the dictionary, but none of that knowledge gave him any insight on what to do in this situation. He knew he couldn't logic his way to an answer. And in that instant, he put his trust in a stranger and shut down every fear receptor in his body that was begging him to call 911.

His nervous fingers dug in his pack for the cantomount. Shaking, he pulled it out and seated it in his hands. Right away, it vibrated and came to life. Bea's hand involuntarily struck his leg over and over. He blinked hard to clear his vision. He thought he had remembered the sequence, but he kept landing back at the view of the Great Hall. Bea started to gurgle, and spit trickled out of her mouth.

He was about to give up and run for help when the viewer projected a window hovering before him with Vaslow's concerned face right in the center of it.

***

Vaslow saw the boy's tear-stained face. The window was shaking because the boy was holding the cantomount in trembling hands. Vaslow could see Bea's quaking body behind the boy; it was further along than he'd thought. His calm words hid his own nerves. "Help me bring her over."

As Vaslow reached his arm through the window, he was bombarded by wave after wave of sensations coming from Bea. Pain, searing pain. Throbbing, cramping in every muscle. Breath, not enough breath. Her whole body was in conflict with itself. These co-feelings were stronger than any he'd ever felt. A vein in his forehead began to pulse; his lungs constricted. The tide of sensations threatened to take him under as well. His eyesight dimmed.

It was his warrior's mind that saved him. The muscle memory of years of mental discipline snapped into play. He fought the urge to shut down the connection; rather, he forced himself to compartmentalize the sensations. Feel them, monitor them, separate them from his own.

He spoke in an even tone. "Calvin." The boy didn't budge. "Calvin. Calvin, I need you to turn her so her head can come through first."

Calvin clumsily worked through his tears, placing his hands on Bayatrice's shuddering body, gently turning her on the smooth linoleum floor. When her head was facing the direction of the viewer window, Vaslow reached through and helped Calvin lift her.

"The viewer window frame isn't solid—you can't lean on it. We'll have to lift her through the center of the window. If you need support, lean on something on one side or the other." Vaslow eased his hands under Calvin's, transferring Bea's body weight into his own weathered hands as they maneuvered her through the middle of the viewer window, from the bathroom and onto his ship. My sweet Jaru, she was so light. He had failed to prepare her for this. He hoped she had enough meat on her bones to sustain her. Could she survive? He pushed that unbearable thought back and concentrated on his task.

"You climb through after I move her out of the way. Bring the cantomount through last or you'll break the connection."

The boy was bawling now. Not listening, Vaslow could tell. "We have to hurry," Vaslow urged as he moved Bea to the back of the vehicle. The boy kept his gaze fixed on Bayatrice's tortured body, her gray face and blue lips. As he reached forward to cross over, he grasped a seat back with one hand to steady himself. Then he reached through with the other hand, the hand holding the cantomount. "No!" Vaslow let out a brief burst of frustration. The cantomount bounced on the firm seat cushion as the window closed. Leaving Calvin behind.

***

Calvin fell back hard against the edge of the stall when the seat he had been holding dematerialized. The projected window disappeared, leaving no trace it had ever been there. Bea was gone. Oh, God, she had to be okay. If she weren't it would all be his fault. What had he done? Why hadn't he just dialed 911? His nose was running and he realized how hard he was crying. In some distant spot in his brain he heard a bell ring. Classes were changing and he was in the girls' bathroom.

He grabbed the backpacks and headed for the door. He could hear the bustle of footsteps and laughter in the hall. Getting closer. He put his head down and shouldered through the door, running into three older girls on their way in.

"Hey," the girls chided. Then, noticing who it was, they added, "Freak!" They yelled what he was sure were more unpleasant things after him, but he heard none of it.

He ran through the hallway, bumping shoulders. He could hear shouts of anger from those he jostled, but he didn't slow. He burst out of the doors into the quadrangle. More shoulders and shouts. Tears blinded him, but he wasn't sure he would have avoided those in his path even if he could have. He was running as fast as he could when he hit a brick wall in the form of Mr. Belk.

"Whoa, Mr. Beech, I think you need to stop and take a breath." If Mr. Belk was thrown by the contact he didn't show it. But when he looked at Calvin's face, concerned filled his voice. "Calvin, what's going on? What's wrong?" He held onto Calvin's shoulder. Calvin tried to shake him loose, but he couldn't budge Mr. Belk's steely grip. He had to hurry, he had to go...but go where? He stopped struggling.

Mr. Belk was talking, but Calvin couldn't process the words. His brain could only focus on one equation: how to get back to Bea. The only thing he could think of was going back to where Vaslow had let them off yesterday.

Calvin shrugged hard, breaking Mr. Belk's hold on him, and took off at full speed across the courtyard and through the buildings. "Calvin! Calvin!" He ignored Mr. Belk's pleading for him to come back. He headed toward the bus stop. Waiting would be torture, but he was sure it would be faster than running. Vaslow would wait for him, wouldn't he? He said Bea needed him.

Calvin looked at his watch and contemplated trying to run the distance. When he looked up, he saw it right across the street. It wasn't there one minute and was just there the next: the burgundy minivan with dark tinted windows. Calvin's heart leapt.

The door to the van opened. "Get in!" Vaslow shouted, impatient.

Thank God. He shot across the street, dodging cars with beeping horns. He climbed into the vehicle, calling out, "Bea?"

He looked and couldn't believe what he saw. The three seats in the back row had been reclined to form a bed, and lying on it was a woman in Bea's school uniform.

Chapter 20: Seeing Spots

The door sealed with a hiss behind Calvin and he lost his balance, hitting his nose on the armrest. "Stop flailing about. I need your help," Vaslow reprimanded. Calvin maneuvered himself into a sitting position as Vaslow drove around the corner into an empty alley and stopped the vehicle.

"I've got to get her stable before we can jump," Vaslow said, springing from his seat to attend to Bea.

"Jump? As in leave? Bea doesn't want to go anywhere with you." Calvin's eyes still stung. He tried to see around Vaslow, to get a look at Bea's face. He could see her arms and legs, but her socks only hit her mid-calf rather than just below her knees as they had earlier, and her wrists were sticking way beyond her sweater. And though she was still skinny, she now had the curves of a woman. Her skin was still pale, almost gray, and her body trembled, though not as violently as earlier. "Is she..." Calvin's voice trailed off. He didn't want to ask the questions that were popping up in his head: *Is she going to live? Is she in pain? Was this really happening? Had he done the right thing?*

"Yes, Jaru willing, she's going to be okay," Vaslow answered as he opened panels and attached sensors and what looked like IVs to Bea's arm. "I need you to watch the middle screen. If you see any red dots, tell me immediately."

Calvin turned toward the instrument panel. The middle screen was a clear blue with white pulsating lines running across it. He watched for a minute and looked back again. "What are you doing to her?" Calvin asked, second-guessing his decision not to call 911.

"Keep your eyes on the screen." Calvin snapped back around. "She's lacking nutrients, nutrients she would have gotten naturally from the food on Vedra." Vaslow moved with a steady determination. "Her body is in shock. I need to stabilize her before it puts too much stress on her heart."

"Are you sure you know what you're doing?" Calvin stretched to try to see Bea's face. They could be in an emergency room right now and real doctors could be working on her.

"The screen," Vaslow snapped, and Calvin spun back around. "She's patounihn—transformed. Her body is now that of an adult Vedrian." Vaslow paused to go through the contents of another compartment. Calvin tried to focus on the screen. "Which means she can be tracked by the soldiers who are hunting her. This ship isn't equipped with adequate long-range sensors. I've modified them, but they must be monitored manually—that is what you are doing. If you see dots, that means they will find us in a matter of minutes. Watch the screen."

Calvin watched the screen, thinking about how mad Bea had been at him. He needed her to wake up so he could tell her he'd just wanted to do what was best for her. No, he wanted her to wake up so he could tell her he was sorry. He just wanted her to wake up. He couldn't take it anymore. Needing to see her face, he took his eyes off the screen and lifted himself halfway to standing. Looking over Vaslow's shoulder, he saw her, eyes closed, looking peaceful. Her color had come back...and then some. The tiny freckles that had dotted her face had grown to the size of quarters and were a dark reddish-brown. They ran down either side of her face and down her neck. Even her hair was different—darker and redder. But she looked more alive, and he allowed himself to believe the danger had passed.

"It must be startling for you, but she's going to be fine." Vaslow closed the last open compartment and made his way to the front of the vehicle. "And I am afraid when she wakes, she will have more of a problem with it than you." He motioned for Calvin to go back to Bea. "I'll watch the monitor now."

Calvin sat down on the edge of Bea's makeshift bed. He couldn't help himself; he took her hand. If she woke up now she'd probably figure out how he felt. Maybe it'd make her mad or not want to be his friend anymore. But it didn't matter—he'd been so frightened he was going to lose her that he didn't care. He had to be near her, feeling that she was alive.

It was still Bea's face, he could see that, but it was so different. He always had thought she was pretty, but now he couldn't take his eyes off of her. She was practically glowing. He leaned in close and whispered in her ear, "Bea, I like you so much."

"She's going to need you to be her friend. The one constant for her in a strange new place."

"What strange new place?"

"Vedra, of course. I'm thinking your stay won't be more than a few days," Vaslow said, moving his fingers across the instrument panel.

"Bea doesn't want to go. I can't let you take her."

"I understand, but the soldiers will come back for her," Vaslow said, looking Calvin dead in the eye. "We need to leave before that happens. That is why she will need you—just for a few days. I was assuming you would want to go, to be there for Bayatrice. Am I wrong?"

He held Bea's hand in his, feeling her fingertips warming. Just leave without telling anyone? Calvin thought of how frightened his G-pops would be. Then he thought about Bea being alone and scared, and he knew he couldn't let that happen. He'd seen her reaction to a small scratch; this could push her over the edge. She would definitely need him. "No...I want to go."

"She's stable. It's time." As Vaslow set his safety straps, Bea gave a groggy yelp and opened her eyes. Calvin let go of her hand and sat back, giving her some room to sit up.

***

"Where are we? What happened? Where's my backpack?" Bea looked around, trying to focus. Her mind was spinning and her arms and legs felt limp. The pain in her head, however, had subsided to a mild throb, and she was hungry—really hungry—for the first time in weeks. She looked around. Calvin was next to her and there were tubes, like IVs, attached to her arms. What were they doing to her? She began tugging and the tubes easily released, one by one, without pain, revealing no puncture marks.

"Bea, don't. You're sick—" Calvin leaned to try to stop her.

"No, it's okay," Vaslow said, placing one hand lightly on Calvin's shoulder. Calvin leaned back as Vaslow reached over and gently released the remaining tubes. "You're stable. The worst has passed." He examined her eyes, not with an emotional concern but with a medical cautiousness.

Bea shrugged his hand off and scooted back on the bed, out from under the old man's touch. She looked at Calvin. "Why did you let him do this to me?" She drew her knees up to her chest and winced as the waistband of her skirt cut into her. "What did you do to my clothes? This is not okay! I want to go home right now! Calvin, how could you just let him do this?" She remembered feeling sick and going into the bathroom at school...and then nothing. She must have passed out, and Calvin just let this crazy old man kidnap her, probably because he wanted another look at the shiny gadgets. The anger swirled in her brain and made it hard to think.

"Calvin did nothing but save your life," Vaslow said to Bea. "You've a lot to process—"

"Process? Process what? Being kidnapped? Drugged?" Bea rubbed her aching arms. "You need to take me home. Now."

"I'm afraid that's not possible—" Vaslow began, but Bea didn't let him finish.

"Take me home. Take me home. Take me home!" Bea squeezed herself into a tight ball and closed her eyes, pressing the hot tears onto her cheeks. Her muscles felt weird and loose. As she moved her arm it felt like she was moving an object not connected to her. What had Calvin let this man do?

"Bea." Calvin slid in close to her. "I think it's too late for that."

"What do you mean too late? I just need—" Calvin put his hand on her chin and turned her face toward the shiny instrument panel next to her. She looked at her reflection and all breath escaped her. "What have you done to me?" She meant to scream the question at Vaslow, but it came out as a raspy whisper. She rubbed at the dark splotches that were now present along her face and neck, trying in vain to wipe them off, but the friction just caused the surrounding skin to redden and sting. It was no use—the marks weren't going anywhere.

"I don't understand." Bea looked at Vaslow, feeling impossibly helpless. "Why would you do this to me?" She couldn't even look at Calvin. As quickly as it had come, her anger was melting, leaving fear to fill in the gaps it left. What if they hadn't done anything to her? What if this *was* the real her? Images of the people in the ballroom on the viewer danced in her head. They all had these spots and Bea could tell it wasn't done with makeup. She fought the memory of Vaslow's words from their last trip, about her body changing and about not being human. Could it be true? The thought made her want to crawl out of her own skin. She buried her face in her knees and just let a wave of sobbing overtake her.

"Bayatrice, now that you've gone through your patou the soldiers can easily track you." She heard Vaslow's words above her sobs. "They *will* find you."

"I just want to go home." She felt light-headed and her thoughts floated about. She just wanted her aunt to hug her and make everything better.

"Then you'll bring those soldiers right to your family's doorstep," Vaslow said.

"Maybe we could just go with him until we get it all figured out?" Calvin offered.

In the parts of her brain that still moved in a logical order, Calvin's suggestion made sense. Every other part of her hated the idea, but she had spots on her face and neck. Her thoughts swam in her head like they did when she had a fever; she couldn't quite pin them down. The only thing she knew for certain was she wanted to be as far away from these two as she could get. If what Vasow was saying about the soldiers was true, she had no choice. Teddy had been inches away from getting shot once. But she couldn't just leave without telling anyone. It hurt to think and cry at the same time.

"Ah, Vaslow." Calvin spoke with a shaky voice. "Red dots. Lots of red dots." Something in his tone made Bea look up.

"I'm afraid we are out of time," Vaslow said. "The soldiers have found us."

Ahhh, Bea screamed in her head, not realizing she was holding her breath.

"Bea?" Calvin looked at her. On the monitor behind him, she saw the red dots getting closer.

"Okay, let's go." She exhaled, making the only decision she could.

Vaslow exploded into action and the ship shimmied and lifted off.

The ship's faint shuddering faded and all of a sudden they stopped moving. Apparently, the diversion scatter, as Vaslow had called it, had worked. The soldiers hadn't followed them. Bea looked out the window and saw that the ship was floating in the blackness of space. But this time it wasn't the Earth she saw. There was a planet suspended before them with yellow-amber swirls wrapping around it. It was huge with a golden aura, not like a ring, but like an envelope of light.

A translucent screen appeared and a voice began speaking. A woman with dark hair pulled into a tight ponytail, showing all her spots, spoke in short clipped way. "Newlight 1, you're clear of inbound traffic. Nice job."

"It was your tech that did the job," Vaslow answered her.

"I'm afraid your little adventure has stirred things up down here, though. We're working through alternate landing sites. This might take some time, so get comfortable. I'll open a com when we've got something." Then her image dissolved, revealing the planet again.

They sat in silence for a long time, Calvin and Vaslow up front, Bea alone on the bed Vaslow had created for her in the back. She tried to sleep, but too much was going on in her head. They both kept looking at her, she guessed checking to make sure she wasn't going to lose it. Calvin looked away when she stared back, but Vaslow just kept looking.

"What?" Bea said. "I'm not going to freak out."

Vaslow turned his chair to face her. "You look like her," he said with a little smile.

"Who?"

"Your mother, you look like her. The very image. You saw her face on the cantomount. Look at yourself again."

Bea didn't move. Was this the moment she'd been waiting for? Was he really going to tell her about her parents? With everything that had gone on, the desire to know had almost slipped from her, but his words brought all those needs rushing back. She didn't want to check her reflection in case he was just saying that to make her feel better. The woman on the viewer—her mother?—was so elegant and graceful; even with the spots Bea had thought her beautiful. No way her scrawny self could ever be like that.

Vaslow answered, not seeming to care if she looked or not. "Your mother was not only beautiful, she was also a great queen, and that is not an easy thing to be on a planet such as Vedra."

"Whoa, you're not only from another planet," Calvin said, "you're also royalty? That is pretty freaking cool." Bea shot him a look, but she saw a look of awe on his face. She wondered if he would think that if it were happening to him.

"This is just too crazy. It just doesn't seem possible." Bea shook her head. Royalty? No way. She stretched her arm out in front of her and saw her sweater sleeve hitting halfway up her arm.

"Maybe I could tell you a little about your parents and where you come from. Maybe that would make it easier for you?" Vaslow asked. Bea nodded. "Vedra's an unforgiving world, dry and hot. We have used all the technology in our grasp to make it livable. But still, it is not an easy existence."

"Yeah, that part doesn't sound so great," Calvin said.

"Let him tell the story." Bea wanted to know everything, good and bad.

"No, he's right. I've started this all wrong. Your parents, Queen Gwynlott and King Solhan—"

Bea cut him off without even realizing it. "Gwynlott and Solhan." She just had to say their names. She said them again. Such unfamiliar words, but as she spoke the names out loud they felt like they belonged to her. "And they called me Bayatrice." She said the name Vaslow called her.

"Yes," Vaslow responded, looking at her tenderly. She still didn't wholly trust this man, but there was something in the way he spoke about her parents that made her want to believe him.

Vaslow continued, "Your parents were on the verge of restoring Vedra to the planet of abundance it had been before my parents were born. They had given the people a reason to hope for a better future. They'd begun to bring back the old ways that had been out of favor for centuries. They had the support of the people, and they were very well loved. Which is why I was able to come back and get you, why we have men on the ground waiting to help us. Wharton, the leader of the Sloan Clan, has assembled an entire militia to try to finish what your parents started. The Sloan are a fiercely traditional people. Once your parents set out to restore what had once been, the Sloan declared their undying loyalty—something they have extended to you."

"To me?" Bea couldn't imagine anyone wanting to give her "undying loyalty." She was just a kid. This all felt like some kind of mistake. Once they met her, they'd realize that.

"Yes, to you," Vaslow said, his face now clouded, as if he were reminiscing. "You come from a great line of royalty." He continued his tale and she let him talk, let the words flow over her, trying to convince herself that it could be true.

He told her of a Vedra that was once lush and green, with trees so wide a full-grown man couldn't even reach halfway around one. He explained that the roots of those gigantic trees had to weave their way down to subterranean oceans to survive the dry seasons. He said that a long time ago the royals used energy that was present in every living thing—zinalha, he'd called it—to bring the weather, the crops, the hearts and minds of the people into balance. Not control them, but bring all the different energies into harmony.

Like everything else today, this seemed hard to believe, but Bea stopped trying to make sense of it and just listened.

"Tapping into the zinalha was changing our entire way of life. People were called together in Zinalha Groups, which existed to teach people how to guide their energy, to call the water. The flow of the subterrainan oceans had started to return, crops flourished, jobs were plentiful again. You could feel the shift as something tangible. The people were relying less and less on commercial water and corporate irrigation."

"What do you mean by commercial water?" Calvin asked.

"It is how the planet survived, how our economy was established. Long before I was born, the rains stopped and the flow of resources seemed to constrict, and the leaders turned to technology—drilling the subterranean oceans. Or perhaps the turn to technology had caused the ebb—the truth of how it all started is forever lost.

"But however it happened, the royals stopped wielding zinalha and turned to manually controlling the flow of resources: drilling, commercial distribution of water, automation of everything. After a while, the oceans no longer kept pace with the drilling. Farming became harder and harder; the trees shriveled and died. I guess you'd say it was a sacrifice to the quest for the water. The people believed they were powerless to stop it—"

"What happened to my parents?" That question could no longer be contained. Bea guessed without Vaslow having to say it that her parents were dead, but she had to know.

"They were making a lot of changes and people have a hard time with change. Commercial water is the cornerstone of the Vedrian economy. What your parents were doing would make it obsolete. It scared enough people to stage a coup." Vaslow stopped talking and looked down at his hands. Bea thought he might start to cry, but then she thought she *had* to be imagining that. "They were abducted when you were a baby. I took you to Earth to keep you safe."

"Then they're dead, aren't they?" Even though she'd assumed that from the beginning, saying it out loud still caused a searing pain.

"After all this time, I'd have to think so, yes. I know this is hard for you. It's hard for me, too. I loved your parents." A wave seemed to pass over him and then it was gone, if it had been there at all. Vaslow looked at her. "I have to talk to you about how your patou has changed you. There are things you need to know about your own zinalha—" Vaslow was cut off by the communications screen materializing behind him.

The same dark-haired woman was speaking again. "I'm uploading the landing coordinates." Bea realized the woman looked like a spotted version of Trinity from *The Matrix*. P.J. had practically forced her to watch that movie. She was so mad at him she had never told him how much she actually liked it. She hoped she'd be able to tell him someday.

As the woman continued to speak, Bea realized she wasn't speaking English, and yet she understood it perfectly. "We've had a breach, so you're going to have to make it fast." Even if she hadn't understood the words, she would have picked up on the sense of urgency being conveyed.

"I've received the coordinates," Vaslow said, furiously tapping things into his dashboard. "Hang on, we're jumping—now!"

The ship lurched. A moment later, they were inside a large building. They'd materialized about ten feet off the ground, and slowly descended.

"We're landing here to avoid the Protectorate Guard," Vaslow told them. "They're the ones who came after Bayatrice at the Parkers' home."

If they'd been on Earth, Bea would have called the place where they'd landed a barn. A very large barn. Dust-speckled light filtered in through small slatted windows on the top level of the enormous three-story space. It looked like it had been constructed out of some sort of metal. On two floors, there were stalls along both walls with something that looked like dark blue hay poking out onto the floor. Near the ceiling some sort of harvest was drying, draped over the rafters that spanned the great expanse between walls.

"Welcome to Vedra," Vaslow said. The airlocks hissed and the door opened, revealing a dozen men in long cloaks with caramel-colored, spotless faces. They were pointing what Bea assumed were the Vedrian equivalent of guns right at them. Bea and Calvin stayed glued to their seats in the ship that had brought them here.

The men shouted and waved their guns in Calvin's direction. The deep guttural voices were loud in the small craft, and Bea couldn't keep herself from screaming. "Ahhh!"

One man leaned in and spoke in an awestruck whisper. "Snarh Jaru. Cadrence Bayatrice." He said the name like a prayer—slowly, with reverence. Everything was still foggy, and Bea was trying to make sense of what was going on. They were speaking, but Bea couldn't understand them.

Vaslow barked an order and waved them back, and quickly came to her side. The men backed off. "It's okay. Bayatrice, look at me. It's okay. They're Wharton's men. They just weren't expecting Calvin. Changes in plans make them nervous, but they're on our side."

"I'd hate to see them if they weren't," Calvin said, trying not to look as shaken as he obviously was.

Before Vaslow could say anything else, explosions ripped through the metal rafters and sparks burst through the barn wall. The men standing outside the ship began shouting and running in different directions.

A young bearded man stuck his head in and called to them. "We go NOW! To the tunnels."

"The girl, we've got to protect the girl," Vaslow shouted.

"We swear with our lives to do that. We've been waiting for her for many years. Trust me. This way-way," the young man yelled back. Another explosion ripped through the lower wall. It was followed by a loud, keening squawk. A dazed animal wandered from its stall. It looked like a long-haired chicken, but it was almost the size of an ostrich. It moved in panicked circles, one of its four small wings dripping a dark purple blood.

Other unseen animals, locked in their stalls, were bleating with fear. Shards of metal sprayed the hard-packed golden dirt floor, sending dust and hay into the air. The scent of dung filled the room. Vaslow leapt out of the ship and accepted a weapon that one of the men offered him. Calvin climbed out after Vaslow and Bea tried to follow, but her muscles wouldn't obey. She collapsed on the floor of the ship.

The young man with the beard saw her fall, leaned in, and lifted her body out of the ship. Vaslow reached to take Bea from the young man. Running men blurred into streaks of dark color, and the deafening sound of tinny booms and ripping metal filled her ears. She saw Calvin's face, pleading and scared, as Vaslow threw her over his shoulder. She wanted to stop him, but she couldn't make her muscles push that hard. With a thud his shoulder sank into her midsection. Her face hit something hard. Her lips were wet. She touched her nose and saw that her fingers were covered, sticky and red, a trickle of blood running up her face. She wished she could faint now.

She watched the ground rush under Vaslow's feet, caught brief glimpses of Calvin frantically trying to keep up. His shoulder dug into her ribs with each footfall; she couldn't get a breath. A man ahead of them pulled open a door that was flat to the ground, like a cellar door. Now they were going down. He picked up the pace with each step, and descending increased the pounding on Bea's ribs. *God, please let it stop.*

She glimpsed dirt walls, dimly lit, and the musty smell of the ground filled her nose. As they hit the bottom step there was an incredible blast and the ground quaked, knocking Vaslow against the wall and sending Bea off the edge of his shoulder, face first into the dirt. The trap door they had come through lifted in a halo of orange and floated back down. It disintegrated in midair as the stairs and the portion of the tunnel they had just fallen across collapsed behind them. Chunks of dirt rained down. She thought she heard Calvin screaming. This had to be a nightmare, the kind where you can't move your body. *Wake up, please wake up.*

Bea's skin scraped across the dirt as Vaslow dragged her back to him. He lifted her weight and flung her over his shoulder again. She saw him reach back and grab Calvin's shoulder, pushing him in front of them. He uttered one word: "Run!" And the world began crashing down around them.

Chapter 21: Homecoming

There was a cacophony of shouts and explosions and crumbling expanses of soil walls and ceiling. The darkness around her, the not knowing what was happening, made it impossible for Bea to get a fix on anything. Where was Calvin? She fought the pounding of gravity and raised her head. Behind them, she caught a glimpse of the young man with the beard who had lifted her out of the van, just as that section of the ceiling collapsed upon him. The cascade of soil knocked him to his knees and continued to flow until all she could see was his flailing arms. She gasped and tried to yell for Vaslow to stop and help, but she ended up swallowing a mouthful of flying grit that made her lungs seize.

They ran and ran, one step ahead of the swallowing darkness. At last the pace slowed and they began to climb back up. She felt Vaslow moving, unsteady on his feet, as he climbed the rough-hewn stairs. His sweat had soaked through to her skin.

She heard a door open at the top of the stairs and craned her head to see Calvin's feet move through the door ahead of Vaslow. Thank God. But then she lost him again. As they crested the top of the stairs, she felt hands lifting her off of the old man's shoulder, turning her upright, and setting her down on the floor. Her head spun and her eyes refused to focus on anything. She pressed her back up against the wall as if that could stop the movement. Slowly, the objects in front of her steadied.

The room was crowded with bustling people, some of them dirt-covered and bleeding. It was dark and the walls were lined with lots of otherworldly devices, like the viewer, but even more sophisticated. She opened and closed her eyes, just catching glimpses of Vaslow speaking to a dark-haired man. "No, tend to the girl first," he was practically shouting.

"Old man, we need to stop that bleeding or you won't be around to bark orders at me," the man responded in a deep accented voice.

"Wharton, I said the girl first," Vaslow said, and the argument was over.

The relief of having Vaslow's shoulder out of her gut was short-lived. Throbbing pain in her ribs quickly took over. At least the blood was no longer rushing to her head.

A boy and a girl pushed their way to her. The girl leaned over Bea and checked her split lip, the pulse at her neck and wrist, looked into her eyes, and then rolled what looked to Bea like stones over her chest. At one point the girl's eyebrows knitted and she sent the boy scurrying away. What did that mean? Was she not okay? Bea felt better for the most part, though now she had bruised ribs and there was a new buzzing in her head.

Bea was cold and scared and wanted to see Calvin. She knew he'd made it, she had seen his feet leave the tunnel. She kept trying to look around the girl, but there were too many people moving about, all stopping to stare at her as they passed. The buzzing in her head was getting more intense. "Calvin?" It was so loud in here, dozens of voices all competing. She added hers to the fray. "Calvin!"

The girl put her hand on Bea's shoulder to still her. "Cadrence Bayatrice, Alhura," she said, pointing to herself and then saying again, "Alhura."

"Alhura," Bea repeated. She guessed it was the girl's name.

Alhura said something about Calvin in an odd language and pointed in the other direction, nodding with an "it's okay" smile that Bea guessed was meant to tell her Calvin was fine. She continued to speak to Bea in a soothing, sing-song tone as she worked. Though Bea didn't understand the words, it was comforting.

She closed her eyes and saw an image of the bearded young man's arms flailing. Her eyes popped back open. Her clothes were tight and wet and she looked down to see that she was covered in blood. She yelped. Oh God, was she dying? Vaslow appeared in an instant.

"I'm bleeding, Vaslow. Oh my God. I'm bleeding." Bea was frantic. She tried to scramble to her feet, but the girl kept her still.

"No, Bayatrice. It's me. It's my blood." Vaslow knelt down next to her.

"What?" She looked at Vaslow. His entire left shoulder was soaked through with blood. That's what had soaked her clothes. He had a gaping wound on his neck that was still bleeding. He wobbled a little and then turned and placed his back up against the wall with a thud.

His words came out softly. "Okay, I guess it's my turn," he said to Alhura as he closed his eyes and slid down the wall.

Bea tugged at the girl's arm. "Please tell me he isn't going to die? He can't die." Bea's emotions seared in her chest. Just hours ago she would have wished him dead, but now losing him was unthinkable. He had to get her home, had to explain things to her. How had things gotten so crazy? She wished she'd never seen that letter in the closet, wished she'd given the device to her aunt and uncle the minute she found it. She wished she and Patty were still friends. And then she remembered the spots on her face and knew that things couldn't have stayed the same. She just wished that she had never dragged Calvin into any of this, but in a small selfish part of her heart she was so glad he was here. "Calvin! Calvin!" she shouted, her voice too loud even in her own head.

Alhura looked at her and spoke sharply, motioning for Bea to lie back down. She addressed Bea in a firm voice, but didn't shout. Whatever she'd said, it was intense enough for Bea to understand she meant her to stop and she quietly leaned back against the wall. The girl turned her attention to the wound on Vaslow's neck. She had an assortment of instruments that looked simple and rustic. The girl worked with confident hands, using a semi-circular blade to effortlessly shave away the beard on Vaslow's face. The bare wound looked ragged and too large. For the first time she saw the spots on Vaslow's cheeks and neck.

Her hands found their way to her own cheeks. Though she couldn't feel anything, she knew the spots were there. She was like him. At that moment it hit her—he had refused treatment until she was checked out. He was putting her life before his own.

The chaotic herds of people thinned and the buzzing in her head had quieted to a dull roar. Several teams of people, some with spots, but most without, worked on technologically advanced devices, flipping through virtual pages with a touch of a finger. She could only understand what the people with spots were saying. Something about raids and fires in the market district and diversion launches. She couldn't hear enough of it to follow the thread of what was happening, to know if the danger would follow them here, but she heard her name coming up frequently in the conversations. She pieced together that they had been waiting for her return, that they were counting on her. Counting on her for what?

Judging by the slowing pace of the people around her, Bea guessed the danger had passed, for now. She watched as Alhura tended to Vaslow. As the girl worked, her air of confidence melted and she'd become tentative and nervous. Her hands now fumbled with her tools. She set her kit down and motioned for a couple of men to come and carry Vaslow away. Alhura trailed behind, barking orders at them as they made their way up the stairs. Though Vaslow was gray and still, Bea could still see him breathing. Where were they taking him? Was he going to be okay? What was going to happen to her?

She sat upright, though her body begged her to lie back down. She wondered where Calvin was, and she missed Patty. Patty would know what to do now, and even if she didn't know, she'd do something anyway. Bea just sat waiting for something to unfold for her. How could people be counting on her? She didn't even count on herself. This was so stupid—she didn't belong here.

The boy who'd been with Alhura earlier came down the staircase across the room from Bea. He was carrying a tray of food and had a dark burgundy cloth draped over his arm. As he cleared the staircase, Bea saw Calvin dressed in a long beige cloak, trailing behind the boy. She had never been so happy to see anybody in her whole life. She stood on rubbery legs and ran to him. Or tried to run. Her arms and legs didn't work they way the were supposed to. She didn't so much hug Calvin as collapse on him.

"Oh, Calvin," was all that she could say, and the hot tears ran down her cheeks. She felt his arms wrap around her, felt the warmth of his body as they pressed together. It felt so good to be in his arms. But then she realized with heart-piercing certainty that she was at least six inches taller than him.

He leaned back and looked into her eyes, and now was looking up at her. Sure and confident and logical, but somehow soft too. Something about him was different. She wondered if he was afraid of her now that she wasn't human. "It'll be okay. I don't know how, but I know it will," he said, like he meant it. He was searching for the words to make her feel better, like he had done the other day. Relief spread through her and hot tears flowed down her newly spotted cheeks.

Calvin and the boy helped Bea back to the pallet where she'd been told to rest.

"This is Si. He's brought food for you." Calvin smiled. "The kid's a talker. Unfortunately, I don't understand a word he's saying."

"Why he no talk pocked-tongue?" Si asked Bea. "You a pocked. You speak, right?"

"I'm not sure what you mean by "pocked-tongue," but I understand you," Bea answered without thinking.

"Hey, that's cool. Can you teach me?" Calvin was looking at Bea, amazed.

"What?" Bea asked.

"You're speaking his language."

"I am?" Bea answered. "Oh. I guess I am." She looked at the boy and back at Calvin. Then somehow something unfolded in her head in a way that had been there all along but she just hadn't seen. There was unseen connection that ran to Calvin, and a different one that led to Si. Like trains switching tracks, she automatically knew which language to speak. The more she concentrated, the more tangible the connections became; the buzzing in her head seemed to lessen as she paid attention to this detail. It was like her head was too full, which caused the buzzing, and she could lessen it by allowing some of it to spill out into these links. All around her she could sense connections—the distance to the wall, the density of objects, the different feelings coming off of the people around her. If she concentrated hard enough, she could actually see these connections—thin lines of…energy. This was all too weird and felt so far from normal it scared her.

"You gotta eat-eat," Si said, pointing to the platter he'd set next to her. "Alhura said if you don't eat-eat you gonna get sick. She said your body is hurtin' itself. It need food."

Yes, she was starving. The mention of food sent the thought of connections and energy and other people's feelings from her head. Her body needed food. Looking at the plate of unfamiliar foods, she pointed to what she guessed was sliced fruit with juicy dark purple meat. "What is this?" It reminded her of a huge ripe fig. Not usually adventurous with food, she was so hungry it didn't matter what she ate.

"That plava," the boy said, smiling. "You got good eye. That my favorite."

She picked up a piece and took a full bite. It was tangy and cold on her tongue. As she bit down, large individual pieces of pulp burst, releasing sweet juice. "It's kind of like a fruit version of bubble wrap," she said to Calvin.

Calvin, looking a bit like an African chief in his flowing cloak, took a piece of the plava and bit into it tentatively. "You're right. That is so weird, but good!"

Si smiled. "He like, right?" he asked Bea.

The three of them ate until the tray was empty. Bea and Calvin savored the strange fruits and meats and black bready crackers—for a moment forgetting Vaslow, the crumbling darkness they had escaped, and the men who were out to get them. Bea ate so much her stomach pushed against her already tight skirt. She tugged at her waistband.

"Oh, I brought this," Si said, handing her a cloth. "You can change there." He pointed to a door off the main room. He stacked all the dishes as he spoke. "You change, I go clean these. I come back."

As Si walked toward the stairs, Bea held up the dark fabric that shimmered from burgundy to ruby-red. It was like a long dress, with a cream-colored inset around the neck and cuffs. Although it was yards of material, it was very light.

Bea made her way across the room, refusing help. The food, or time, had made her steadier and her limbs were starting to obey her commands. She entered the small room and closed the door behind her. It was a bathroom. Though it was not like any bathroom back on Earth, she could figure out what everything was and how it worked.

She took off her now too-small top and threw it in a heap in the corner. Holding the dress up, she searched for a zipper or some way to get into the thing. Her eyes drifted down to her legs. Then she ripped off her skirt and her undershirt and looked at her stomach and chest. The spots didn't stop at her neck. They ran down the entire length of her body, getting larger and larger until they finally merged together at her stomach. She had breasts—that was certainly different—but they were a mottled pattern of half brown and half her normal creamy color. Her whole stomach was brown, brown like Calvin. The color ran the length of her thighs and tapered back off to spots at the knee. She sat looking at her body. She touched the dark patches of skin, dragged her thumb hard across them as if maybe they were just painted on. Did everybody with spots have them on their bodies, too? It didn't feel like this body belonged to her. Her emotions spun in her head like a blender, like they were chopping into her brain. She couldn't run away from this, but she didn't want to look at it anymore either.

She slid the dress on over her head and it stretched to allow her to get it over her shoulders, then tightened again. The material was soft against her skin. On the front there was a kind of mesh lacing attached that made the torso of the garment form-fitting and gave support to her brand new breasts. The fact that she needed that support was new and different too, but, as frivolous as it seemed in this moment, she was excited about that part. She let the gown fall into place. It was so light and gave her such a range of motion, she almost felt naked.

She made her way back over to Calvin, nervously smoothing the already smooth bodice, thinking of the skin under the fabric. Her own body was some alien thing she couldn't escape.

"Bea, you look—" Calvin began.

"I know, stupid," Bea answered, looking away.

"I…was going to say beautiful." Calvin stared at her in a way he never had before.

"You don't have to say that." Bea wanted to cry. She didn't want to be lied to.

"I'm not just saying that." His eyes darted to her face and then away again. "I mean, I always thought you were pretty, but now…I mean…you're really…I don't know…beautiful."

He had always thought she was pretty? He had to be lying, but she had never seen him so nervous. He'd never been like that around her. No one had ever called her beautiful; she didn't know what to say. Bea gave him a half-smile and quickly sat down, noticing the way the fabric poofed around her as she sank to the ground. She could feel him looking at her, but she felt too nervous to look back at him. Instead, she looked down at her dress, pretending like it was the most interesting thing she'd ever seen. She squeezed a handful of fabric as tightly as she could—it refused to wrinkle.

"It's amazing stuff," he said. "I've never felt anything like it. It seems to have a temperature-regulating feature. I wonder if it's nanotechnology."

Bea laughed. That was so like Calvin. "I was just thinking it was pretty." As they sat there waiting for word on Vaslow, or for someone to tell them what to do next, the woman who had given Vaslow the landing coordinates, the one who looked like Trinity, walked over to them.

"Vaslow asked me to give this to you." She handed Bea her cell phone.

"Uh, thanks, but I don't think this planet is in my coverage area," Bea said. She took her phone anyway, happy to have something familiar.

The woman gave her a strange, questioning look. "It is a simplistic technology and I was able to alter the frequency. The use of the magnetic wormholes causes too great a time delay for voice communication, but you can send typed messages."

"Are you saying I can text?" Bea asked incredulously.

"Ah, I think so, yes. It can function in a typing-only capacity." The woman looked like she was about to leave, but she paused, turning to Bea. "My name is Dahreen; I'm tech support here. If it isn't working properly, let me know."

"Thank you," Bea said.

Bea explained to Calvin what the woman had told her.

"That is totally unbelievable," Calvin said in awe. "We can at least let your family and my G-pops know we're okay."

Bea switched on the phone. It made a chime and the little track ball glowed in multicolor—she used to think *that* was so futuristic. As soon as it came on, it started vibrating. She was receiving dozens of texts, one after another—all from Patty.

Bea where are u? 3:45 PM the first one read. Then she looked at the rest.

R u ok? 5:30

Really u ok? Mom's calling the police. 6:29

I'm sorry. 7:15

I'm so sorry. 8:04

Bea I'm sorry. 8:38

I miss you. 8:39

I'm so sorry. 8:40

It went on and on. All these millions of miles away and this was the closest she'd felt to Patty in a long time. She held the phone to her heart.

Me too. We're fine. Can't get back. She hit send. "What else do I say?" Bea looked at the phone in her hand. "We're in the middle of a war on another planet, might not make it home for dinner. And oh, by the way, I've morphed into an alien being."

"Just let them know we're alive," Calvin said. "Bea, they love you no matter what. You'll see."

Bea wasn't so sure. Maybe Teddy would be frightened of her. Maybe Aunt Lucy wouldn't want her around. Maybe she wouldn't want to live on Earth looking like a freak anyway. She was still thinking as Patty's texts were coming in. Suddenly, there was a tiny pop and the phone sizzled and sparked in her hand. Bea yelped and threw it up into the air. It came crashing down in several pieces.

Dahreen rushed over. "I guess it wasn't as able to handle the frequency as I thought. Did you get a message out? Vaslow was pretty adamant that you do that."

Bea just stared at the shattered phone, her lifeline to the life she'd left behind in pieces. "I don't know. I think one went out before it blew up."

Dahreen bent down and collected all the pieces. "Well, Vaslow will be glad about that," she said.

Bea snapped back to her current reality. "Have you spoken to Vaslow?"

"Not since they took him," Dahreen responded.

"Do you know where he is? If he is okay?" Bea asked.

Dahreen shook her head. "No, I'm sorry, I don't. But I will try to fix this and make sure your message was sent." She walked away, looking at the pieces in her hand and shaking her head.

"We need to find Vaslow," Bea told Calvin. As she spoke she saw Si coming back down the stairs. Bea had made up her mind. As soon as he made his way over to them, she blurted out, "Take us to Vaslow."

"I can't," Si said slowly, shaking his head and looking down. "The old man is...gone-gone."

"Vaslow's dead?" she repeated in English, and sank to her knees in a puddle of red fabric.

Chapter 22: A Borrowed Move

"He can't be dead." Calvin's eyes welled up, face twisted in disbelief. "How will I get home?"

Bea started to cry—not for Vaslow, not for Calvin, but for herself. She heard it so clearly: "I" not "we." Calvin had accepted the fact she couldn't go back. She wanted to fight, to yell at him for being so selfish. She'd gotten used to always having him around and hated that it felt like he could leave so easily.

Si, confused by their reaction, said reassuringly, "He gone-gone, but Alhura said he be swift as sand soon."

"You mean he's not dead?" Bea said almost accusingly.

"No." Si spoke fast, hoping to correct the misunderstanding. "Alhura say he need real doctor. Popi took him to Uncle."

"He's alive," she said in English.

Bea looked at Calvin, wanting to believe her feelings about this had been all wrong. Calvin was here with her, not safe back at home. He had traveled across the galaxy, risking his own life for her, just like Vaslow had. Then the face of the young bearded man buried in the tunnel flashed in her mind. Things were being blown up around her, people were dying and she didn't know why, but she knew it was *because of her*. She didn't understand this, didn't want this, hadn't chosen this. But it was real just the same. She was so tired of having these feelings. She had to do something, but she couldn't trust her own heart. The thought came to her, *If I just think like Patty I can figure it out.*

One thing she was sure of, Patty wouldn't sit around here waiting. Bea stood up. "Come on, we're going."

"What you doing? You sit back down. Rest-rest," Si said, shaking his head. "No, Miss-Miss. We stay here."

"You're taking us to Vaslow."

"That tunnel be broken. We can't go there. We stay here," Si kept his seat. "I can't. Popi be very mad-mad."

Bea ignored him and headed the way she'd seen them take Vaslow. "And bring a cantomount. Calvin needs to learn the language."

The boy rose and led the way, up the stairs and through the house, muttering curses the whole way. Si had given Calvin a cantomount, tucking it into one of the many pockets Calvin hadn't known were on the inside of his cloak. On the way out the side door, Si handed them both capes, calling them outercloaks, insisting they wear the hoods despite the warm temperature. Bea had offered no resistance to the request to hide her face.

They walked through the shaded alley and out onto a street. The sunlight was blinding after being in the semi-darkness of the basement for so long.

"Bea, check it out," Calvin said, pointing to the sky. "Two suns."

Bea looked up, squinting at the alien sky—blue, but a greener shade than that of Earth. Her hood slid back on her head, revealing her face. Si grabbed her arm and turned her toward the wall.

"You want that dark guard to shoot you now?" Si demanded, motioning over his shoulder to a small patrol of uniformed guards that were going the other direction. Bea could tell he was trying to sound angry, not scared.

She pulled her hood back on and they crossed into what was clearly a marketplace. Though she didn't exactly have a headache, her brain felt fuzzy and her thinking was dulled. She grabbed Calvin's elbow and felt a funny flutter in her stomach as they walked arm in arm, following Si through the bustling market.

Though she hated that he was in danger, she didn't want him out of her sight. The flood of scents coming from animals, spices, and the throngs of people, all familiar but exotic at the same time, enticed Bea to sneak a glance here and there. She tried not to gawk at the highlighter-colored fruit, at shiny chrome vehicles hovering a foot above the ground, animals with two heads and moving spots. Si kept them walking and made sure their hoods stayed in place.

Si cut at an angle from between the vendors' stalls and down an alley—very similar to the one they'd started on—and led them down a dead end into the very narrow space between two small buildings. Calvin and Bea kept close on Si's heels. As they came out from between the buildings, two men on a balcony trained their weapons on the three of them and began shouting. Instinctively, all three of them raised their hands in the air—Bea thought that this was truly a *universal* symbol. Si shouted back to the men and told Bea and Calvin to pull their hoods down.

The back door of the house opened and a dark figure urged them inside. No sooner did they step in than the dark-haired man from the compound, Wharton, began yelling at Si and whacked him on the back of his head. Not viciously, but more out of frustration.

Si just kept repeating, "Sego, Popi, sego. Popi, sego."

Bea put herself between Si and Wharton. "I made him bring us," Bea said, speaking in Vedri. The man let go of the boy.

"You?" He looked at the boy. "Is this true?" Si nodded. He continued in an even harsher tone to Bea. "So it is you who are the fool? You would risk my son's life? Risk all of our lives, our futures?"

Bea was stunned—was that what she had done? It didn't matter what planet she was on, it seemed she was good at making bad decisions. It wasn't an answer to his questions, but it was the only answer she had. "I need to see Vaslow."

"You may look like her, but you do not share the soul of your mother." Disgusted, Wharton turned and walked away.

Her mother. The words shocked her into silence. All her life, Bea had pushed every thought of her mother back to the dusty recesses of her mind. Her aunt and uncle would never tell her anything about her parents, and now she knew why. They'd never known them, and they weren't even really her aunt and uncle. She knew that, but it was like she had to keep reminding herself that it was really the truth. Thoughts were all jumbled up in her mind at the idea of having to reimagine her life with this new perspective. And people were talking about her mother, expecting her to be like this woman she'd never met, someone she knew nothing about. Talk about a pendulum swinging from one extreme to the other. Her thin grasp on composure was slipping, and going completely wack was right on the other side.

Si had led them into what Bea would call a living room. It was both rustic and futuristic at the same time. A large fire pit with an elegantly curved metal chimney hanging from the ceiling above was the centerpiece of the circular room. Tapestries and rugs woven in brightly colored metallic fibers lined the walls. There were a number of large, overstuffed low chairs. Si had told Bea that when his father was ready he would take them to Vaslow, and not a moment before. It was his way. The only thing they could do was wait.

The three of them settled into the well-cushioned chairs. Calvin pulled out the cantomount and began diligently studying. Si peppered Bea with questions about Earth, but she couldn't concentrate and her answers trailed off. Si gave up and they fell into an impatient silence that was only occasionally broken by Calvin practicing his Vedri aloud.

Chapter 23: Clearing the Fog

Bea sat on the armrest of a padded chair with her feet hanging over the side. She hated her newfound extra height. She was so used to trying to be shorter at school. And now these extra inches only made her body feel even more unwieldy and foreign. At least she didn't feel like Lurch here, far from it. Everyone she'd seen on Vedra was tall, as if the whole population had been stretched.

Bea watched a strand of hair as she twirled it round and round, imagining she was giving her finger a dark auburn dress. Ugh, even her hair was different. A booming voice broke the silence and made her jump.

"To dinner," Wharton barked, and left as quickly as he had entered.

"Where's Vaslow?" Bea called, following after him.

Si jumped down and ran in front of her, shaking his head. He spoke in a hushed voice. "Please, Miss-Miss, you no ask. Just go to dinner." His face was pleading.

Calvin trailed behind and he shrugged at Si. He managed a few words in broken Vedri, "There's not much...luck...to change her mind."

"I really need to see Vaslow," Bea pleaded to Wharton's back. She just had to know if he was okay. Was that so much to ask? He'd almost died because of her, and she'd been such a brat to him. She just wanted to say thank you and that she was sorry.

Wharton continued into the dining room without so much as turning to look at her. "Please, Mr. Wharton—" Bea crossed the threshold into the dining room and twenty pairs of eyes turned to her. The buzzing. The buzzing was so loud, crippling. She grabbed her head and sank involuntarily to her knees. There was a collective gasp.

Wharton wheeled around, bent, lifted her, and carried her from the room. He motioned to the others to keep their distance. He took her back to the living room and laid her on multicolored pillows. Si and an ashen-faced Calvin followed Wharton and then knelt beside her. As soon as her body hit the cushions, she sat back up and shook her head.

"I'm fine, really. It's just this strange buzzing that comes and goes," Bea said, rubbing her temples.

"Well, if you're so fine, can you lay off this fainting business? I can't take much more of it," Calvin said, sounding stressed. He looked at Wharton. "Is she really okay?"

Wharton, ignoring Calvin, stared at Bea in disbelief. "Snarh Jaru, Bayatrice. *You really know nothing.*" Wharton stood, staring at Bea, or more accurately staring through her. He had the air of someone who was shaken at his core. The way he looked at Bea made her feel tiny and insignificant. She wished that were really the case. After a long moment, he simply turned and left the room.

"What did I do?" Bea called, not expecting anyone to answer. Was she supposed to sit here and wait for him to return, for him to possibly explain? What didn't she know? Well, everything, of course. Maybe it was time for her to find out. She turned to Si. "Where do you think Vaslow is?"

"Oh, no, Miss-Miss, no," Si said in futile protest as he stood.

Calvin shrugged again, using his Vedri as best he could, "No use… to argue."

Si led them into another room where Wharton was standing inside the doorway. One look from his father and Si blurted out, "Sego, Popi, sego!" And he scampered back out of the room.

When Bea peered inside the room, Vaslow was there, lying in the bed, alive. She was so happy to see him she rushed past Wharton.

"You see! She has no sense of what is right." Wharton's anger boomed.

"Wharton, her weaknesses are my fault." Vaslow spoke in a dry gravelly voice. He was propped up to a half-sitting position. His face was pale and his arms looked limp, but there was a spark in his eye when he saw her. She leaned over and hugged him, relief welling up in her.

"You indulge her too much," Wharton continued, his veneer of anger cracking. "We expected someone who could fill the footsteps of her mother. And you bring us an ignorant child?"

"My friend, please give me a moment with her?" It was a question and a gentle command at the same time.

Wharton wheeled around and came face to face with Calvin. As he was leaving, he looked back at Vaslow as if to say something more, a storm of emotions passing over his face. Wharton swallowed whatever deep thought he had and simply said, "We need to talk about my investment." He left the room, beckoning Calvin to follow him.

"Vaslow, I am so confused. What do they want from me?" Bea took the seat at the side of Vaslow's bed and put her head on his hand. Her hot tears wet the back of his hand.

"Bayatrice, please don't cry." He lifted his other arm and placed his palm gently on the back of her head. "Shhh. It's all right," he soothed her in a soft warm voice.

"I'm sorry I was such a brat. I'm sorry I didn't believe you." She swallowed hard. "You almost died because of me."

"It's okay, Bayatrice. I'm okay," he repeated.

"What does he mean about my mother's footsteps? And why," Bea swallowed a sob, sat up, and looked up at him, "are people willing to die for *me*?"

"Poor Bayatrice, this is so much all at once. But I know you have the strength inside you to handle it," Vaslow said with a certainty Bea didn't have within herself. "It is time for you to take your place on the throne. To pick up where your parents left off."

"What? I'm not even planning on staying." Even as she said the words, she didn't know if they were true. Where did she belong? Certainly not on a throne. Was everybody here crazy? The way he looked at her was maddening, like he expected her to be someone she wasn't. He was trying to make her into something she would never be. And worse, she could tell that he thought the future depended on her. She couldn't manage her algebra, much less rule an entire planet!

"You belong here. You'll feel it, you'll see. If you don't feel it by the time you hold the scepter, you'll feel it then." He spoke in that expecting way, as if his words could mold her into the vision he had of her in his head. "The Protectorate is a Scepterus De Facto government, and by law can only exist in the absence of a person of royal blood—until an heir returns. And you've returned." He continued talking as if he expected her to just go ahead and take the throne. Like it was a test for AP math or something, rather than something impossible, like trying to turn a frog into a swan. Which all the magic in the world couldn't do.

Vaslow continued, "There's a scepter at the palace that proves the royal bloodline. It has been used for centuries. It gives the bearer answers beyond imagining—if he is of royal blood; if not, it will cause instant death. So you can see, there aren't many challenges for the throne. That scepter is your birthright. As sole heir, you need to claim the throne, Princess Bayatrice."

"Princess Bayatrice?" Bea spoke the title for the first time. Princess Bayatrice. Was that really who she was? She was so many things: the kid who was good in English; the one who always read to Teddy; Patty's shadow. How could this be her destiny? She wasn't like Patty, the one who always wanted to be followed, always wanted to be in the spotlight. That just wasn't the kind of person Bea was. But now, with these spots and her height, she also wasn't the kind of person who could be Patty's shadow anymore. She felt adrift and didn't know which way to steer this boat of her life.

"Vaslow, I'm sorry. I know you want this. I know now how much you risked to bring me here." And she did know that, even if she hadn't asked for any of this. "But this is a mistake. I'm no leader. I can't be something I'm not. If my mother was as wise you say, even she would see that." As she spoke, hot tears rolled down her face. This wasn't fair. She felt like a failure and a disappointment, and it wasn't even her fault.

"You are wrong, Bayatrice. She would be proud of you." Bea whimpered in protest. Had he not seen her make the wrong choice at every turn? Was he blind? Vaslow continued, "You are fierce like she was. You have a great deal of fight in you—you just need to learn where to aim it." Bea could hear the smile in his voice.

"I'm not fierce," Bea said, practically shouting at him.

Vaslow laughed. "Even in your most desperate hour, you still argue with me. Yes, you are like her."

***

Vaslow paused in thought. How could he think of Bea's mother without thinking of that night? He couldn't stop it; the whole memory just flooded back into his head.

Dust swirled in the air of the summer evening , so soft and warm you barely noticed it until your cloak was coated. In his off-duty hours he had gone to the officers' club in Tanloo and the effect of the drink had snuck up on him. Why had he even gone? He vaguely remembered being coaxed by someone.

There had been no blasts in the sky, no explosions that shook the ground, but the world had been thrown off its axis that day just the same.

Groggy, he had awoken in the middle of the night to the sounds of running in the corridor, muffled voices. He ran to the sovereigns' bedchamber. The door had been bolted from the inside. Five men were trying to break it down.

A primal scream rose up from deep within him. He ordered the men away and began firing until the door was nothing more than shards. Inside, the room was in shambles, a guard unconscious in the corner. Two trails of blood, the kind of marks bodies leave when being dragged, was all that remained of the sovereigns. The tracks stopped in the middle of the room; obviously they had been taken through a cantomount window. No ransom, no demands—just vanished. He forced this memory to end and pulled thoughts from a happier pool.

"She was strong and passionate and kind. And loved you more than anything in the universe." Vaslow told stories of her mother insisting on making Bea's baby booties herself, accidentally sewing the soles to her tablecloth; of lullabies she'd sung, and how she never wanted baby Bayatrice out of her sight. He told her the meaning of her name, Bayatrice. It was a small white flower that grows on cliffs above the sea. Experts on such matters had said, as the planet's water decreased, it would be one of the first species to become extinct. But instead, the little plant sent its roots farther down into the soil, breaking through the rocks of the cliffs if it needed to. It found a way to survive and bloom. "You see, even from birth it was predicted that you would prevail."

His voice trailed off as sleep overtook him, and for the moment there was an unfamiliar warmth in his heart.

Chapter 24: Sacrifice

Bea must have dozed off as well. The next thing she knew Wharton's deep voice was booming in the room again. "Run along now, Bayatrice. Vaslow and I have important business." Wharton was gruff and sounded angry, but there was something more—he seemed sad.

Bea sat up and glared at him. "I want to stay with Vaslow."

"What I have to say is not for your ears." Wharton motioned to the door. "Go." Bea kept her seat, straightening her back to full height.

"Let her stay. She's heir to the throne. It is her right to know," Vaslow said, gently squeezing Bea's hand.

Wharton scoffed. "If that is your wish, but I have no desire to insult her more," Wharton said. "Vaslow, when our paths joined I staked this mission on your faith in *her*. I bet our hope for just rule, my entire Clan's future, my family's lives…" he choked on his words for a brief moment, caught himself, and then continued. "On…on what? On a girl who hasn't been trained to rule." Wharton spoke as if Bea wasn't even in the room. "It is the tide of the people that will win this war, one way or another. If we back her, we will have two battles on our hands: one to overthrow the Protectorate, and one to win over the people. The rumors of her existence are running like fire over paper through the whole of Pleet. They are hungry for her, but they will turn on her like gurdrus on rotting meat when they see she's not able to lead them."

"You underestimate her," Vaslow responded, undisturbed.

Bea was confused. She wished she hadn't stayed. She didn't want to rule, but hated the way this man was talking about her. She might not be ready to rule a planet, but that didn't mean she was as insignificant as he made her out to be. This was crazy. She should be in biology, worried about dissecting a frog, and wondering if she was setting a good example for Teddy. Hoping that Aunt Lucy would take her and Patty to the mall to get new jeans.

"I think it is you who have the wrong idea about this girl," Wharton responded, shaking his head. "Your heart has swayed your eyes from the truth. She knows nothing. She can't even control the zinalha. That alone could be her demise. She called it 'buzzing.'" Wharton said the words as if they tasted bad in his mouth. "How can she lead if she can't wield her zinalha?"

"She'll learn to master her gifts. There is greatness in this one, Wharton." Vaslow's tone was unshaken. He continued with a certainty that couldn't be moved. "And that can't be taught. It's what is already inside her that will make your faith in her justified."

"There are those who began their zinalha studies at birth who failed to wield it. And she is past her patou with no training at all? I am sorry, Vaslow, I have no faith in her." Wharton words slowed, and his volume dropped to a whisper. "I lost my oldest son in that tunnel because of her. She only brings misfortune and broken dreams with her. It isn't her fault, but we are in danger because she is here. All of us, our lives are in danger simply because of her presence."

His words rushed through Bea like quiet daggers slicing a path to her heart. She hadn't wanted to come, didn't want to be here. Of course it wasn't her fault. But that thought didn't ease her guilt. The young man who had lifted her out of the van, the one she'd seen with his arms flailing as the tunnel swallowed him, had been Wharton's son? His hating her made sense now. Even as the despair flooded her and threatened to drown her, something else stirred inside her. A well of desire buried deep—a desire to fulfill this destiny Vaslow spoke of, to live up to his expectations of her—came alive inside her. A seed planted long ago, unseen until now, that now wanted to bloom.

No, she chided herself. How stupid to think, even for a minute, she would be capable of living up to Vaslow's belief in her, of being anything other than a social misfit, a wannabe, a curse. Her eyes welled up. She wouldn't cry in front of Wharton, the man who had already lost so much. She stood up slowly and quietly left the room.

Vaslow, helpless and unable to go after her, called out, "Bayatrice, we will make it work. I promise you. Bayatrice…"

"You shouldn't make promises you can't keep, old man," Bea heard Wharton say as she walked down the hallway.

Bea made her way back downstairs, through the halls. At the bottom of the stairs she could hear voices and the clatter of dishes from the dining room. She stood at the doorway and listened to the few words she could understand. *It wouldn't be long now. There are forces gathering in the market.* Si and Calvin were at the far end of the room eating. As she stood, a number of men and women noticed her, looking hopeful and awestruck, then more and more faces turned toward her. She wanted to go in, but the buzzing in her head got stronger and more painful. The pain seemed to grow worse with each gaze that fell upon her. It was finally so strong that she backed across the hall; as she reeled clumsily forward, the buzzing lessened with each step away from the crowd.

She made her way through the living room and out into a vestibule. *They were all in danger simply because she was here.* She paced in front of a door with a heavy latch. The soldiers were hunting *her.* She'd made Si take them through the streets—who knew if they had been seen? Maybe men with guns were on their way here now? Just being here was putting them all in danger. She heard Si and Calvin enter the living room. Calvin was awkwardly trying to put words together in Vedri.

She propped up the heavy latch on the doorway and pulled hard until the door swung open, creaking on its hinges. Wharton had already lost one son. She hurried through the front yard to the gate.

"Bea? What are you doing?" Calvin shouted from the doorway behind her. "You've got to come back inside."

"Come back, Miss-Miss!" Si's voice was practically a squeal.

"No." Bea spoke through tears. "You need to be as far away from me as possible." She broke into a run, her muscles now doing what she asked them to do, and turned into the market. Into the buzzing.

As she ran through the market, she heard Calvin yell. She turned to look behind her and saw Si's face frozen in a tortured scream. She turned back around, still running, and slammed full-force into the bulky frame of a Protectorate guard.

The guard grabbed Bea's arms. She saw his dark eyes flash as he realized the prize he had captured. She thought she heard him start to chuckle before a rock flung by Si hit him on his left brow, splitting the skin. Before the guard could react, Si cranked his arm back again, throwing the stones with a contraption that reminded Bea of a sling-shot. This time the small sharp rock landed with enough force to knock the huge guard down, and he let out an ear-splitting bellow.

People in the market had come to the edges of the stalls to watch the commotion, staring at Bea. The buzzing in her head was stronger than ever. Bea couldn't make the world stop spinning. Wharton's prediction that this buzzing—the zinalha—could be her "demise" echoed in her head. She was terrified at what was happening in her own body, terrified at what would happen to Vaslow, Calvin, and Si if she stayed near them.

The guard writhed on the ground, holding his head, blood running between his fingers. As he rolled to a sitting position, Si and Calvin grabbed Bea's arms and pulled her, despite her protests, into an alleyway that led back toward Si's uncle's compound.

Bea tried to dig in her heels, but she had no traction in the sandy soil. "You have to let me go! It's not safe for you."

"Get her back in here!" Wharton shouted from the other end of the alley. "Hurry."

Si, Calvin, and Bea tumbled back down the street and through the gate to the compound.

"Let me go." Bea tried to shake loose. "You should just let me go." If they heard her, they didn't show it.

"Did the Protectorate guards see you?" Wharton asked Si as he bolted the door behind them.

"Yes!" Si yelled.

"Get her downstairs, to the south tunnels." Wharton was emotionless as he barked orders. "The men down there will tell you which way to go. Make sure the three of you stay together."

They heard the noises in the street before they saw them, the sound of feet marching in lockstep, the rattle of weapons in holsters. The dark guard were approaching.

"Aaaiiiiiiieeee!" Wharton let out a loud high-pitched yell that warbled in his throat. *A war cry,* Bea thought. Before they made it out of the vestibule, men came from all over the house, all armed and ready to fight. As Wharton barked his first commands, an electric pulse ripped through the front wall. Sparks and tiny embers rained down on Bea. In her effort to make things better, she had done nothing but make them worse—again. She had brought danger and fire and death right to those she had been trying to protect by leaving. Couldn't she do anything right?

Si led Bea and Calvin toward the basement stairs.

"I can't go without Vaslow!" Bea turned toward his room without waiting for an answer. "Don't follow me. Get to the tunnels."

The boys followed anyway, Si groaning but keeping up. "Popi say we stay together."

Vaslow was on his feet when Bea entered the room, shaky but standing. "We've got to go!" Bea went to his side.

"Go! To the tunnels. I'll be right behind you." Vaslow waved her off.

Bea spoke through her tears. "I know this is all my fault, but I won't leave until I make sure you're safe! I won't!" She grabbed hold of his torso and slid up under his arm to support him.

Calvin took the other side and said, to no one in particular, "Like I've been saying, there's really no use arguing with her."

As they maneuvered Vaslow down the first set of stairs they got into a quick-step rhythm, all their legs working together, Si leading the way. They picked up speed in the straight hall and made their way down to the basement, entering a control room similar to the one at Wharton's, though this one was much smaller. There was a Sloan rebel soldier keeping order as dozens of people moved through the metal-rimmed doorway. Bea thought she saw Alhura kiss him on the cheek before moving between two older women and disappearing down into the tunnel. Escape. They all needed to leave because of her.

The sounds of the battle were closer now. Screams and explosions. The house shook. They fell into a line of people, all heading down. The rebel soldier guiding the people called to Bea. "Miss-Miss, I am Rham. I fight for you. Please go down now." He tried to usher her to the front of the line of people.

"No, not until they are safe." She kept her place in line. The house shook again. Bea thought of the crumbling tunnels and the flailing arms, Si's brother disappearing in a cloud of dirt. "I thought the tunnels had collapsed?"

"Only north of the market. These tunnels are strong," Rham replied.

"There must be another way out?" Bea was pleading. The thought of being underground in darkness made her shudder.

"No, Miss-Miss. This is it." Rham shook his head.

Another group of Sloan rebels had their backs to the basement, guarding the group and shooting rounds at the invading dark guard. Si was already in the tunnel; Calvin would be next, followed by Bea, still clinging to Vaslow. A shot tore across the room. It struck the left side of the heavy metal tunnel doorframe, twisting its regular shape and sending it collapsing on itself, separating Si from Bea, Calvin, and Vaslow. Shards of metal sprayed them. "Si!" Bea yelled. She and Calvin dug at the dirt among the twisted metal, but it was no use—the doorway was sealed. "Si!" It was so loud around her, she couldn't hear if Si was calling back to her. *Dear God, let him be okay.*

Rham was on the ground, bleeding from his arm and shoulder, but conscious. They were bleeding and dying because of her. She had to do something. Bea shouted to Rham, "There has to be another way!" He just shook his head.

"I've got it!" Calvin shouted, fumbling around in his cloak for the cantomount. Calvin explained to Bea what Vaslow had told him back on Earth about the device. If it has a linked unit synched with it, you could open a window on the other end with no one needing to activate it. "We can use this!"

"It needs a mate. We can't open a window without one," Vaslow said, a darkness coming over his weary face.

"It has one. To Si's," Calvin said as another shot whizzed between them, searing the edge of his wrist and knocking the cantomount out of his hands. They all dropped to the ground in unison, taking cover behind the dense metal workstations. Now Calvin was edged up against the useless doorway with Rham. Bea and Vaslow were positioned farther back. The cantomount had landed out in the open, between them. Smoke was filling the room. Small fires burned on all sides.

"Use your weapon, cover fire so the boy can get the cantomount!" Vaslow shouted to Rham. Bea heard a groan and saw the soldier raise his weapon awkwardly in his left hand over the lip of the table. He fired rounds, high, over his own men, while Calvin reached forward and grabbed the cantomount.

Calvin quickly seated the device and moved his fingers deftly over its surface. A window opened to Wharton's control room, chaotic and equally loud, though the battle had not yet reached them.

"Cover fire!" Vaslow shouted again. Bea and Vaslow quickly crawled on their bellies to Calvin.

The fray on the stairs was more intense. The Protectorate Guard was advancing down into the control room. "Bayatrice, go!" Vaslow pushed at her back.

"No, you first. You need our help." Bea shrugged Vaslow off.

Vaslow opened his mouth to protest, but Calvin cut him off. "Might as well go. She won't change her mind." Calvin and Bea helped him through the window. Dahreen noticed him coming through and helped on the other end.

"Okay, you go now," Calvin said to Bea.

"No, injured first," Bea said, pointing to Rham. "Help me with him," Bea said, lifting Rham's shoulder as the soldier groaned in pain. Calvin shook his head, but lifted the man's other shoulder, helping until the wounded man was on the other side. The room was so full of smoke now that they couldn't even see the battle. Shots rang out, hitting all around them.

"Now go, Bea!"

"No, you're injured, too!" Bea surprised Calvin by popping the cantomount out of his hand. "You know there's no use arguing."

"Bea," Calvin was frustrated, but moved forward. "Make sure to bring your body through first, before the cantomount, or you'll break the connection." Calvin cleared the window.

For a moment the smoke cleared at the top of the stairs and Bea saw the Protectorate guard from the market. His brow was cut and dried blood was dappled on his cheeks, alternating with his Cass markings.

Vaslow looked in horror from his side of the window at the Protectorate guard. "Islook!" Vaslow said, panic crossing his face. "Bayatrice, you have to come over *now!*"

"I love you both, I really do," Bea said, knowing for certain that this was true. As she looked at them, she thought, *But it's me they're after.*

"No, Bayatrice!" Vaslow screamed as she smiled sadly and threw cantomount through the window, breaking the connection. She turned, alone, to face the battle.

Chapter 25: My Way

Vaslow and Calvin stared in utter disbelief as the window disappeared. The cantomount bounced on the hard floor and slid up under a workstation. "No, no, no!" Vaslow shouted into the air. "Not this way, Bea," he said more quietly, using her familiar name, the one Calvin called her. All these years she had been an ideal, a quest, a vow he needed to honor. But now she was real. A young woman, a force of her own. He wanted to see her step into the power he knew she had inside her. He wouldn't lose her, not now.

"We need to get back to Bayatrice," Vaslow said to Dahreen.

"But you can barely walk," Calvin said.

Dahreen added, "And there is a barricade of Protectorate guards in the center of the market. You'll never be able to get through on foot." She paused, looking at a battle on the screen. "With the tunnel sealed, I really see no other way."

"Is there another cantomount connection?" Calvin asked hopefully, using his Vedri more confidently.

"I don't know of any, and I'm the administrator of those devices," she replied solemnly.

"Think. Think." Vaslow spoke the words out loud, but was speaking to himself. His mind raced, trying to come up with options. "Is there another house near here with tunnels that are still open?"

Dahreen flipped through pages that were projected before her until she came to a map. As she used her fingers to zoom in, Vaslow recognized Sloantown enlarging and coming into focus. There were lines running under the market area, leading in all directions out of Sloantown. These, Vaslow assumed, were the tunnels. Dahreen pointed to an area highlighted with flashing red lines. "This whole section was collapsed by the last explosion," she explained, starting to shake her head. But then, as if an idea had come to her, she pointed to the translucent screen. She moved the map to the right with her hand then circled another area with her finger, leaving a pulsating circle of blue where she had touched. "But you could go west." She enlarged again and moved the virtual map until she found what she was looking for. "Here," she said, tapping the projected image and creating another blinking dot on the hovering page. Her finger traced a green line of light down. "It will take you right inside the barricade—if that's where you really want to go. I can get a sled to take you west, but you'd be on foot in the tunnels."

"You'd never make it that far on foot," Calvin said, looking at Vaslow.

"I'll make it," Vaslow said, knowing that for Bayatrice he would find a way.

***

It was hard to breathe. Bea's eyes watered from the smoke. What now? She couldn't try to be Patty or her mother or anyone she was not. Her next move had to come from inside her. This torn heart of hers would lead her. It had to. She wanted what Vaslow believed about her to be true, wanted to believe those qualities he saw were really a part of her. But ultimately it didn't matter; either way, she would see the killing stop, even if she had to stop it with her own life. As these lofty ideas floated in her head, two guards grabbed her, one on either side. She kicked at their shins and they tightened their grip, practically cutting off the circulation in her arms, until she stood perfectly still.

As she stood completely immobilized by the two guards, Islook made his way down the stairs toward her. This was the man that had been fighting with Vaslow the first night the viewer window opened in her bedroom. She'd seen the panic on Vaslow's face when he'd recognized Islook at the top of the stairs before the window closed. Now his black eyes bored into her, and the buzzing in her head was so loud she could barely concentrate.

The room around them became eerily quiet. Bea watched as the last two Sloan soldiers stood with their hands raised, backs to the wall. A Protectorate guard raised his gun to finish them. The two guards squeezing her arms were now dragging her forward.

Islook pulled papers from his pocket, speaking loudly and forcefully, addressing all his fellow soldiers. "I carry orders directly from Commander Falstoff." As he spoke, he flashed the papers above his head. Bea could see some kind of official seal on the documents. The guard pointing his weapon at the rebels stopped to listen, and those holding her loosened their grips. "All rebels are to be taken into custody for questioning." The guard with the gun pointed at the two rebels nodded, lowered his weapon, and forced his prisoners to the stairs. "And I have orders to bring *her*," Islook spoke as if it would be too distasteful to speak her name, "to the commander personally."

Oh, God, Bea thought, *maybe this was a mistake.* As bad as these two were, she'd take them over this dark-eyed giant of a man. But the guards holding Bea didn't release her. Bea thought of Teddy and Patty, and the rest her family. She would die here and they would never even know what had happened to her, never know how much she loved them.

There was no way to run, and in a matter of seconds she would be in Islook's grasp.

The guards looked at each other, puzzled. "Why would the commander send a junior officer to bring in Princess Bayatrice?" the older of the two guards asked Islook.

"Commander Falstoff needs his best men at the barricade—now. He doesn't need them nurse-maiding a…child!"

At this the guards nodded and relinquished Bea. Islook took her arm with less force than she'd expected. He addressed the guards that released her. "Your orders are to return to assist in securing the barricade." At that, the two soldiers hustled up the stairs and out of the room, leaving her alone with Islook.

"Finally, Princess Bayatrice," Islook began in a low voice. He released her arm. His hand went to rest on his weapon, but he didn't take it from its holster. "You are brave to stay behind."

She didn't feel so brave. Her muscles were trembling and she felt blanched, wondering how white her face could possibly look with her new marks. Was he going to kill her? Would she never get the chance to say goodbye to Vaslow? Or to kiss Calvin? The thought of that surprised her, but she realized how strongly this desire was true: she'd like to kiss Calvin goodbye. A real kiss, like she'd seen in the movies.

Bea looked down, afraid of what this man might do to her. Then the thought came to her: this was her decision to stay behind, and it was the first decision she had made that actually felt good—like she was taking some initiative for a good outcome. Vaslow and Calvin had made it to someplace safe. She had made those she loved safer. Straightening to her full newly extended height, she met Islook's eyes.

Islook stared back with his dark eyes. Bea could smell the blood and sweat on his body. She braced for whatever he would do, and promised herself she would not cry out.

Islook took a step back and then bowed his head and dropped to one knee. "I, Islook, of the Sloan Clan of Mahlid, son of Wharton, pledge my allegiance to you, Princess Bayatrice. I hereby vow that I dedicate my deeds to serve your will." Sitting in her bedroom, what seemed like a lifetime ago, she had heard those words on the cantomount, spoken by another subject to her mother. She knew these pledges were not given lightly.

Bea was still, frozen. Islook stood and raised his head, smiling at her bewildered expression.

"I don't understand," she responded. This man who had fought Vaslow and who'd come after her was now pledging to serve her?

"The orders were forged," he said, dropping the papers that had called the other guards off. "Wharton is my father."

His eyes, yes, there was something about them that reminded her of Si's, but he had Cass markings on his face. How could this be?

"Nice tattoos, huh?" He fingered his Cass markings. "Even my own brother, Simoud, doesn't know who I am." He gingerly touched the crusted wound on his eyebrow. "It was decided after my patou that I would take this path to help our cause of overthrowing the Protectorate. I was to be someone on the inside, someone who could know their mind. It has served us well."

"But I saw you fighting Vaslow, that night the window opened to his room."

"Vaslow has been the hardest part. He is a great man and I have disappointed him. But that night I was there to warn him. If I hadn't, he would have been killed." Islook stared directly into Bea's eyes as he spoke.

His words came from his heart and Bea wanted to believe him. But Vaslow had been so distrustful of him. Could she trust her gut? Islook could have already killed her three times over if he had wanted to. Bea held his gaze and then simply nodded. She had no choice; he would either help her or hurt her, and she couldn't control which it would be. "Okay, then, let's go." She headed toward the stairs.

"Forgive me, but not that way. We'll go out the side door. The alley is our best chance. I'll find you a cloak." Islook moved quickly, only stopping short when he realized that Bea was not following him.

"We're going out the front. And I don't need a cloak." Bea waited for him.

"I am afraid you don't understand. There is a barricade in the market. Everyone, I mean everyone, is looking for you. It would be suicide to go out the front." She could tell Islook was forcing himself to be patient.

"You may as well get used to it. I never do what people want me to." Bea smiled to herself as she spoke Calvin's words, thinking for once that perhaps this was a good thing.

"I'm afraid not. We're going out the side if I have to put you in a sack and throw you over my shoulder to make it happen," Islook said. He was clearly not amused.

Okay, so now was the time to see if he was true to his word. "Look, I think it would be safer for you if you stayed here, but you can come with me if you want," Bea said. She saw nothing but truth in those dark eyes that reminded her so much of Si's. No matter how deeply she looked, only truth. "I believe you just swore your allegiance to me. I'm guessing that wasn't a pick-and-choose-which-parts-you-like kind of oath?" She turned and continued toward the stairs, knowing only that he would follow, not sure of what would happen next.

As Bea stepped out the front gate, she felt the warm sunlight on her face. *Sunslight,* she thought. It felt good and right. Now that she had chosen to listen to herself, she saw that she was indeed being led by an inner voice, one that had always been with her, guiding her, but one she hadn't ever really been able to hear, or perhaps she just hadn't listened. It was louder now, more certain than it had ever been. She dug down inside herself, calling up the courage to make her shaky legs follow it, moving her tentative feet forward. The distant sounds of battle filtered through the air on plumes of smoke. Islook reluctantly followed as she headed into the fray. What would she do when she got there?

The market was deserted, the stalls empty, the wares nowhere to be seen. All was quiet except for the sounds of creaking shutters as a few Sloanfolk snuck glances out their windows. She felt the weight of their gazes upon her. Bea tried to get glimpses of those who were watching her. She knew they had heard rumors about her coming. Wharton had said it was the people, those who hungrily stole glances now, who would win this war.

A door slammed behind them. Islook whirled around, aiming his weapon. "Put your gun away," Bea said as they saw a figure scurrying toward them.

It was an old woman in a patched cloak, her cheeks tear-streaked, her gray hair sticking out from its wrap. Her gait was uneven, as if one side pained her, but still she ran. The old woman grabbed Bea's hand and kissed it, speaking loudly in Sloan. Bea couldn't understand her.

Islook translated, "We knew you'd come, we knew you would. Our hopes and prayers go with you." As Islook spoke, more shutters opened.

Bea gave the woman a weak smile, though the buzzing tore through her head, getting stronger. "Thank you. I will try to be worthy." The woman let go of Bea's hand and stood, watching Bea, waiting. That was it! The people would win this war. "Islook, how do you say, 'I am here for you' in Sloan?" He translated and she repeated with all the volume she could muster, "Mod, Cadrence Bayatrice, esh nom hany-hany!" She shouted it again, letting the words flow out from her soul, feeling it was more true than anything she had uttered before.

She continued on, surefooted, the reluctant Islook in tow. One by one, the people came down from their hiding places until the whole neighborhood was filling the streets behind her. Shouting prayers and hopes and allegiance.

"They are saying they are with you," Islook told her.

The buzzing was so loud now, Bea could barely think. She smiled as she looked at them all, but she felt the tug of their words as if they were pulling at her very flesh. The buzzing was too much. The buzzing would be her demise, she remembered Wharton's words again. She desperately wanted to quiet her aching head.

"Princess Bayatrice, do you want to stop?" Islook was asking her, though she couldn't make out his face.

"No." She shook her head and forced her feet to keep moving. She realized she was digging her fingers into Islook's arm, but she couldn't loosen her grip.

At the end of the block in front of her she could make out the barricade: sheets of slick metal that had been linked together to make a structure. The barricade was clearly a staging area, a base of operations in unfriendly territory. It looked like it had just been assembled and plopped down, out of place on the dusty street. Several panels were not quite connected, leaving gaps. It was twice the height of a man, with little slits for viewing and shooting. She could catch glimpses of the many soldiers behind it, along with vehicles, probably full of extra weapons.

In front of the barricade, she could see a few rebel soldiers crouched behind barrels or stacks of crates, darting out to shoot at the gaps, and then retreating.

As they saw her approaching, the fighting stopped and all eyes were upon her.

***

Calvin and Vaslow came up from the tunnel and out of a house at the south end of the market. They were covered in yellow dust. Blood was seeping around the edges of Vaslow's bandage, but he was moving well, powered by sheer will.

The scent of smoke and electric fires hung in the air. They could hear a commotion, but it wasn't weapons fire. It was voices. They stepped out from between the houses and into the market, and saw the street filled with hundreds of people, shouting and crying. The depth of emotion the crowd was pouring out was amazing.

"We have to see what's going on. Help me up." Vaslow stood at an empty stall. Calvin gave Vaslow a hand up onto the counter and climbed up after him. They could see Bea in the center of the street, walking with Islook. They were walking straight into the Protectorate barricade.

"Sweet Jaru, no! Islook has her!" Vaslow was frantic.

"No, look. She's holding onto him. Not the other way around." Calvin watched Bea. "If she didn't want to be going that way, she'd have to be dragged. And he doesn't have his weapon out."

Vaslow tried to sense Bea's emotions. There was fear, but that wasn't her strongest emotion. The boy was right. Whatever she was doing, it wasn't against her will. He felt her zinalha. It was too strong, an electric shock in his brain threatening to tear him apart. He had to break the connection. She wouldn't be able to withstand it. He called out to her, but his voice was lost, joining with the others shouting her name. He had to get to her, to help her. He jumped down from the table, ignoring the pain that raged in his body. Calvin followed close behind, pushing their way through the crowd. Bea was in sight but he couldn't reach her. He saw her stumble. Islook reached behind her to keep her from falling, but it was too late.

***

The noise in her head clouded all Bea's senses. White light filled her vision. It started small, a simple pop in the back of her skull. Then hundreds of tiny explosions tore paths through her brain. Her body shuddered on the gritty soil beneath her.

Islook had his hand on her quaking shoulder. They were steps away from the Protectorate barricade. Weapons were trained on them, but no one moved. The crowd was silent and still. Bea's body was wracked by an undulating tremor that made her torso twist and then snapped her body back upright.

She blinked. The buzzing was gone—more like, disseminated. Instead of staying bunched up in her head, she could feel the energetic vibration, like ropes reaching out from her. She could see, but her vision was sharper, colors richer. Her arms and legs felt stronger, somehow more solid. Through Islook's hand on her back, she felt his rapid pulse. She was now tangibly connected to the ground she sat on, the crowd around her, the guards before her, the air she breathed. As she looked around she could see a fleck, an energetic spark, at the center of everyone, everything. The buzzing had been like a tightly wound ball of yarn. She guessed she was supposed to use her mind to unwind it and cast the lines to make the connections to this spark, this light, in those she chose. Instead, the onlookers, with all their expectations of her, had pulled the connections from her all at once. She was a part of them and they were a part of her, forever entwined.

She closed her eyes and felt the sensations coming to her in rapid succession, so much to process she couldn't separate them. She resisted the urge to fight against this unfamiliar happening in her brain, instinctively knowing that if she held back it would ball up and she would be in pain again. She remembered to breathe, deep slow breaths. With each breath she tried to untangle the energetic cords, keep the flow of sensations moving. And with each exhale her body calmed.

Chapter 26: Destiny

Vaslow and Calvin broke through the crowd. "Bayatrice?" Vaslow said her name. "Sweet Jaru, let her be all right." A prayer whispered under his breath.

She opened her eyes slowly and gave him a wisp of a smile. "I'm okay," she muttered. She stood and hugged Vaslow. Though her mind was still moving slowly, her body was sure and strong and incredibly receptive. There now was another sense active in her. She could feel his relief, though no emotion showed on his face.

Calvin just looked at her. His heart was beating hard in his chest; she could feel it. Calvin—she was so happy to see him, her heart leapt in rhythm with his. She leaned forward to give him a real kiss, but at the last second she chickened out and placed her lips on his cheek. "Thank you. Both of you. I have to finish this now." She turned away from them and closed the remaining distance between her and the Protectorate guard, still holding their armed stance.

The men and women of the guard looked to Islook, who stood silently by Bea's side. Finally, one guard stood up from behind the barricade, his weapon trained on Bea. "Okay, plebe, I'll take her from here," he said, motioning for Islook to stand down. Bea held her breath. Would Islook really go against all these men with guns to protect her?

"I have pledged my allegiance to Princess Bayatrice," Islook said, drawing his weapon and aiming it at the guard who spoke. There was a collective shuffling behind the barricade, and Bea could feel a sense of confusion wash over them and then settle into a hair-trigger tension.

The guard reacted quickly, adjusting his aim, ready to fire on Islook. Bea moved between them.

Bea reached over and gently pointed Islook's weapon down. "Not that way," she said, stepping forward. "You may take me if you need to." Bea put her wrists together and held them up to the guard who spoke.

"If you do, you'll have to take me too," Islook said, stepping forward and making the same motion. Vaslow stepped up behind Islook and clasped his hand on the man's shoulder, as a proud father might, and nodded. Then he raised his arms as Bea had. Calvin did the same.

From the far side, Bea could see someone trying to make his way through the throng of people. The crowd at the front parted and Wharton stepped up behind Bea, followed by Si.

"Si." Bea hugged the boy, who was scraped up but was otherwise unharmed.

"We, too, stand with Princess Bayatrice," Wharton said without looking at Bea. He continued in a softer voice, just for her to hear, "Rham told me what you did during the attack. You saved his life, and the lives of countless others. I have underestimated you."

A woman stepped from the crowd and shouted, "And I, too, stand with Princess Bayatrice." One by one the crowd moved behind her, forming a silent wall. She was buoyed not only by the strength of their conviction, but by the wave of energy they brought forth. Bea could feel the strength in her body increasing.

The guard leader looked at the numbers in his own ranks, then looked back at the hundreds who stood quietly in opposition. "Hear me! All of you are committing a treasonous, punishable act! If you stand down now, we will let you return to your lives."

"The law clearly states that the Protectorate only has authority to rule if there is no surviving member of the royal family." Islook spoke loudly. "So, it is you who are on the wrong side of the law."

"I'm a member of the Guard. I follow orders. I don't make them. We have no idea who this girl is." The guard swallowed his rage and addressed the crowd. "Last chance." No one moved. "Well then, you all are under arrest for treason." Looking at Bea, he continued, "You know the penalty for treason is death. *You are condemning them to death,* but you have the power to save them. Just tell them to stand down. No one else has to die. Our orders are to get you, no one else."

Condemning them to death? Was this feeling of certainty, this voice that was speaking so loudly inside her, just as wrong as so many of her decisions had been lately? She wasn't just risking detention; this was life and death. She searched herself for what was most true in this moment, and she realized she had to ask the people to stand down. She would go alone, and everyone else would be safe.

"Islook, would you translate for me?" she said. She climbed onto a crate at the base of the barricade and faced the crowd. "I feel your support and I thank you. It means more than you know. I want you to know I'll fight to my last breath to make right what the Protectorate has made wrong. But you need to go home now. Go back to your houses and be safe."

As Islook translated, Bea thought the emotion of his words matched her own, but the crowd still didn't disperse.

"Please, I won't let anyone else die because of me!" Bea was pleading now. She felt fear and the weight of responsibility heavy and growing inside her, twisting her stomach, making her heart pound. It seemed that wherever there were negative feelings in her body, the energetic connections could not be made.

Islook translated a shout that rang out from the crowd. "We cannot be safe if we are not free!" Cheers of agreement rang out. Followed by other shouts. "We are staying with you." And, "They will not steal you from us again!"

The guard behind the barricade swore under his breath. He shook his head and said to Bea, "Okay, I'm calling for transport."

Should she beg them to go, make them listen to her? Bea felt the fear in her like a solid object, dark and ugly. She also felt the threads that connected her to those around her, light and alive. She had to choose, and this wasn't a decision she could make with her head. The lightness was leading her in a way her head didn't want to go, but as she moved toward the energy, she knew it was right.

"We won't need transport. We'll walk," Bea said, feeling the energy rise in her. The crowd around her let out a roar of approval.

"Don't be crazy. That would take hours." The guard was clearly angry now.

"We will walk," Bea said again. "Let's go." The crowd followed her around the barricade like sand pouring out of a bottle.

They walked through the streets, Bea leading, Si and Calvin happily flanking her. Vaslow leaned heavily on Islook. And the crowd grew. One by one. They would see her, do a double-take, and then fall in behind her. They were hungry for what she represented, as if the soul of the planet had returned. The heaviness of that responsibility was too much for her to bear, so instead she decided to make it about something outside herself—hopes and dreams of the people, that she symbolized for them. They followed her, followed what they hoped she'd bring them. And with each person that joined their ranks, Bea felt the energetic connections increase.

Protectorate Guard ships hovered above the crowd. Guard presence on the street grew, but they were still no match for the numbers who followed Bea. Step by step, the masses bridged the distance from the market to their destination. Bea was mesmerized as she witnessed the low sand-colored buildings give way to more sophisticated buildings as they left Sloantown. But even as they forged on, the numbers following her increased. Bea was reaching her physical limits. Her newly transitioned body needed rest and quiet. She was tired and thirsty, but she wouldn't stop.

A shop owner pushed his way through the crowd carrying a heavy box. He handed Bea a small silver pouch. "For you, Princess Bayatrice," the man said, bowing his head as he handed it to her.

"Thank you," Bea replied, not knowing what it was or what to do with it.

Si must have read the confused look on her face. "It's water, Miss-Miss." He pointed to the top edge of the pouch. "Put your mouth here and squeeze."

She did as he directed and cool sweet water poured into her mouth. When she pulled the pouch from her lips, it sealed off again. "Oh, thank you!" she said to the man again, and he began handing out pouches of water to all those around. Si explained to her that here on Vedra this was like giving out free money.

Vaslow was so pale by this point that she was certain that Islook supported more of his weight than he did himself, but the younger man didn't complain. Bea was grateful for Islook, and grateful they all had the water.

Along the way, people came bearing gifts of water or meat or fruit, not just for her, but for all those who followed. And when their boxes or bags were empty, they joined the march.

After what must have been at least another couple of hours they finally approached the gateway of Verlona City. It was an amazing sight. Bea had to bend backwards to see the top of the arch. As they approached, she could see the shimmering, multi-colored reflection of the people in its glistening surface. They passed under it, and the crowd quieted as the weight of the image reflected back to them sank in. It was as if this gateway had been built for this day, to show all those who passed through it the power of their combined strength.

On the other side of the gateway, the buildings were even more sophisticated—taller, with green flowering vines descending from their heights.

Vaslow raised his hand and pointed down a long tree-lined boulevard. "Up ahead," he said in a raspy voice. Bea could see that the road ended at a great expansive building with colored flags waving in front of it. The palace.

The swell of followers crested in the thousands as they reached the end of their walk.

There were no drums, no markers of celebration as Bea had seen on the viewer, yet she sensed the Protectorate knew she was coming. She could feel the dark energy seeping out from inside the palace, a wall she had to walk through. But the energy freely given by those around her surrounded her like a bubble, giving her both strength and protection.

As they approached the entrance of the building, Vaslow put his hand on her shoulder and she stopped to look at him. She could feel his emotion: he was proud of her. The feeling was overwhelming—warm, and comforting. He simply said, "You are your mother's daughter."

"Thank you." This time she wouldn't argue; she would try to make it true.

She entered the building and moved through the antechamber into the great hall. She was taken aback by the familiarity of the room, the translucent ceiling, arched windows, effortless sculptures. The viewer had spared no detail. The crowd flooded in behind her, filling every crevice, flowing out onto the portico, into the street, filling the square and trailing all the way out to the next district, she suspected.

She looked around the room. This was where she'd heard her mother tell jokes, listened to her father's words of wisdom, where she had laughed as a baby. On the platform where her parents once sat were the five members of the Protectorate. They began to speak, first one, then the next, in random order.

"Who is
it that
dares
invade
our sanctuary
unannounced?"

The chilling voices, the highs and lows. It was the voice from her nightmares. It wasn't one person, but five separate people. A wave of the fear from those nights she'd spent curled up in the middle of her bed washed over her. She ran her hand down her forearm to where they had touched her in the dream. It was cold and throbbing, and as she approached them the cold began to move up her arm. Everywhere the cold touched the bubble of energy faded. The more it faded, the quicker the cold moved. The icy flow moved through the veins of her arm and up her shoulder, heading toward her throat. It was like being thrown into a pool of ice water. She tried to speak, but no words came out.

"Clear

this

hall.

Take her

into

custody."

The Protectorate blasted the words and guards went into motion. Bea heard their pitch-black thoughts in her head, unmistakable.

Kill her.

Then send

out proof

she was

a fraud.

Bea fought against the paralyzing cold that invaded her body, the ice picks that pierced her mind. She felt the threads of energy slowing as the chill overtook her, bringing along with it a mind-numbing pain. *No, no, this can't happen.* But her body wouldn't respond and her legs faltered beneath her. The world around her swirled, threatening to disappear into the darkness of unconsciousness. How could she possibly fight them? She couldn't even speak to say she needed help.

"When confronted

the imposter

will

crumble."

From the corners of her consciousness she heard footsteps coming toward her. Islook was speaking, encouraging her. It was all blurring together. And the pain was now burrowing into her head, begging her to close her eyes. *No, Bea, you can't close your eyes.* She instinctively knew that would be the end.

She listened to this internal voice. *Pull.* It spoke to her. *Pull.* Pull what? And then she realized the connections were still there, reaching out to her, brushing the edges of the new doors in her mind. They weren't gone or frozen; they were just moving in slow motion.

She concentrated on those behind her, around her, but mostly her friends beside her, for those connections were the strongest. She reached for their hopes—their energy—like she was trying to grab a rope to keep her from tumbling into an endless abyss. One strand stood out, stronger than the others: it was Vaslow's. She tugged it with all the strength in her mind. The energy reverberated and cracked like a whip. Then she was able to grab another and another until she had remade hundreds of connections. The effect was like snapping a towel covered in ice. The dark energy that enveloped her shattered like thin glass, falling away and releasing any hold on her. The feeling reverberated in her body and she shook her head as the warmth returned to her. She heard a single, dark, icy thought:

She

is

too

strong.

With that their onslaught was over, the hold they had on her shattered like brittle ice. Bea ascended the steps and spoke loudly, without hesitation, half-turning toward the seated five. "I, Bayatrice, daughter of Gwynlott and Solhan, thank the Protectorate for the safe keeping of Vedra, for exercising my duties while I was not yet able." She turned and faced the crowd. She wasn't sure where the words were coming from; they just seemed right, like those she'd heard spoken over and over on the cantomount. "I am now ready to accept my responsibilities and reclaim my family's rightful place."

At that, the silent seal that held the crowd ripped open and a deafening cheer burst forth. The volume ebbed and flowed for what seemed like an eternity, until it finally receded into silence.

The Protectorate did not move.

"We have

had claims before

and all have

proven false."

They stepped in unison, closer to the edge of the stage.

"We will take

her into

our protection

and verify her

claim."

The crowd was mute. One lone voice in the back shouted, "No!" Then someone yelled out, "The scepter! Give her the scepter!" The crowed joined in, all chanting, "The scepter! The scepter!"

Bea felt a shift in the icy energy from the Protectorate—surrender? They nodded in acknowledgment.

An aide stepped onto the stage carrying a carved wooden box. He opened it and stood in front of the Protectorate. One from the middle reached in and pulled out a long object wrapped in a purple flannel cloth. As he held it, careful not to touch the object itself, the top of the fabric fell open, revealing the jewel-topped scepter. Its dark pewter-blue surface looked as cold as the Protectorate felt to Bea. This was the scepter that Vaslow had told her about. If she wasn't really who he thought she was, touching it would kill her. She'd come too far and seen too much to doubt him now. She looked at Vaslow and saw nothing but assurance in his eyes.

She smoothed the perpetually smooth bodice of her gown, climbed the steps and stood toe-to-toe with the Protectorate. The one holding the dark scepter extended it to Bea. Time seemed frozen, and she swallowed hard and looked back at Vaslow one last time. Was this her destiny? She slowly reached forward and accepted its icy weight, heavy, but not quite solid. As it touched her skin, it began to glow and then got hot. Had she made a mistake? She kept her grip firm as the heat welled to the point of being almost unbearable, then finally subsided. The glow pulsed and then sent out a steady beam of light, illuminating all the gems on its surface.

"Yes,

she is

of the

royal

bloodline."

The surface of the scepter was constantly moving in her hand, though it maintained its shape. She held it tightly, faced the crowd, and raised it high up into the air. Again the crowd erupted, triggering another burst of light in her head. Images, memories, someone else's memories flashing across her mind. She got a brief glimpse of two faces, dear to her though she had never seen them in person, lying motionless but alive. Glimpses of thoughts and plans and something important that she needed to remember.

All this came rushing at her for an instant, swirling bright and clear. And then poof, it was gone as quickly as it came. She tried to reach for the thread of the images, the thing she was supposed to remember, but she couldn't catch it. It was still with her, just packed into the back of her mind, beyond her reach. As she tried to sort out what was happening to her, her focus was drawn back to the energy of the Protectorate. Anger and outrage consumed them. It bubbled up, vile and sticky, threatening to lash out at her. But then, as if they'd collectively swallowed a bitter pill, she felt them rein in this noxious force. An all-consuming thought repeated in their heads: They needed to leave and protect their assets. Whatever that meant.

The Protectorate took one step back and spoke in the emotionless hive-speak:

"We who
have served
your lineage
rightfully
return your
throne."

With that they backed off the stage in unison with a slight, deferential bow. Bea heard their words, but as they retreated she also felt their emotions: a ugly righteous anger. Though it wasn't visible on the surface, the malice in their hearts and their indignation ran as deep as the sands of Vedra. This wasn't the end of the fight. Their paths would cross again.

Chapter 27: The Beginning

As soon as the Protectorate left the room, the crowd exploded with excitement. Vaslow called to a guard to make sure the five were escorted from the palace to a holding cell. He told Bea he was sure they still had a lot of friends in powerful places, but he would do his best to help her make sure they paid for their crimes. Bea motioned for her friends to join her on the stage. Everybody in the room was hugging and laughing, whooping and dancing. Bea heard the distinctive Sloan "aaaieee" cry coming from the throng. But it wasn't just Sloan in the crowd. There were people of all colors: some like her with brown spots, some with red skin, and some with skin that was almost translucent. All different, but all sharing the same moment of victory. Somewhere in her body she understood that this shared emotion was special and unique, that she should catalog this feeling, that she might need it in the future. It didn't make sense to her at the moment, but she was beginning to get used to that.

Bea let the energy of all those in the room wash over her. It grew so strong inside her she felt like it might lift her up off the stage. As the crowd began to settle down, Bea realized with an almost paralyzing stage fright that they were looking to her for...she didn't know what. The certainty she had felt about leading the people here had evaporated, and now it was just plain ole Bea standing before them. This was worse than having one of those dreams where you suddenly realize that you're standing in the middle of class naked, because this was real.

There was scurrying on the stage behind her. The five thrones were removed and replaced with one: her mother's. Tears came to her eyes. Her mother had sat in this chair. Bea had seen it through the cantamount. If she sat in that chair, it would put her on a path to knowing who her mother was. With a pang of guilt, images of Aunt Lucy swam through her head: being hugged and sung to sleep when she had the flu; her English paper hanging up on the fridge for weeks; perfecting their chili recipe. All the little things she had never really paid attention to but had always counted on.

The crowd's jubilation waned and now all she could feel was expectation. It pulled at her, physically drawing her to the edge of the stage, so strongly she felt she might just tumble off. She wondered what Vedrians would think of stage diving? As she tried to resist the force that drew her forward, the buzzing came back, more painful than ever.

"Are you all right?" Calvin asked.

"Yes." Bea tried to smile. "Just hold on to my arm, okay?"

And then, like someone had turned down a dial, the pull at her core lessened. She looked out over the crowd and saw a path being split down the center. All eyes turned to see what was happening. It became clear to her that when the crowd's expectation shifted off her to something else, the pull on her decreased as well. She saw what they were looking at: a line of men and women in long white robes with different patterned collars making their way to her from the back of the room.

Vaslow leaned in close to her. "These are the Cenates—rulers of all the countries on the planet. They are here to pledge their allegiance to you, to align their power with yours." He was doing his best to maintain his warrior façade, though not succeeding. He wasn't bleeding, but he was pale and weak-looking. At the same time she'd never seen anyone so satisfied, so proud. She wanted to draw that feeling in, but was afraid to open up in case the pull of the crowd overtook her again.

"Take your seat and call to them. Do you understand the ceremony?" he asked.

She was about say no, she had no idea how to do this, when all of a sudden she realized she did. All those rewinds and replays had etched the whole scene permanently into her brain. She nodded to Vaslow and walked to the throne. Was this really happening? It seemed unbelievable that her biggest worry a week ago had been kids in the caf singing "K-I-S-S-I-N-G." She looked at the throne, noticing the ever-so-gentle indentation in the cushion and the worn surface of the wooden hand rests. It called to her, told her she belonged. But in her heart she missed her family back on Earth. No matter what she chose, her decision would end up leaving some part of her behind.

She stood for a long time with her back to the crowd. The silence was alive: the shuffle of feet, the increasing rustle of fabric, the energetic pull at her core, strong and painful. So many people counting on her.

She rubbed the velvet arm of the chair. Where she brushed it, the red fabric lit up gold and changed colors as her touch faded. Everything here was all so different, so unexpected, yet it felt so right. Her heart was telling her this was her destiny. Could she trust it? She took a breath, turned, and sat in the chair. Closing her eyes, she let the words come to her.

"Heysay, heysay," Bea said, addressing the crowd. She tried to make her voice loud and strong. As the focus shifted back to her, the buzzing increased. She knew now not to resist. If she let it back in and allowed it to flow it wouldn't rip her apart. She swallowed and continued.

"I am here to serve you. I am in your presence to be judged. I accept your will whether it be yea or nay." She noticed Vaslow struggling to hold back the tears, Islook on one knee beside him, head bowed. Calvin was staring at her with an awestruck expression on his face.

***

Vaslow watched Bayatrice, who sat as her mother and grandmother had done before her. He struggled to keep his emotions in check and to keep the pain in his body at bay. His whole life had been leading him to this moment. And in this moment, having succeeded, he felt his sins forgiven, a weight lifting from him that he had carried too long.

He watched as Bayatrice breathed in the life of the room around her, instinctively knowing how to control the zinalha. All his hopes and dreams had been brought to life by this girl, this child of amazing strength. His faith in her hadn't been misplaced; if anything, his expectations hadn't been high enough. She had united the people in a way no one could have predicted, moved aside an enemy without a single bullet. Yes, there was greatness in this one.

***

"I am here to serve you," Bea continued. "I only have the power you give to me." She paused as her mother had done. "Will you give me that power? Who is to be the first among you to speak your will?"

"I shall," a voice rang out from the front of the line.

"Who stands before me?"

"I, Eltahn, daughter of Rehanna, First Cenate of the District of Colhan, stand before you." She genuflected on one knee, touching the back of her hand to her forehead, keeping her head bowed.

"Stand, Eltahn, daughter of Rehanna, and speak your will." She hoped she was getting all the words right. They had seemed so clear a minute ago, but as spoke them, they were starting to escape her.

The woman stood. "I, Eltahn, recognize your authority to rule. I pledge my allegiance to you and accept your authority as Queen. I hereby vow that I dedicate my deeds to serve your will."

Queen? She wasn't even used to "princess." The words hit her like a hammer. Instead of pulling at her, they pushed with such force she had to struggle to keep the air in her lungs. The room was silent. She was supposed to say something. Then the words came to her; she spoke them as loudly as she could. "I hear your pledge and humbly accept your vow."

Eltahn stood aside and another Cenate took her spot. By the third Cenate she didn't know if she could continue. The weight was so heavy on her chest, she wondered if this was what it was like to have a heart attack. With what seemed like a bone-crushing surge, all the resistance she'd been holding onto was pushed out of her. The tide swamped her; her lungs struggled against the onslaught. As the energy entered her body, filled every inch, she let go. Unable to resist, she gave up trying. With a terrifying certainty, Wharton's words came back to her again—the buzzing would be her demise.

As the last of the breath left her body, her vision started to dim. If she'd been standing, she would have collapsed. She didn't even try to take another breath, but her body didn't give up. And then, like being at the bottom of the ocean and discovering you could breathe, her lungs filled and her vision cleared. The weight shifted; instead of crushing her, it became a part of her, slipping between the cells of her muscles and intertwining with her molecules. The pain subsided. Her mind settled. Her body's strength grew to even greater heights. The new energy in her body had been like a cord plugged into an outlet— and now someone had turned on the appliance. The electricity was set into motion in and out of her. She felt energized, on fire with the feel of it running through her. Of course, it made perfect sense! She understood what Vaslow meant: They were here to literally give their power to her. The Cenates would give to her so that she in turn could give back to the people. And they would give to their Cenates. It was a complete cycle of energy and she was at the center of it. She had a long way to go to figure out how to really use it, but she wouldn't let the fear in any longer.

One after another they came and she accepted their gift, their tangible allegiance. Each Cenate's pledge was different; some fierce and strong, some polite, some an outright lie. She tried to memorize those faces. Once she stopped resisting, the energy moved like the wind when you hang your head out of a car window, speeding right through to her very core.

Vedra had 203 Cenates and every one of them had shown up. By the time the last pledge was made it was the middle of the night—on Vedra. She'd lost track of how many hours she'd now gone without sleep. Had she really only been here for just over a day? *How could your world change that much, that fast?*

Vaslow had nearly collapsed, but refused to leave; his only concession was he let the attendant bring him a chair. The crowd, the entire crowd,

had remained until after Bayatrice had left the stage and the lights in the great hall were dimmed.

Her small band of friends and their families were escorted to the Royals' receiving room in the west wing of the palace. A small contingent of guards remained outside the door. Bea was told they were her personal security detail. They would be with her everywhere. That would take some getting used to.

The receiving room was cozy—for a giant room with servants lining the walls. A fire burned in the enormous hearth, sending golden hues glinting off the lush fabrics that adorned the walls and furniture. Bea noticed there were no windows in this room. At first she thought that was odd, but then realized, like everything else here, there had to be a reason.

The long table in the center of the room was covered with platters of foods Bea had never seen before but was anxious to try. This new body of hers was always hungry, it seemed.

Wharton and his entire family were here, including Alhura and Si, standing next to his newly discovered brother, Islook. Si's uncle was here with a few men from the compound that Bea recognized. There were several Cenates that Vaslow had called "loyalists." Calvin had stayed close to her. Every time it seemed too overwhelming, she reached out and took his hand. It steadied her. But she could tell that he was dying to explore. Every new light switch, medical gadget, and access panel sparked a twinkle in his eyes. She finally sent him off to look around.

The energy roiled in Bea's body, which still felt foreign and mysterious. She had so much to learn about this zinalha, about her birth family, about everything actually.

She sat with her plate of food, trying to stuff her face and make polite conversation with well-wishers at the same time. Across the table, in a small cluster of chairs in a nook, she could see the official palace doctor working on Vaslow. He was a long-faced man who reminded her a bit of a spotted version of a Père Noel she'd seen in French class. As his instruments moved over Vaslow, she could see the color come back to his cheeks.

The doctor had come to her first after the ceremony, requesting she "retire to chambers" for an examination and rest. But she told him she would remain in the receiving room and refused to be seen until after Vaslow; it seemed only fitting. The doctor wasn't pleased, but hey, she was the queen, right? She wondered if she'd ever get used to that.

"Miss-Miss, you do really good today." It was Si, with Alhura by his side.

She shifted her focus from Vaslow to these two brave kids. Yes, she did end up doing good today, she'd give herself that. But she had no idea what she'd been up against when they started. These two knew what they were getting into and went eyes-open into danger.

"Si, today would never have happened without you two." She wished she could find the words to tell them how she really felt. "You're both so brave." She was about to ask Si to translate when she realized a few Sloan words had stuck in her head. "Alhura and Si, trod donny-donny." They both burst out laughing. "What? I was trying to say you guys did great."

Si tried to stop his laughter. "We know, but you'd better work on your Sloan."

"What? What did I say?" Bea felt her face flush. Si just giggled.

Wharton came over and put his hands on his children's shoulders. "Our lives are in your hands now." He bowed his head as he spoke. "I am happy to be your servant."

Bea was speechless. This man who she'd thought would never trust her was now bowing before her. He had risked so much, given so much, and suffered so greatly for her to be here. How could she ever make up for the loss of his son? "No, I owe you. More than I could ever repay," she replied. Wharton raised his head to look at her in surprise and Bea continued quietly, "It's I who am your servant."

"Ah, Bayatrice, you constantly surprise." He nodded to the other side of table. "Tell the old man I know I was wrong." He smiled and ushered his family from the room.

When it was her turn to be examined, the doctor moved his light over her, nodding as he did so, seeming pleased with the results. "Your Majesty, with your permission," the doctor said with a slight bow, eyes down. "It is time I get you an escort to your chambers. A minimum of a week's bed rest is required after one's patou. And after today," he smiled, "you have some catching up to do."

"We have one more task before I can rest," Bea said with a sad smile. "We need to get Calvin home."

Chapter 28: Goodbye

Bea, Calvin, and Vaslow sat in plush chairs facing the fire, talking about what to do next, how much to tell her family and Hal, how to get in and out without causing a scene. The rest of the party stood around the table or sat in little clusters, jubilation giving way to fatigue. From time to time someone would come to Bea to ask for a blessing before they left. Vaslow explained it was a courtesy the queen would provide, and he gave her the words to say: "May blessings flow into your life as water flows to the sea." Bea thought that was kind of a strange blessing for a desert planet, but maybe that was the point: a blessing for more than they could imagine.

A servant stepped forward and whispered into Bea's ear, "There's a woman at the palace gates requesting entrance. Claiming she's here at Vaslow's request. Her name is Dahreen Romneck." He stood and waited for a reply.

Bea just stared straight ahead. She was exhausted and her brain was so tired she didn't think she could make even one more decision.

The young man leaned in again. "Should I allow her entrance?"

Dahreenromneck…it sounded so familiar. Yes, Dahreen, from Wharton's compound. "Yes." Bea was afraid to say more for fear of sounding stupid. The young man turned and left the room.

Quietly Bea confided in Calvin, "I have no idea what I'm doing. I don't know what's expected of me. I'm not even sure I know the proper way to answer a question."

Calvin smiled back at her. "Just be yourself. It seems to have been working for you so far."

Bea wouldn't have recognized the woman who walked in if she didn't known who she was. The pants she'd been wearing had been replaced by a gown, not unlike Bea's but in dark shades of blue. And her hair, which had been pulled back into a severe ponytail, was now done up in soft curls. She looked like an entirely different person.

"You look beautiful," Bea said, without thinking if that was a proper thing for a queen to say or not.

"I meant to make it for the ceremony," Dahreen said, nervously fiddling with her dress. "But this took longer that I'd expected. It's almost as if this thing was built to fall apart. But it's working now." She extended her hand; Bea's phone rested in her palm. "And I'm fairly certain I've fixed the frequency issue."

"Thank you," Bea said as she took her phone back. The plastic was charred and melted on one corner, but it flipped open as it was supposed to. "Time to let them know we're coming."

Bea opened her eyes and stretched, having slept nearly the entire six-hour trip back to Earth. She'd had the strangest dream, and morph man—the Protectorate—was nowhere to be seen in it, thank goodness. She was laughing and running through the trees, enormous green-topped trees that rustled and whispered in a light breeze. But it wasn't on Earth—it was on Vedra.

"We're almost there," Vaslow said from the front passenger seat. Islook was driving.

She sat next to Calvin and another guard. Two guards was the absolute minimum the Commander of the Guard was willing to let her leave with. He'd wanted to come himself, but Vaslow had convinced him to stay and begin sorting out the loyalties among the troops. Bea didn't even want to think what that was all about.

The ship bounced as they jumped into Earth's atmosphere. She saw it brilliant blue and green, like a gem floating before her. That's when it hit her—she was saying goodbye to a whole planet. How could a person do that?

Since none of the adults knew how to text, they had given all the details to Patty: she and Calvin hadn't been kidnapped; they'd arrive back home at 2:15 AM; don't involve the police; have Hal meet them there; they'd explain everything when they arrived. Bea hoped they would follow the instructions about the police. But Vaslow had a plan B to make sure they were covered. He probably had a plan C, too, knowing him.

The streets were dark and empty—not much trouble finding a place to land. They chose a spot a few doors down and drove into the driveway at precisely 2:15 AM. They parked Vaslow's "minivan" in the driveway right behind Aunt Lucy's.

No sooner had they landed than the front door of the house flew open and her entire family and Hal came spilling out, Aunt Lucy leading the way, running. Before Bea had time to get out of the van, her aunt threw her arms around Bea's half-sitting body and squeezed. She could feel Aunt Lucy's hot tears on her cheek. No one had noticed yet that her body had changed. She could see her whole family standing, waiting to hug her. She savored the moment, wondering if they would still want to hug her once she got out and they saw how much she had changed. She didn't want this illusion to be broken, didn't want to let go of her aunt.

She heard Uncle Pete ask, "Where have you been?"

"What are you two wearing?" Aunt Lucy asked, moving back to let Bea out of the van.

Vaslow stepped out from the other side of his vehicle.

"Ed?" Uncle Pete said, as Vaslow made his way around the front of the vehicle. "What's going on?"

Bea stood up. Patty was the first to notice. "Oh my God, Bea, what happened to you?" Her face was twisted with shock.

"Bea, my God, you've grown six inches." Aunt Lucy was dazed. "And your face …"

Teddy asked, "Bea, what's that on your skin?"

Bea's hand flew up and touched her face where she knew the spots were. This was it. They wouldn't want her now.

"I think it would be best to explain inside," Vaslow suggested.

They all moved toward the porch, up the steps, and into the house. Islook and the other guard remained outside the front door. The living room was exactly as it had been just two days ago. It was all so familiar, but as much as she loved it, it was no longer home. That thought felt like a stone in her heart.

"I'm not who you thought I was," Bea said, looking away.

"Hey, he has them too? Are they contagious?" Teddy asked.

"No, they are not contagious. They're like birthmarks," Bea said, searching for a way to make Teddy understand. She was so afraid that the wrong words might send them all farther away from her again.

She looked at Vaslow, pleading for him to fill the gaps. Vaslow nodded.

"But Bea wasn't born with these," Patty interjected. "Bea, you look so…different."

"How can Bea have grown like this overnight?" Aunt Lucy asked with a knitted brow. "Ed, what's going on here? How is it possible you haven't aged a day in thirteen years? In fact, you look younger."

"What have you done to our children?" Hal spoke up, his anger unmasked.

"G-Pops, I'm fine. Really." Calvin put his hand on his chest and motioned at his body, careful to cover his wrist. "Hardly a scratch on me. Let Vaslow explain."

Vaslow began in a quietly commanding way, "Please sit down." Everyone looked anxious but didn't move. He urged them again, and one by one they sat. Teddy, much to Bea's surprise, snuggled up close to her. Vaslow started at the beginning with the night her parents had been abducted. He told more of the story than she had heard before.

In the chaotic aftermath of the abduction, a band of fifteen Cenates risked their lives to save the baby Bayatrice from the same fate as her parents. For weeks they hid the baby with a loyal nursemaid in the caverns below the city and allowed the world to believe she, too, had been abducted. When it finally became clear there was no safe place on Vedra for the child, the loyalist Cenates had elected Vaslow to take Bayatrice offworld until she was of age to rule. He didn't hesitate, and would've given his life to save the royals if he could have. He'd been off-duty the night it happened, but as Commander of the Royal Guard, he held himself responsible for their abduction. He officially resigned his commission the day he accepted the mission.

In the dead of night, knowing nothing about caring for a child, much less a baby, Vaslow had set off with Bayatrice to a world he had never been to. There were other planets with more advanced technology where being an offworld alien wouldn't have mattered, but Vaslow chose Earth. Hoping that since it would be more difficult to blend in there, the Protectorate would search there last. But as everyone knew, it hadn't happened that way. He had left "Bea" with the Parkers, knowing she would pass for human until close to her fifteenth birthday.

Hal interrupted, asking if this was some kind of a joke. Bea lifted her skirt to just above her knee, revealing the cream-color skin that gave way to a sea of spots and then eventually to a solid dark brown.

"This is no joke," Bea said, and let her skirt fall again. But Hal just looked at her with a blank expression.

"Wait, I've got it," Calvin said excitedly, and he pulled the cantomount from the pocket of his cloak. He held it while it hummed and grew. He pressed a few buttons in specific order and opened a window into Wharton's command center. Dahreen was at her station, eating dinner. Everyone in the living room gasped.

"What can I help you with?" Dahreen asked nonchalantly.

"Do you mind?" Calvin asked in broken Vedri as he reached through, took a bit of plava off her plate and pulled it into the living room.

"Hey, actually, I do mind," Dahreen said, looking a little miffed. "I haven't eaten since yesterday." And with that she moved her plate out of reach of the cantomount window.

"Sorry, I was just trying to explain," he said, and went to put it back.

"Well, you can have it now."

Calvin shrugged and popped the piece of fruit into his mouth.

"Thank you, Dahreen," Vaslow said. "Sorry we interrupted you."

Calvin closed the window. Though her family hadn't understood the conversation, his point was made.

Vaslow finished his tale of the Protectorate, Bea's bravery—which she blushed at—and the fact that she'd stopped a war. No one questioned its truth. Bea was afraid to meet anyone's gaze for fear of not finding the emotion she wanted in their eyes. When Vaslow was finished, everyone just sat stunned and silent.

"Bea's a queen? Like a real queen?" Patty was first to break the silence. "Wow, you jumped past wannabe right into queen bee."

Bea looked into each of their faces as their questions started to pour in.

"You were being shot at? People died?" Uncle Pete asked.

"This was all too dangerous," Aunt Lucy said.

"I don't understand," Teddy was looking scared. "I don't understand. What's happening?"

It was Patty who answered him. "Bea can't be with us anymore," Patty said, and then looked at Bea with tears in her eyes. "She has something really important to do." She stood up and hugged Bea like her heart was breaking.

"No, no," Aunt Lucy said, crying and shaking her head. "She's just a child. She's still my baby." At those words Bea's fears melted. She rushed over to Aunt Lucy and hugged her like she had never hugged anyone before, a hug that she would remember forever. "You're here to say goodbye?" Aunt Lucy managed between her tears.

Bea nodded.

"Are you sure, honey?" Uncle Pete asked with pleading eyes. "You don't have to go. They can't make you. We won't let them." Even P.J. welled up.

How could she explain to them? It was a path laid out for her before she was born. When the molecules came together to make her body and sent her spinning off into her future, they'd pointed her down this path. She could choose not to go this way, to stay here on Earth and do her best to fit in. Or she could choose her destiny, which was alive in her body and heart. She had to go where her fate led because somehow she felt if she didn't, she'd be walking away from the best parts of herself she had yet to discover. She would do this for herself because it felt right in her bones. And now she would willingly return to Vedra, knowing that no matter who—or what—she was, her *family* loved her. The warmth of that knowing filled her.

Teddy curled up with this head in her lap, sound asleep. Safe and warm in their love, it was time to tell them her story: how unsure she had been about what to do, how she had realized she had to look inside herself to figure things out, how much she missed them, about feeling the energy in her body and feeling like it connected her to all of Vedra. Bea sat with them until the sun was inching up on the horizon.

"We need to be going," Vaslow said to Bea.

"No, not yet," Patty said.

"When will we see you again?" Aunt Lucy asked.

"Calvin will have the cantomount," Vaslow assured them. "We'll figure out a way to vary the signature so your authorities don't detect reoccurring transmissions. I'll get Dahreen on it right away."

"You mean just like open a window to your planet?" P.J. asked.

Vaslow nodded. "Yes, something like that."

"Totally cool," P.J. said, nodding.

They walked her outside to Vaslow's ship. She stood in the driveway hugging each one of them, one at a time. When she finished, she started over again. "I'm going to miss you all so much," she said over and over, because that was the one thought in her head. How could she leave them? She'd spent the last month trying to get them back. And now that she had, she was walking away from them.

"I'm sorry," Islook said, putting his hand gently on her back. She could feel his energy willing her back to the ship. "We really need to get going."

The feeling reminded her she belonged someplace else. "Okay." She nodded to Islook, seeing Vaslow and the other guard already onboard.

As she climbed into the ship and sat in her seat, she remembered that this time Calvin wouldn't be getting in with her. A sob caught in her throat. She reached out and grabbed him by his funky garb and pulled him through the door to her. She went to kiss him and this time she pressed her lips right on his, felt the warmth, and tasted the salt of their combined tears. And she felt a new tingle, one that started in her toes and moved up. As soon as she did it, she wished she hadn't. "I'm sorry, I just wanted to—" Her words were cut off by him leaning in and kissing her back. When the kiss ended she tried to make the words she wanted to say come out of her mouth. But she didn't have enough breath to form them. It was just about the nicest thing she'd ever felt. But she was leaving.

How could making the right decision feel so bad? She would miss them all terribly, but she'd miss Calvin most of all.

"Vaslow said I can come visit," he said, trying not to cry. "I'll tell my G-Pops it'll be like a super-stellar summer school program. He'll love it."

"And you can stay the whole summer?" she managed to eke the words out.

Calvin nodded. She leaned into his ear and whispered. "I want to wait until I can make sense of what all has happened. You know, know for sure. But when I held the scepter, I saw things. I mean it just made me know things...I don't understand exactly, but I'm pretty certain my parents are still alive."

Calvin stepped back and looked at her, shocked. "What?"

"I know, crazy, right?" Bea said, shaking her head. "That's why I don't want to say anything to Vaslow yet. It's all a jumble in my head. I was hoping you'd help me figure it out."

"I think it's gonna be one heck of a summer." Calvin smiled. And Bea smiled back, looking from Calvin to her family, knowing that no matter what she had to face in her future, she was loved.

Hope you enjoyed reading this book!

To get bonus materials and sneak peeks of Bea's next adventure,
Like **The Intergalactic Adventures of Queen Bea** FaceBook page
or visit www.jeannegranseebarker.com to join the mailing list.

If you liked this book, it would be fantastic if you would write
a review on Amazon or Goodreads. It's the best way to
introduce Bea to more readers.

Thanks for coming along on this adventure.
It wouldn't be the same without you.